I0606638

The nightmare has returned. People are being slaughtered, people with a direct connection to me. Is it happening all over again? And am I somehow responsible?

I went to my locker to put my stuff away before meeting Shaniqua and Watts for lunch. When I opened my locker, there was a folded note sitting on top of my Biology book. At first I thought it was from Shaniqua, and I eagerly opened it up and started to read.

*I know what you are. If you want the killing to stop, meet me in the meadow a mile and a half east of Cailleach Canyon. There's a large oak tree at the entrance. A wolf's head is carved into the trunk. Meet me there on Sunday at 6:00. **DO NOT BE LATE** or you will be sorry.*

It didn't seem possible. Who could have figured out my secret? And why would someone write a note anyway? Why not just tell me to my face?

I was going to have to meet whoever it was and see what they wanted.

I just hoped they didn't bring a gun with them.

Especially loaded with silver bullets.

Two years ago, James Manarro risked his life to kill the werewolf that stalked Wolf Creek. Now sixteen, James struggles with the pressures of being a teen: dating, math, and the knowledge that he, too, is a werewolf. Then the murders start again, and the victims are all tied to James, who worries that he just might be responsible. When his favorite teacher discovers James's secret and tells James he can help him learn to control the wolf, James jumps at the chance. But things are becoming more and more suspicious to his girlfriend Shaniqua and her friend Watts, who set about trying to uncover the truth. Little do they know that the killer has arranged to meet James in a brutal showdown that will shock the entire town and leave James wondering if he will ever be able to restrain the wolf…

KUDOS for *Moon Watch*

In *Moon Watch* by Lisanne Harrington, James Manarro is now two years older than he was in the last book. He also knows that he is a werewolf. Now the killing has started again, and people with a connection to James are dying. He killed the last rogue werewolf who was terrorizing the town two years ago. That werewolf had a virus that made her kill, but why is this one killing? James is having a heck of a time dealing with all the changes in his life, even without being a werewolf, like fighting bullies in high school, falling for a girlfriend—to tell her or not to tell her, what should he do? Sometimes, life just isn't fair. I enjoyed this second installment of the story very much. Harrington introduced a lot of new characters, but we also saw a good deal of growth in the ones who remained from the last book. I can't wait to find out what happens in the next book. ~ *Taylor Jones, The Review Team of Taylor Jones & Regan Murphy*

REGAN MURPHY SAYS: *Moon Watch* by Lisanne Harrington is the sequel to *Moonspell*. Two years have now gone by since the end of *Moonspell*, and our young hero, James Manarro, is still hurting from the loss of his best friend to the rogue werewolf that terrorized the town and killed so many people. But life moves on, and James is trying to do the same. He is sixteen now, and though he discovered he is a werewolf at the end of the last book, he is learning to control it. He now has a girlfriend—a new girl who has just moved to town—and James is trying to decide if he dares to tell her his secret when all hell breaks loose, and people start dying again, just like two years before. Harrington's character development is first class. I really like how James struggled with his condition and how much he grew over the course of the story. His character has a real ring of truth to it. You just can't help caring about what happens to him. ~ *Regan Murphy, The Review Team of Taylor Jones & Regan Murphy*

ACKNOWLEDGMENTS

I have to thank James for sharing his story with me and trusting me to tell it *as it really happened* to the world. And thanks to Shaniqua and Watts for coming to me fully formed and ready to tell me their side of the story.

Thanks to my family for putting up with me once again as I was spirited away to the world of Wolf Creek. I know how difficult it was when I would forget something important, like Mom's birthday (sorry again, Mom) or otherwise seem to blow them off. I wasn't, really, but the world of the writer is a mercurial thing, demanding of an author's full attention when *it* wants, and leaving them stranded when it doesn't. Writers are at the whim of their characters, who aren't always cooperative. In the case of *Moon Watch*, though, not only were they cooperative, but sometimes, they just wouldn't shut up!

My buddy Jamie Parker gave me lots of inspiration with her beautiful, sometimes haunting, pictures of the moon.

A special thanks to the folks at Black Opal Books, who worked with me to get this book out so quickly: Lauri, for her willingness to take a chance on the entire Wolf Creek series, and me; Faith, who spotted the holes and helped me fill them; Jack, the mind-reading artist whose cover was even more than I could have imagined; and Arwen, who pushed it all along. Thank you so much for all y'all do. I look forward to a long and happy relationship with each and every one of you.

And as always, my special thanks go out to you, my Most Important Reader, without whom all this would be superfluous. I hope you enjoy James's story.

You can contact me through my website, http://www.lisanneharrington.com, or shoot me an email at Lisanne@lisanneharrington.com.

I would love to hear from you.

MOON WATCH

BOOK 2 OF THE

WOLF CREEK MYSTERIES

LISANNE HARRINGTON

A Black Opal Books Publication

For Mom
Welcome to the dark side.
Now that we have our fangs
firmly embedded in your flesh,
We will never let you go.
Mwahahahahahaha!

The moon can appear reddish because of the sultry haze of August. This month is also known as the Dog Days of Summer, so it is sometimes referred to as the Dog Moon.

CHAPTER 1

The boy ran frantically through the heavily wooded park. Trees seemed to reach out and grab him, ripping the flesh on his arms and bloodying his face. His breath came in short, hard bursts. His skin was on fire, as though he'd been stung by a thousand pissed-off hornets. Blood pounded through his veins, his heart beat like a crazed drummer, and he felt as though his head would explode.

He glanced over his shoulder, searching for what— he didn't know. The moon dueled with the sun to see which one glowed brighter. As he looked forward again, he tripped over a tree root, stumbling several steps, but managed to keep to his feet. The boy paused to catch his breath.

That's when the pain hit.

His bones snapped. The skin across his shoulders stretched and shifted like angry snakes fighting over a rodent. Hair grew from every pore, covering his face and arms, like wild ivy in a neglected garden. It was more than he could bear.

Then just as suddenly, it ended.

He gazed up at the moon again. But this time, there was nothing creepy or sinister about it. Instead, there was an affinity. A familiarity. An understanding.

A deep and profound joy.
And the werewolf howled his devotion.

CHAPTER 2

Tuesday, September 8, 2015,
Twenty Days to Full Moon:

Two years ago, when I was fourteen, I thought killing a rogue werewolf would be the hardest thing I'd ever have to do in my entire life. It had killed several of Wolf Creek's townsfolk, including Riff, my best friend, and Donna, the woman who'd helped me kill it—and the monster's final victim.

But then my parents told me the awful truth.

Werewolves are real.

And I'm one of them.

How's a dude supposed to deal with that?

"James Manarro."

"Huh?" I had slouched down in my desk and wriggled around to sit upright. "What?"

"First day of school, and you're already off in la la land," Mr. Hansen said. He cocked his head and squinted over the top of his half-glasses. "This going to be an ongoing problem, Mr. Manarro?"

I shifted uneasily in my seat. "No, sir."

Not the best way to make a first impression. And I really wanted to make a good impression on Mr. Hansen. I'd need his recommendation to take Creative Writing as one of my electives next year. I wanted to be a writer when I graduated, and I hoped to learn a lot from him. *Who knows? Maybe I'll become the world's first bestselling author werewolf.* I chuckled at the thought. Then felt the heat rise up my neck when the teacher glared at me again.

I sank lower in my chair, vowing to pay attention for the rest of the class. But as Mr. Hansen told us what we were going to study this semester, my mind wandered. I thought about how I'd grown up with all the same monster myths and legends as my human friends. Gone to movies like *Daybreakers, Abe Lincoln: Vampire Hunter,* and *Ginger Snaps.* Watched *Teen Wolf* and *Vampire Diaries* on TV. Even read that stupid *Twilight* book, laughing over the shimmery vampires. The subplot with Jacob and the rest of the Quileute werewolves was much more interesting.

How was I supposed to know they were real?

□

The kids at her old school all thought Shaniqua was weird. She preferred unique. While other sixteen-year-old girls were concerned with what the next YouTube phenom was up to, or which Kardashian they most wanted to emulate, or which movie star was the hottest, she would rather spend time working on her graphic novel—drawing was her life—maybe curl up with a good book, or even nuke some popcorn and put on a DVD of a B-movie horror flick. It sure beat hanging out with the Neanderthals who populated the school's sports teams or the Mean Girls, who thought they were the fashion police, there expressly to pass judgment on anyone who wasn't them.

Her parents had worried about her because she didn't

have many—or any—friends, until just before what happened that got her sent to Wolf Creek in the first place. Oh, sure, she'd had friends when she was little, until the day she tripped running around the bases during a school softball game and knocked Meghan, the most popular girl in school, down, accidentally breaking her nose in the process. Since then, she was persona non grata.

Today, Shaniqua decided as she woke up and stared at the ceiling, was going to be different. Like her Uncle Roshaun told her, today is what you make it. You could either slink around with a big black cloud over your head raining down on you wherever you go, or you could make sure the sun shined on you every day. It was your choice. She'd decided she'd rather live in the light.

Yes, today was going to be the day everything would change.

Aunt Lydie made her a big breakfast, with pancakes, sausage, and scrambled eggs. All her favorites. She'd done her best to eat as much as she could, but there wasn't much room, what with the boulder rolling around in her stomach.

The whole way to school, she clutched her backpack to her chest, periodically checking to make sure her art pad and charcoals were tucked safely inside. Her aunt and uncle talked about things that didn't matter—what time they'd be home from work, what time she should be home from school by, if she was ready for her first day at a new school. All she could think about was staying invisible and not pissing anyone off. Not the first day, anyway.

When they pulled up in front of school, Shaniqua opened the door. Before she could bolt, her aunt turned around in the front seat and regarded her. "Sure you don't want us to walk you in?"

Oh, sure, that's all I need. A personal invitation to Dorkdom, courtesy of my auntie.

She shook her head vehemently. "No. Thanks."

"Well, have a good day."

Shaniqua dutifully kissed her goodbye. Uncle Roshaun took her by the hand.

"Just relax," he told her. "You'll do fine."

She flashed what she hoped looked like a genuine smile, even though she felt like throwing up. She got out of the car, slammed the door, hurried past some kid plugged into his ear buds, and was pretty sure those were Mean Girls sitting on the wall lining the walkway into campus, stuck together like Pringles. Honestly, did anyone ever see just one?

Trudging past them, relief flooded through her when she got all the way to the end of the walkway without incurring their wrath—or even their notice. When she got to the office, she went in and waited at the counter. She was supposed to get her schedule, books, and locker information before class, and a glance at the wall clock behind her showed it was already seven-fifty. Five minutes till the bell rang. She tapped her fingernails on the counter. The frizzy-haired woman sitting at a desk didn't even look up. Shaniqua cleared her throat. Still no response.

"Excuse me?" If the secretary, or whoever she was, didn't get a move on, Shaniqua was going to be late to her first class. "I'm supposed to get my schedule and books?"

The woman, whose nameplate announced that she was Sheila Lambert, finally glared up at her.

Shaniqua smiled. "I'm new here."

Mrs. Lambert seemed unimpressed, returning her gaze to the computer screen.

"I'm going to be late."

The woman sighed and pulled herself away from Facebook, or a stupid cat video, or whatever had her so interested on the computer. "Name?"

"Shaniqua. Shaniqua Robinson."

Mrs. Lambert tapped a few keys on her keyboard, looked at the printer across the room, and waited. Once it spit out a piece of paper, presumably Shaniqua's schedule, she strolled over to it and yanked the paper off the tray. Then she went into a file cabinet, pulled open a drawer, and walked her fingers slowly across several file folders before pulling out a second piece of paper and disappearing into another room.

Shaniqua glanced at the clock again. Seven fifty-three. No way was she going to be on time.

"You lost, young lady?"

Shaniqua turned to find a balding older man with a significant beer belly standing with his hands on his hips. He had a patchy brown moustache that seemed more like it belonged on one of his students than on a man his age.

"I'm waiting for that lady…I think her name is Mrs. Lambert? I'm waiting for her to get my schedule. I'm new."

"Well, okay then. I'm the principal here. Mr. Petrellis."

"Hi."

He smiled. "Hi."

Shaniqua was surprised to see that his teeth were gleaming white, and she wondered if he chewed Crest White Strips when he wasn't at school. She stifled a giggle.

"Here you go." Mrs. Lambert dumped a stack of books on the counter in front of Shaniqua and handed her the schedule and locker information. "I see you met Mr. Petrellis."

"What's her first class, Sheila?"

"Language Arts. Mr. Hansen."

"Oh, a Junior. I see. Well, come along." Mr. Petrellis turned on his heel and left the Office.

Shaniqua struggled to pick up her books and hurried after him.

〇

I was busy writing in my notebook when the classroom door opened and Principal Petrellis walked in. Trailing along behind him was the most interesting-looking girl I'd ever seen. She wasn't beautiful in the traditional sense, but she had this thick reddish-brown hair that curled around her head like a nimbus and the most unusual green eyes I'd ever seen.

"Class," Mr. Petrellis said. "This is Shana." He motioned for her to stand next to him.

She mumbled something to him. He frowned. "What?"

"Shaniqua," she told him. "My name is Shaniqua." She shifted her pile of books to the other hip. A drawing pad stuck out of the top of her pack.

"Shaniqua, then." He sounded like he was pissed about something. What a jerk. "Welcome. Shaniqua." He overemphasized her name. "You can take a seat over there."

He gestured at the only empty desk, three seats and two rows away from me, and everyone watched as she walked over and sat down. She pulled out a notebook and pen and sat quietly, watching Mr. Hansen. I wondered how I could meet her.

The rest of the class was pretty much lost to me. Between sneaking glances at the new girl and pretending to take notes while trying to figure out what to say to her, I had no clue what Mr. Hansen said. I only hoped he hadn't assigned any homework, or I'd be screwed.

Maybe I could offer to show her around school. Find out what classes she had and see if we had anything else together. Or—

The bell rang and people filed past me. No one spoke to Shaniqua while she put her things back in her backpack. *Might as well talk to her now, while I have a chance.* I took a deep breath, pulled my backpack off the desk, and lugged it over to her.

"Hi," I said. The back of my ear started itching, and I scratched it quickly.

She looked up at me and smiled. I was hooked. "Hi," she said.

"I'm James."

"Shaniqua."

Kids were starting to come in for the next class, so we headed for the door. "You new here?"

Heat rose up my neck and I knew that I was blushing. What a stupid thing to say. I wouldn't have been surprised if she laughed and got away from me as fast as she could.

Instead, she giggled. "Yeah."

I couldn't help but grin back. "What's your next class?"

She studied her schedule and made a face. "PE. Ugh."

"Can I walk you?"

She tucked a strand of wiry hair behind her ear. It looked like those scrubby things my mom used to clean the sink. I wanted to touch it to see what it felt like. "Sure," she said.

We walked to the gym. I opened the door for her and followed her inside. A glance at my watch told me I had less than two minutes to make it to my own class in the next building over. Hopefully, I would make it before the tardy bell rang.

"Here you go," I said when we got to the girls' locker room.

"Thanks."

"Well, see you around."

"See ya."

I started toward the main door but stopped and turned back around. Shaniqua was standing there, holding the locker room door open for the stream of chicks flowing inside. She was watching me. My stomach fluttered a little bit.

"Hey," I called to her. "See you at lunch?"

She smiled but didn't say anything. Then she disappeared into the locker room.

▯

I could barely sit still during Geometry while Mrs. Falcone droned on and on about quadrilaterals, parallelograms, and rhombus. Even if I'd been paying attention, it would have gone right over my head. A math whiz I'm not. That's why I had to take the two-year course to cover Algebra One instead of the one-year course. The written word was my thing. Short stories in particular, although really, I'd write just about anything. Someday soon, I hoped to write a novel. No matter what my father said.

Shaniqua seemed different, not like all the other girls I'd gone to school with. Definitely not a Beautiful Person, although she was pretty cute. Looked kind of like Demi Levato, but with darker skin. She didn't seem like someone who would fit in with the popular cliques. At least I hoped not, because if she did, I was screwed. If she was, once she found her own group, there'd be no way would she even talk to me, much less be my friend.

It would be useless to look for the new girl during Break, which only lasted ten minutes, but I kept my eye out for her anyway as I strolled over to the vending machines. Hoping the School Board hadn't hitched up to the wagon train and filled them with "healthy" snacks over the summer, I scanned every face in the crowd as I waited in line for my much-needed Pop-Tart. I'd just dug my money out of my pocket and was about to make my choice when I was bumped from behind so hard, I crashed into the glass. My money went flying.

I didn't have to turn around to know who it was.

"Logan." I hitched my backpack up onto my shoulder and prayed he'd go easy on me, seeing as how it was the first day of school. Chase, Boy-O, and Liam, his crew, flanked him.

"Dickweed." He sneered at me and I wondered for the bazillionth time why girls and even teachers found it so charming when all it did for me was creep me out. "How's it hangin'?" His fan boys guffawed like that was the funniest thing they'd ever heard.

When I tried to leave, Chase, Logan's number one boy, stepped in front of me, blocking my way.

"Where you think you're going?"

"Just leave me alone," I mumbled, feeling like the world's biggest wimp. This had been going on for as long as I could remember. I'd had a bit of a reprieve for a while because Logan was almost eighteen and we'd gone to different schools for a couple of years, but I could tell this year would be business as usual.

"Oh, look it," Boy-O said. "Widdo baby's gonna cry."

Logan crossed his arms and eyeballed me. "That true?" His sneer was malevolent. "You gonna cry, widdo baby?"

I straightened my shoulders and looked him in the eye. "No, I'm not going to cry. I'm going to go to class." People were milling around, and I hoped to be able to disappear into the crowd once I got away. But when I tried to go around him, Chase pushed me back against the vending machine again and pinned me there by the throat.

Then he squeezed.

And squeezed.

Black spots formed in the corner of my vision. Faces around me seemed to elongate and wobble, but no one rushed in to help. I was on my own. I grabbed Chase's hands and tried to pry them apart, but he was too strong. My eyes felt like they were going to pop out of my head. I couldn't breathe. I think I was close to passing out, and I wondered if I could convince Mom to keep a steady supply of Pop-Tarts at home from now on so I wouldn't have to use the vending machines.

Everything started to go dark.

"Hey, what's going on here?"

Air flooded into my lungs, and I coughed. My sight came back and I tried to find the source of the voice. People were leaving and, as the crowd thinned out, I spotted an adult standing there with his hands on his hips, looking from me to Chase to Logan and back.

"Nothing, Mr. Sanderson." Logan gave him his winningest smile. "Just saying 'sup to my homie, here."

Mr. Sanderson scrutinized me, his head cocked to one side. "That true?"

I had two choices. Rat Logan and his crew out and spend the rest of the year dodging him and hiding in the shadows, hoping he wouldn't ever find me. Or I could lie and say everything was fine. Never was much for the dark, anyway.

"Sure." I resisted the urge to rub my throat. Instead, I nodded at Logan. "'Sup."

We all stood there grinning at each other while the teacher looked us over. At least I hoped I was smiling. My whole face was numb so it was hard to tell.

The bell rang. Break was over, and what was left of the crowd dispersed.

"Go on," Mr. Sanderson said. "Get to class." As Logan turned to leave, the teacher put a hand on his arm. "Maybe next time, you say hello a little less…boisterously, okay, Logan?"

"Sure thing, Mr. Sanderson," he said, his eyes never leaving my face. As soon as he left, Boy-O shoved me. Right into Logan, who went sprawling.

Logan got up slowly, brushed himself off, and picked up his backpack. He slung it over his shoulder and smirked. "You're gonna pay for that, jack off. You're gonna pay for that *big* time."

I waited a few seconds until he and his crew entered the Science building before heading to class.

That's when I saw Shaniqua watching me from across the Quad.

❑

The bell rang, and Shaniqua hurried to her next class: Manufacturing Technology-Metals. She was really looking forward to learning how to use a welder. Her plan was to make metal sculptures of her graphic novel characters. If she could only find a partner who could write the story. Not her forte, writing. But she thought she had some pretty solid ideas for characters.

When she got to the shop, it surprised her that she wasn't the only girl. She'd figured all the other girls would opt more for some silly Home Ec courses—Foods, Creative Needlecraft, something called Clothing, whatever that was. Nothing that interested her, that's for sure. It was probably sexist, or politically incorrect or something to think that, but true was true.

She nodded to the other girl, who grinned an intolerably big smile and motioned for Shaniqua to sit by her. Feeling trapped, Shaniqua glanced around, saw a few other empty desks and briefly debated heading for one across the room, but didn't want to piss anyone off her first day so she relented and took a seat at the desk behind Grinny McGrinnerson.

"Hi," Grinny said. "I'm so glad to see you. I was afraid I was going to be the only one." Impossibly, her smile widened even farther. "Girl, I mean."

"Hi."

"I'm Watts."

"Watts?"

"On account of my smile. My daddy always said it was brighter than a hundred watt bulb. You know—"

"Watts," they finished together.

"Yeah, I get it," Shaniqua said. Watts's smile was bright. And contagious. Shaniqua couldn't help but grin back. "I'm Shaniqua."

Watts tilted her head. "That's so pretty. I never heard that before. Is it…Black?"

"What?"

Watts snapped her fingers. "Oh, sorry, is that not the PC thing to say any more? I guess I mean African American."

Shaniqua shrugged. She opened up her notebook and began doodling in the margins. "Don't really know. We're English."

Watts's face flushed a deep red. "Oh."

Shaniqua got a good feeling from Watts. Maybe they could be friends. "It's okay. No worries." When the girl refused to look at her, Shaniqua nudged her gently. "Really. It's okay."

"Oh, whew." Watts drew her hand across her forehead in an exaggerated way then waved off the imaginary sweat. "Thought I'd really blown it, there."

"Hey, whaddaya know. We got two real live dykes in class this semester."

Shaniqua turned to find two of the same boys who had hassled James by the vending machines sitting a few rows over, and groaned.

"Oh, shut up, *Boy-O*," Watts said. "Look who's talking. What kind of name is Boy-O, anyway?"

Boy-O came out of his chair and charged toward her. "Listen, you bitch," he exclaimed, getting right up into her face. She didn't budge an inch. "You don't want to make fun of my name."

"Or what? You gonna beat me up? Didn't your daddy ever tell you not to hit girls?" Watts flashed a smile at him before clucking her tongue and shaking her head. "Oh, yeah, you don't have a daddy, do you? 'Cuz it could be any one of several guys, isn't that right? Boy-O."

Boy-O lunged at her, tripping over one of the desks that stood between them. As he scrambled over it, the teacher walked into the room at the same time as the other kid grabbed Boy-O's arm.

"All right, everyone, take your seats," the teacher said. He stopped when he saw what was happening and spoke to Boy-O's friend. "Brody, what's going on here?

"Nothing, Mr. Sanderson." He turned to Boy-O. "Knock it off," he whispered. "You wanna get us kicked out of class on the first day?"

Boy-O shook him off and glared first at Watts then at Shaniqua. "This ain't over," he said quietly. "Not by a long shot."

□

Shaniqua and Watts left Shop class and walked out of the building. "Do you think that guy meant it? About not being over, I mean," Shaniqua asked.

"Who? Boy-O?" Watts snorted. "Don't worry about him. He's all talk. Look, I gotta go to the bathroom. Want to meet up at lunch?"

"Sure." Shaniqua hated to eat alone. She'd had more than her share of lonely lunches. "Where?"

"There's some tables next to the office. I like to sit in the one in the corner."

Shaniqua raised an eyebrow, and Watts grinned at her.

"It's a position I'm familiar with. From when I was little."

Shaniqua chuckled and patted her new friend on the back. "Yeah, I'll bet. See you." She watched Watts head towards the girls' room and then pulled out her schedule to check the room number of her next class. M123. Trig. Well, she liked arcs and radians and angles and stuff like that, even if it did make her a weirdo. She hoped the teacher was decent.

The room was down the first corridor of the Math building, fourth from the end. She walked inside and headed for a desk in the back of the room. A quick glance around showed that it was mostly nerds and geeks, as she suspected it would be. She'd fit right in.

"Well, fancy meeting you here."

Shaniqua looked up. Watts jammed her Jansport under the desk next to her and slumped down into the chair.

"Watts!" Shaniqua was genuinely happy to see her new friend, and that surprised her. She wasn't one to make friends all that easily, and here she'd made two on her first day. "What are you doing here?"

"I know, I know. I don't exactly look like a math whiz."

Embarrassed, Shaniqua felt her face flush. "No, I didn't mean—"

Watts giggled. "It's okay. Everybody thinks that. No

big deal." She lowered her voice and leaned towards Shaniqua. "Can you believe we got Terwilliger the Troll?"

"Who?"

"Ugh." Watts gestured toward the man standing at the front of the room, his back to the class. He wrote *Mr. Terwilliger* on the whiteboard. Or rather, scrawled. Shaniqua could barely read it, and she wondered if he'd flunked out of medical school because he wrote like a doctor. "This dude is so boring. No personality whatsoever. I had him for Algebra in Middle School. Just my luck he transferred over here in time to torment me again."

"Maybe he won't be that bad," Shaniqua said.

Watts pulled out a pencil and began chewing it in the middle. She looked like a dog with a skinny bone, and Shaniqua giggled.

"What?" Watts asked.

The bell rang. Mr. Terwilliger turned around and studied the class. He seemed to glare at each individual student, and, when it came to her turn, Shaniqua did her best to hide behind the girl in front of her.

It only made him narrow his eyes and seem to focus in on her.

□

As soon as the lunch bell rang, I bolted across campus to the lunch tables. I didn't want anyone else to get to Shaniqua before me. Not that I would be jealous, exactly. Just wanted to make sure we established a friendship before anything happened. And if I was lucky, it might even be something more.

But I was worried that she'd seen what happened with Logan and them at Break, and that it had put her off.

After all, what did I know about her? Maybe she'd been popular at her old school. Maybe she'd be charmed by Logan's smile like everyone else seemed to be. Maybe she'd even go out with him. Who knew for sure?

By the time I got to the lunch tables, someone else had beaten me to it. There was a weird-looking girl sitting next to Shaniqua at a table in the corner. The sides of her head were shaved, and there was a spiky purple Mohawk down the middle. Her eyes were heavily lined with some sort of black gunk. Her tee shirt had one sleeve ripped off, and there was a heavy silver cross hanging from her neck on a chain that seemed like it belonged on a pit bull. What, was she trying to ward off vampires? Would she start wearing silver if she knew I was a werewolf?

As I headed toward them, Shaniqua looked up from unpacking her lunch. When she saw me, she smiled and waved. I waved back, glad I'd have a chance to talk to her, even if she wasn't alone.

"Hey," I said and sat down across from her.

"Hey."

I nodded at Mohawk girl, who grinned back at me. She actually had a nice smile. Her teeth weren't even filed down to sharp points like I'd expected.

"This is Watts," Shaniqua said. "We have Shop together. And Trig. Watts, this is James. He's in my English class."

"Hey." Watts stared at me with a funny expression on her face. "Aren't you—"

"So how was your day so far?" I quickly interrupted.

Shaniqua shrugged. "It was okay."

I pulled out my sandwich and took a big bite. Looked around. Avoided eye contact. Risked a glance at Shaniqua, who was nibbling on her sandwich with a slight smile on her face.

"What?"

She tilted her head but said nothing. Her eyes twinkled, and I wondered what she was thinking.

I glanced around again, hoping I wouldn't see Logan. Or better yet, he wouldn't see me. One potential disaster a day was just about all I could handle.

When I peeked back at Shaniqua, she'd put down her sandwich and was looking at me. She wasn't staring, exactly, but she barely blinked. It made me fidget. The bench had never seemed so hard and uncomfortable.

I cleared my throat.

Took another bite of my sandwich.

Dug through my backpack and pulled out a bag of Fritos.

Opened them.

Offered them to her.

She reached into the bag and pulled out a handful. She wasn't shy about taking food someone offered her, that's for sure.

She popped one into her mouth and chewed, never taking her eyes off mine.

"Thanks." Watts also snagged some chips. "Don't mind if I do."

"So," Shaniqua said, popping another chip and winking at Watts, "we going to talk about it, or pretend it never happened?"

"Pretend what never happened?"

She shrugged, put the rest of her sandwich into her baggie, and stuffed it into her backpack. "If that's the way you want to play it." She picked up her Diet Coke and got up to leave.

"Wait!" I reached out and grabbed her arm. "Don't go. I—I'll tell you about it."

"Good." She sat down and popped a couple more chips. "I was hoping you would."

"Logan's kind of a…" How could I explain it without sounding like a big wimp?

"Jerk? Bully? Douche bag?"

I laughed. "All of the above."

"Yeah, I kind of figured." She sipped on her soda. "Back home, his name was William."

"Back home?"

"Chicago."

"Oh. I guess every school has a Logan."

"Logan, William. They're all the same. Think they're God's gift to women."

"And that they own the whole world."

"Yeah." She went silent and dark all of a sudden, like she'd thought of something terrible. What could I say to lighten the mood again?

"Are you okay?" It was all I could think of.

She kind of set her shoulders and looked me in the eye again. "I'm fine. So what do you do for fun around here?"

Had I heard her right? Was she asking me out? Sweat broke out on my upper lip and I wiped it hastily away. No one had ever asked me out before. What was I supposed to do? Ask if we could go somewhere? Wait for her to come right out and ask me?

It made my head spin.

"Hello?" She waved her hand in front of my face. "Anybody home?"

"Oh, sorry."

"Where'd you go? Didn't think it was that tough a question." She giggled, glancing at Watts again, and it sounded just like my mom's stained glass wind chimes. Sweet and a little high-pitched.

"Just trying to think of things to do. There's really not much. The movies, library, a little shopping. There used to be a mini-golf course, but that shut down when—

uh, two years or so ago. The diner has pretty good food. And there's always school stuff going on. Football games and dances and stuff."

"Dances?"

Now I'd done it. I could no more dance with my big feet than I could fly. It was just my luck that she'd pick up on that.

"Yeah. Bet Chicago had lots of stuff to do."

"Uh huh."

Watts shook the last of my chips out of the bag and popped them into her mouth. "Tell her about MORP."

"MORP? What's that?"

"It's kind of an anti-prom," I explained. "MORP is prom spelled backward."

"I saw some signs for that. Isn't it in a couple of weeks?"

"The eleventh, I think." *Please don't let her want to go. Please, please, please.*

"Sounds like fun. But isn't there something we could do before that?"

"We could do something this Saturday, if you want."

"Deal." She stuck out her hand, and we shook on it.

The bell rang, and we gathered our things. I picked up her trash and Watts's along with mine and tossed it into the trash can.

"See you guys later," I said.

She waved and headed across the Quad with Watts. I couldn't help but watch her until they disappeared around the side of the Science Building, where the lockers were located.

Shaniqua wasn't like anyone I'd ever met before.

It wasn't long before I would find out just how different she was.

□

"You are unbelievable," Watts said as soon as they rounded the corner of the Science building.

"What?" Shaniqua had pulled out the paper she'd been given, the one with her locker number and combination on it, and was searching the numbers on the lockers to see which one was hers.

"Don't give me that. You know what."

Shaniqua stopped and put her arm on Watts's forearm. "No, I really don't."

"Dude, don't freak out. It's okay, really. It just that…"

"It's just what?"

"I've lived here all my life. Never been asked out. Not once. You're here, what? Five minutes? And you have two dates lined up." She shook her head. "Unbelievable."

Shaniqua didn't know what to say. She felt bad for Watts. She liked her a lot. But she liked James, too. Was she going to have to choose between them? Because she honestly didn't know who to pick. It would be nice to have a boyfriend, but it had been a long time since she'd had a best friend.

Her emotions must have shown on her face, because Watts punched her lightly on the shoulder. "Hey, I told you, it's okay. Really. I mean, get a load of me…" Here she gestured toward herself, a dopey grin on her face. "And then you." She waved at Shaniqua, who looked down at herself, making Watts giggle again. "Hey, girlfriend. I got eyes. If I were a dude, I'd pick you over me any day."

"Oh, Watts, you're cute, in your own way."

"If you're into freaks."

"Nuh uh."

"Give it up, Shaniqua. This is one argument you won't win. Gotta jet. See you tomorrow."

It seemed like Watts was okay with it. Shaniqua hoped so. She was such a unique person, at least on the surface. Only time would tell, she supposed, if she was as different from everyone else deep down.

☐

Shaniqua wondered what her aunt would say when she told her that she'd been asked out for not one date, but two. She'd probably tell her she couldn't go. God forbid she have any fun, especially with a boy. Especially after what happened in Chicago.

Maybe she wouldn't tell her. Maybe she'd have James meet her somewhere instead of picking her up at the house. But where? And how would she get there?

Maybe Uncle Roshaun would help.

Probably not.

Going to high school was a lot like being forced to get up and run head first into a concrete pylon at seventy miles an hour, day after day. It was the place where Darwin's Survival of the Fittest played out each and every day, where evolutionary advantages like perfect teeth, perfect hair, perfect clothes and perfectly perky boobs worked in tandem to catapult you to the top of the food chain while kids like Shaniqua were left to fend for themselves against the demons who fed on the fear of those less fortunate.

What was it her father said about the definition of crazy? That it was like doing the same thing over and over again but expecting a different result each time. Well, she certainly wasn't crazy because she pretty much expected life to suck here in Wolf Creek like it did back in Chicago. She'd long ago faced up to the fact that she was invisible when it came to the other kids at school, which wasn't necessarily a bad thing. It kept her relatively free from ever angering the Gods and Goddesses of Popularity.

Until she'd become the most highly visible kid in school.

But with any luck, she'd remain invisible here and no one would ever find out what happened.

And as long as she didn't commit any serious faux pas, she should be okay. It was one thing to grow up and go to school with all the same people and all the same rules, but moving somewhere new, somewhere with a completely new social structure, was a challenge. She'd have to watch her step until she got the hang of things.

She couldn't worry about it anymore right now. She had to find L167, her assigned locker, dump off the books from her morning classes, and get to Biology before the tardy bell rang. When she finally reached it, there was a couple locked together by the lips draped across it. Ten to one they were the school's "it" couple. They had that quality.

"I'm going to miss you so much," the girl said, once they'd come up for air.

"I'm gonna miss you more," the boy murmured.

Shaniqua rolled her eyes. *Geez, she's not going to the moon. She's only going to fifth period, you know.*

When they both turned and glared at her, she realized that she must have said that out loud. So much for invisibility.

"Could you move over a little? You're blocking my locker."

"Jealous much," the girl said.

The boy snickered. "Obviously never had a boy-friend."

The girl looked Shaniqua up and down. "And never will. Skank."

They walked off with their arms wrapped around

each other like mating octopuses, hands tucked into their mate's rear pockets.

"Not one like you, that's for sure." Shaniqua put away her books from her morning classes, which lightened her backpack by about seven hundred and fifty pounds or so.

□

Shaniqua chose a stool at a table in the back of the Biology class. She hoped no one would notice her. Being the new girl really sucked, but after what happened at her last school, she guessed it was better than the alternative. The stares and whispers and not-so-nice comments she'd heard most of the other kids making as she walked down the halls had gotten to her, but she could have gotten used to it, she supposed, if only her own parents hadn't started treating her like some kind of freak. Then, without any hint or even consulting her, they'd decided "it would be best" if she went to live with her aunt and uncle for a while, and she'd been shipped off to this suburban nightmare.

It wasn't that she didn't love Aunt Lydie and Uncle Roshaun. She did. They were pretty cool, as far as adults went. But it felt weird living with them and going to school here. Wolf Creek High? Seriously? It wasn't even on the same planet as Chicago, was it?

The teacher, a small gnome with a severe case of bed head, wrote his name on the board, pronouncing each syllable as he went. "Miss…ter," he said. "Row…mohn …e…oh." He dotted the "i" and underlined his name with such force that the chalk broke. Several kids tittered until Mr. Romanio turned around and glared at the class.

"That's enough." He picked up a stack of papers off the desk and tossed several onto the first lab table. "Here is the syllabus for the semester." He tossed the next several onto the second table. "Pass these back." He moved on to the third row. "Now, I expect you to—"

The classroom door flew open, bouncing against the wall. Startled, Shaniqua dropped her pen on the floor. In barged the school's main Mean Girl. Of that, there was no doubt. Blonde, thin bordering on anorexic, wearing what Shaniqua could only assume was the height of fashion. Her own fashion sense was a hybrid of nerd girl and tomboy.

It was that Mean Girl, the mating octopus who'd blocked her locker. She actually had an entourage who followed her into the room. The four of them breezed through the door and paused. Were they waiting for applause?

Mr. Romanio grimaced. "Take your seats, ladies."

After glancing around the room, Mean Girl locked eyes with Shaniqua. A slow smirk spread across her face. "Come on, girls," she said, her eyes never leaving Shaniqua's. Mean Girl and company strolled down the aisle toward her, even though the only available seats were two rows over. When she got to Shaniqua's table, she stopped, one hand on her hip, and flipped her hair.

Shaniqua pretended to look at the wall and rolled her eyes.

"You wanna move your shit?" Mean Girl said. It wasn't a question.

"What?" Shaniqua asked, confused.

Mean Girl's eye flicked down and up again. "Do you not speak English? Seems like a simple enough request. We don't speak Skank here." Her smile broadened. Shaniqua wondered if it had ever had even a passing acquaintance with her eyes. "Or ghetto." The Entourage giggled appreciatively.

Shaniqua looked down and realized that her notebook was lying on the floor. "Oh, sorry," she muttered and reached for it. Mean Girl casually put her highly pedicured, Jimmy Choo-wearing foot on top of it just as Shaniqua's fingers grabbed a corner. She looked up and, to no surprise, saw Mean Girl sneering at her. She tugged on the notebook but the foot remained planted in the middle. She tugged harder, freeing it, and couldn't help but snicker when Mean Girl took a step backward.

"You want to watch yourself, skank," Mean Girl said.

"There a problem, Alexis?" Mr. Romanio asked.

Mean Girl turned and gave the teacher what Shaniqua supposed was her winningest smile. "Not at all, Mr. Romanio." She turned back to Shaniqua. "I was just welcoming the new girl to our school."

"Well, take your seat then. You can chat with your friends later."

"Oh, we will," Alexis said softly, her eyes narrowed into tiny slits. "We will." When she walked past, she made sure to knock Shaniqua's backpack off the table and kick her pen God knows where. "Oh, my bad. So sorry." Then she continued on to one of the empty lab tables in the middle of the room.

Shaniqua sighed. Some things never changed. Seemed like there was a Mean Girl at every school on the planet. At her old school, she'd been named Tiffany.

Shaniqua picked up her backpack off the floor. She thought about James and Watts and smiled then looked around quickly to see if anyone noticed, especially Alexis, or anyone in her posse, or whatever they called them at this school. But, fortunately, Alexis was too busy flirting with the guys sitting around her to notice. Shaniqua didn't want Alexis to think she was laughing at her. Too much chance that would make her Alexis's Target of the Year. There'd been too much of that at her last school.

Her thoughts turned back to James. He had a cleft in his chin like Cary Grant, that old-time actor her mom always swooned over. But what Shaniqua liked most was James's long, wavy golden hair and soulful, milk chocolate eyes. She couldn't help but wonder who he was and what he was like. He seemed really interesting, if just a bit nerdy, but that was all right. She was a bit of one herself. Besides, so far, he and Watts were the only ones to say anything nice to her. Or at all. *His being a hottie certainly doesn't hurt, either!* She grinned bigger then covered her mouth with her hand and glanced around again, just to make sure.

Maybe there was hope for this place after all.

□

Watts headed to her last class of the day with what she felt sure was a dopey grin on her face. She'd been thinking about Shaniqua ever since lunch. It felt good to have a friend again. For reasons unknown to her, she seemed to lose friends easier than she made them. Things had pretty much been okay until about fifth grade. She'd had two best friends back then. They'd done everything together, until one day, neither one would talk to her. Watts had had no clue why.

It happened again the next year. She and Trish were close, closer than she'd ever thought possible. They spent all their time together, walking to class together, eating lunch together, going to each other's house every day after school.

Until the day Tommy Campbell, a.k.a. Boy-O, called them lezbos. After that, Trish wouldn't even look at her.

So Watts had spent the next several years alone, gaining a rep as a freak. She didn't mind so much—who wanted to be friends with those losers anyway?—but it did get a little lonely sometimes. She hadn't realized it, though, until she'd met Shaniqua. They'd hit it off right away, and Watts hoped they would be good friends. Digging in her backpack, she rummaged around until she found a broken rice cake, pulling it out with a grimace. Why couldn't her mom ever buy cookies or even chewy granola bars? At least she could handle those. But this health food kick she was on bugged Watts beyond belief. Her only hope was that it would end soon.

She'd just opened the bag's zipper with her teeth when someone knocked into her shoulder, hard enough to send her into the row of lockers lining the hallway and her snack flying. "Lez."

She turned to see who banged into her, but the corridor was crowded and she couldn't tell who it was. Several people were laughing at her.

"Wow," Watts said to the crowd. "I see none of you gained any IQ points over the summer. Big surprise." She bent down to pick up the biggest piece of the rice cake. She was hungry, after all. "Three second rule," she muttered then blew it off and took a big bite.

Someone bent down in front of her and put their hand on hers. Watts's first instinct was to yank her hand away. Until the someone spoke. "Hey, you okay?"

Watts squinted up into Shaniqua's smiling face. The instinct passed, replaced by delight. "Sure." She shrugged. "No big."

They both stood and grinned at each other. "What are you doing here?" Watts asked.

Shaniqua gestured down the hall. "Going to class, silly." She giggled and Watts felt her own grin widen. Shaniqua glanced at her schedule. "Room LA104. Animation Projects."

"Cartoons. Cool."

Shaniqua cocked her head.

Watts nodded. "Personally, I like the old-school 'toons. Tom and Jerry, Road Runner, things like that."

"Porky Pig?" Shaniqua grabbed the rice cake out of Watts's hand and took a huge bite. And grimaced. "How can you eat this crap?" Instead of spitting it out, she let it sort of dribble out of her mouth and down her chin. Watts laughed.

"You get used to it."

"Guess I'll have to. What class do you have next?"

Watts screwed up her mouth and wrinkled her nose. "Spanish. Room 110. Right down the hall from you." She didn't want to tell her that while she was good in math, her Spanish grade last year sucked, and she was having to repeat the class. She just didn't get it, conjuring all those verbs and what-not. Made no sense to her at all.

Shaniqua frowned. "You don't like it? Spanish, I mean."

"Only taking it because I need it to get into college. I have the worst accent in the world." Watts crossed her eyes. "May yama Watts. Much as grassiass." Shaniqua giggled as Watts uncrossed her eyes and grinned. "See?"

"You're making that up."

"Unfortunately, not. Three years of Spanish and I can't speak it any better than the first day I walked into class. Sad but true."

The warning bell rang. They had less than two minutes to get to class before the tardy bell rang.

"Come on. We don't want to be late." Shaniqua looped her arm through Watts's and they headed off down the hall.

CHAPTER 3

Saturday, September 12, 2015,
Fifteen Days to Full Moon:

I'd wrapped a towel around my waist after getting out of the shower and was standing in front of the bathroom mirror. After wiping off the condensation, I leaned forward and peered at my reflection. Popped a pimple on my chin. Rubbed my fingers up my cheek. Even though there was more than two weeks until the next full moon, my stubble was growing thick again.

I turned on the faucet and let the water heat up while I smoothed shaving cream over my face. It went on pretty thick and I wondered if that was what I looked like when I transformed.

"Who are you kidding?" I asked my reflection. "Probably just look like a hairy beast." I wet the razor and started shaving. "Or maybe like the Wolfman in that old Bela Lugosi movie." I flicked the cream off the razor into the sink and lifted my chin to start on my Adam's apple.

"Do wolves even have Adam's apples?" I wondered.

There was a knock at the door. "James, can I come in?"

"Sure, Dad. Just getting ready for my date."

Dad opened the door and waved away the steam in front of him. "Hot in here."

I took a peek at him in the mirror, wondering what he was up to.

He stood in the doorway and watched while I kept shaving. Finally, after I'd finished my neck and was about to start on my upper lip, I casually ran the razor under the water while watching him in the mirror.

"What's up?"

"So, you're going on a date, huh?"

My eyes narrowed and I tried to figure out where this was going.

"Yeah."

Dad nodded but said nothing. I kept shaving.

I had just finished the last stroke and was cupping my hands under the stream of water so I could rinse off my face when he spoke again.

"What's she like?"

I splashed my face, grabbed the hand towel from my neck and dried off. "She's pretty cool. She's got all this wiry red-brown hair…"

"Auburn."

"What?"

"Auburn. Red-brown hair is called auburn."

"Okay. Auburn." I hadn't gone on many dates before, but he'd never quizzed me when I had. So why was he chatting me up about this one? "Her name's Shaniqua."

"Ooh. I don't think I've ever heard that name before. It's kind of pretty, isn't it?"

I nodded and took a step toward him. "Dad, what's up with all the questions? If I don't get dressed soon, I'm going to be late."

He put his hand on the top of my shoulder. "I want you to be careful tonight."

"I know, Dad. I'm always careful."

"I know you are. But now that you're sixteen, it's especially important."

So that's what this was all about. Relief flooded through me. "Because I'm transforming now."

"Right."

"But there's still a couple of weeks before the next full moon."

"Sit down, James. There's something you need to know." He backed me over to the tub and gently pushed me onto the side. He flipped the lid down and sat on the john.

He was starting to freak me out. "What is it?"

"When a young wolf gets…intimate…with a girl—"

Oh, God, here it comes. The Sex talk. "Dad!"

"Just listen for a minute." He rubbed his face vigorously, then stopped and sighed heavily. "When a young wolf gets intimate with a girl, it can bring on certain changes in his body. Changes that he might not be able to control. Changes that might be dangerous, for the wolf *and* for the young lady. Especially if she's human."

I gulped. "You mean, it could bring on the transformation?" My voice squeaked like it used to when I was thirteen.

Dad nodded. "So it's vital that you make sure things don't go too far. Not until you are better able to control the wolf."

"Okay, Dad. I will."

"And don't forget the things I taught you about controlling it. I know it wasn't much, but at least it should give you a decent starting point."

"I know. I won't forget."

"Well," Dad said as he stood up and walked to the door. "I'd better let you finish getting ready."

It never occurred to me that the Transformation

would get in the way of my love life. As if first dates weren't hard enough.

◻

Shaniqua sat in the living room drawing while she waited for James to pick her up. It was kind of a drag to have to walk everywhere—one more reason to hate California—but then again, it was also kind of sweet. It made her feel somehow closer to James.

When the doorbell rang, she hurried to answer it before her aunt beat her to it. "Hi." She smiled at James and fingered her necklace.

"Hey," James answered. "You ready?"

"I have to introduce you to my aunt and uncle before we can go."

James shrugged and followed her inside. "Okay."

Uncle Roshaun poked his head around the corner where the hall opened up into the living room. "Well, who do we have here?"

Shaniqua led James down the hall. "Uncle Roshaun, this is James."

"Hey there, young man."

James grinned. "Hey." He turned toward Shaniqua and raised and lowered his eyebrows quickly in a "that went well" expression. She barely suppressed a giggle. Had she actually laughed, it would have been cut short by the appearance of her aunt, who seemed unusually irritated and made an exaggerated show out of crossing her arms tightly across her chest as if to ward off the evil that was James. Apparently.

"Auntie Lydie, this is James Manarro," she said quietly. "The boy who asked me to the dance."

James extended his hand to her aunt. "It's nice to meet you, Mrs. Robinson. And you too, sir."

Shaniqua could see how uncomfortable James was, and wanted to get them out of the house as quickly as she could. "Let me just put my stuff away and then we can go. Okay?"

"Sure," James agreed.

She dashed into the kitchen, grabbed her drawing pad and pencils, and went to toss everything into her room. "Be right back," she exclaimed as she rushed past them.

"'kay. No rush." But she could tell by the tone of his voice that James was anxious to get out of there, too.

"Where are you taking our girl tonight, James?"

The antagonism in Aunt Lydie's voice came through loud and clear, and Shaniqua tossed her stuff onto her bed and hurried back to James.

James licked his lips and glanced at Shaniqua. "Well, I'm not sure. We were going to figure it out on the way."

"Hmpf."

"Now, Lydie." Uncle Roshaun patted her arm. "We should let them be on their way. I'm sure James will protect her and keep our girl safe." He studied James, his eyes narrowing slightly. "Won't you?"

"Absolutely." James licked his lips again, and then scratched behind his ear.

Shaniqua slipped her hand through James's arm. "You ready?"

"Yep."

"Curfew's ten o'clock, Shaniqua," Aunt Lydie said sharply.

"Ten? But—"

"Better do as she says, 'Niqui," Uncle Roshaun said. "Ten o'clock. Okay?"

"Fine," she said with a heavy sigh. Maybe someday they'd trust her. "Whatever."

She and James left, and when she accidentally-on-purpose slammed the door, she figured that if they ever asked, she'd just tell them it slipped.

□

"Wow. That was, uh, confuzling, to say the least." What I really meant was why is your aunt such a hard-ass?

"I'm so sorry," Shaniqua said. "I don't know why she's being such a hard-ass about you."

I snickered, covering up my mouth with my hand. But when I glanced at Shaniqua, I laughed so hard, I doubled over.

She looked confused, but there was the beginning of a smile on her face. "What?"

I shook my head and tried to compose myself. "Nothing."

"Yeah, right." She wriggled her fingers in a hand-it-over gesture. "Give."

After wiping the corners of my eyes with the edge of my palms, I gave. "We are so made for each other."

She cocked her head. "How so?"

"I was thinking that exact same thing."

"What? That my aunt is a hard-ass?"

"Uh huh."

We'd stopped on the sidewalk in front of the house, and we both saw the curtains move a little. Shaniqua slipped her arm through mine again. "Come on," she said. "Let's get out of here."

"Where would you like to go?"

"Somewhere we can talk."

"Talk?" I stopped and frowned, curious. Had she heard something about me? Something about that night two years ago? "What about?"

"Don't look so worried, James." She flashed that

smile of hers, that one that could make me forget my own name if she wanted me to. "I just want to get to know you, that's all."

"Oh, okay. How about we go to PJs for a little snack? Diane makes a monster chili cheese fries."

"That and a chocolate banana shake and you got a deal."

I made a face. "Yuck."

"You no likee?"

"Chocolate banana? No, thanks."

"First thing you need to know about me? That's my favorite flavor. The second thing? I'm always hungry." She squeezed my arm with hers. "Now, take me to this Diane person."

I chuckled. "Yes, your Highness."

We headed towards town and a mountain of chili cheese fries.

And I might even learn to love chocolate banana.

☐

It was a perfect first date. Or would have been, if Sheriff Riggs hadn't shown up and nearly ruined the whole thing.

Riggs hated me. I'd gotten into some trouble when I was little and even though I'd apologized and spent an entire summer doing community service to make up for it, here it was five or six years later and he still hadn't forgotten about it. And he never let me forget it, either.

Shaniqua and I were on the way home from gorging ourselves on chili cheese fries. I couldn't quite bring myself to try a sip of her gross shake and ordered my usual Coke instead.

"Ow," she groaned, holding her stomach and fake-stumbling along. "Why'd you let me eat so much?"

"What?" I feigned innocence. "Like I could stop you?"

She sidearm punched me in the stomach. "Hey!"

I grinned. "Just kidding."

"But seriously, I ate way too much. Never should have let you get a second order."

"Could have been the extra chili that did it, you know. You ordered that."

"Yeah, yeah, blame the new kid."

"Easy target." I started to chuckle when I saw something out of the corner of my eye. Without turning my head to actually look, I could already tell what it was by the way my stomach was tightening. It was totally obvious that it had nothing to do with Shaniqua's punch.

My radar had engaged full force.

We were being followed.

I could feel Shaniqua frowning up at me so I grabbed her hand and pulled her along. "Come on, let's go."

"What's wrong?"

"Tell you later." Sweat trickled down the side of my face and I resisted the urge to wipe it away. I couldn't afford to let Riggs see me getting nervous or he'd only make things worse.

We walked quickly down the sidewalk. Hopefully, we'd get to her house before Riggs decided to pull any funny stuff. She must have also felt his presence because she started to turn her head to see who it was but I yanked her along. "Don't!"

"James, what's going on? Who's that following us?"

Before I had a chance to respond, Riggs started in with his usual jeering. You'd think after all this time, he'd learn some new lines, instead of harassing me with the same old, same old.

"Hey, punk. What're you so nervous about?"

I kept walking, trying to keep my pace even. Shaniqua took my cue and matched my steps, staring straight ahead without saying a word.

"Hey, asshole, I'm talking to you." Riggs didn't bother waiting for me to reply. He gunned the car and ran it up over the curb, blocking our path. When he threw open the door and stepped out, it bounced back and knocked him in the shoulder. Just like always. You'd think he would have learned by now.

It was obvious what was coming, and I pulled Shaniqua over behind me. When Riggs poked me in the shoulder with two fingers, like he did every single time he saw me, I couldn't help myself. It was all so pointless. I rolled my eyes at him.

Wrong thing to do.

"Don't you roll your eyes at me, you little prick. Have some respect."

"Respect is earned, Officer...Riggs is it?" Shaniqua had stepped back around me and was peering at his badge.

Riggs sniffed and shifted his duty belt. "That's Sheriff Riggs." He gave her the once over. "I don't think I know you."

She started to answer him, but I interrupted. "What do you want, Riggs?"

"What are you doing out here, this late at night?"

I pulled out my cell phone. "It's only a little past nine thirty. Not so late."

Riggs grabbed me by the arm. "Maybe I should take you in. How would you like that?" He gestured to Shaniqua with his head. "You and your little whore."

"Hey!" Shaniqua got right up into his face. She reminded me of Beth, my cousin, who had stood up to Riggs more than once. "Who you calling a whore? I should report you."

"Yeah? You and who else?" He yanked my arm up

behind my back, but I wouldn't give him the satisfaction of groaning, even though it really hurt. "This little bitch?"

The radio in the squad car crackled. "Sherriff? You there?"

At first, Riggs did nothing, and I wondered what he was waiting for.

"Sherriff Riggs, this is base. Can you hear me?"

Riggs shoved me away and reached into his cruiser. He pulled out the mic and glared at me as he spoke into it. "Yeah, I'm here. What do you want, Charmoose?"

Charlese was a nice lady, and had recently started as a dispatcher for the department. What could she have done to get Riggs mad enough to make fun of her name over the airwaves? Knowing Riggs, it probably hadn't taken much.

"There's been a report of a missing child. A…" You could hear Charlese flipping pages and I figured she was trying to find the code number.

"Don't got all day, Charmoose."

"Right. A nine twenty c."

"Got a name? Description? Anything?"

"Caucasian female, seven years old. Blonde hair, blue eyes. Name's Timothea Richland. Goes by Timmy."

"Timmy? What kind of name is that for a little girl?"

"Dunno. She was last seen leaving Wolf Creek Elementary about two twenty. She was wearing a green and white striped tee shirt, jeans and blue sneakers with green light-up soles. Also had on a red baseball cap."

"On my way. Out." He stepped into his cruiser, slammed the door, and turned back to us. "This isn't over."

"Is it ever?" I muttered, but not loud enough for him to hear me.

I just wanted it to be over this time so we could get home. The last thing I wanted was to get Shaniqua home late and have her aunt decide I was a creep and never let us go out again.

We watched Riggs back the car off the curb and speed off, laying rubber as he went.

Shaniqua turned to me. "What the hell was that all about?"

I puffed up my cheeks before blowing the air out of my mouth. Ran my fingers through my hair. Scratched my side.

How could I tell her the truth on our very first date?

"James?"

"Yeah."

She frowned at me and waved both her hands sharply in a "What the hell?" gesture.

"It's a long story. Let's head home and I'll tell you all about it."

CHAPTER 4

Monday, September 14, 2015,
Thirteen Days to Full Moon:

So, how was it?" Watts asked.

She and Shaniqua were sitting on the wall that surrounded the Senior Quad, waiting for James to arrive for school. Watts was dying to know what they'd done, what they'd talked about. If they'd kissed.

Shaniqua was sketching on her pad and didn't bother to look up. "How was what?"

Watts rolled her eyes. "What do you think?"

"Oh, the date?"

"Yeah, the date. Geez."

"It was fine."

"Fine?"

Shaniqua shrugged. "Yeah, fine."

Watt nodded sympathetically. "Bad kisser, huh?"

That got her attention. "What? No!"

Watts grinned. Shaniqua blushed.

"So what's up, Buttercup."

"What're you, like, eighty?"

"Just something my dad likes to say."

"The date went fine. We had fun. It's just…" She shook her head. "Nothing. Never mind."

"What?" Watts demanded. Shaniqua was beginning to bug her. "Come on." She poked her in the ribs with her elbow. "Give."

"We had this thing—this run-in, I guess you'd call it—with Sheriff Riggs."

"Over what?"

"That's just it. Over nothing. We were just walking home, and he started hassling us. For no reason."

"That's so random."

"That's exactly what it was. Random."

"What did James say?"

"I guess he got into some trouble a while back. Logan and them put him up to it, and he stole a VCR or something."

"A VCR? What did he want with one of those?"

"Maybe it was a DVD player. I don't know. He also threw a brick through a car window. Turned out to be Sheriff Riggs's car. Anyway, he felt bad and gave it back, and even apologized to Riggs, but James still had to do community service. And apparently, Sheriff Riggs has never forgiven him."

Watts studied her fingernails. She'd had her own altercations with Riggs. "So, you going out with James again?"

"Of course. How could I resist that gorgeous hair of his?"

Watts smiled, but was filled with reservations and doubt. One of the reasons she didn't have many girlfriends—or *any*—was because they always seemed to find boyfriends and then forget about their girlfriends.

"Hey." Shaniqua patted her arm. "Don't worry. You and I? We're going to be fast friends. I can feel it."

"Yeah." Watts grinned. "Me, too."

But she still wasn't sure. She had a feeling something was going to happen.

And soon.

CHAPTER 5

Thursday, September 17, 2015,
Back to School Night,
Ten Days to Full Moon:

Back to School Night in high school was lame. No one could figure out why they even bothered, since pretty much only freshmen parents went. Most were burned out from all the junk they had to suffer through when their kids were in elementary and middle school, and by the time they got to be sophomores, it was no longer important to either the kids or the parents.

Except when you had parents like mine, who assured me that they wouldn't call attention to themselves or let anyone know who they were. They just wanted to see what I was working on, they said. Or like Shaniqua's aunt and uncle, who insisted on going because they hadn't been to one in years, ever since their son was killed by a drunk driver, and they wanted to make sure Shaniqua was doing "well," as they put it. How teachers were supposed to figure that out after only a week and a half was beyond me.

Since we had first period together, I figured I'd have to introduce Shaniqua to my parents. We couldn't very well ignore each other. At least, I hoped not.

"Who's your first teacher, James?" my mom asked as we got out of the car and headed toward the gate.

"Mr. Hansen." I scanned the people flowing onto school grounds. No sign of her yet. "Language Arts." Maybe they weren't coming after all. She'd told me she was going to try and talk them out of it. For her sake, I hoped so, since it was what she wanted. But, to be honest, I also hoped she hadn't been able to, because I was looking forward to seeing her.

I'd just opened the door to the English building for my parents when I thought I caught sight of Shaniqua, a flash of hamster-car green in the crowd. She'd told me she'd be wearing a green scarf, but I hadn't realized it would be so…bright. There was no way I could miss it, which I hoped was the point. But they were still all the way across the Quad, and I'd look like a total tard if I stood there holding the door open until they got to it.

Following my parents down the hall, I directed them to Room LA117. "In here, guys."

We found seats in the middle of the room. The clock on the wall told me that there was only five minutes left until the official start of the night. A smattering of parents occupied random desks, maybe a third of all the seats in the room.

Maybe someday, the administration would give up on this whole farce. Hopefully by the time I had kids.

Every time the door opened, I checked out the people who came in. Where were they? The bell to start the evening was about to ring. And as it did, the door opened and there she was, wearing a pink tank-top thing and jeans, the green scarf wrapped around her shoulders and trailing down her side. It flowed behind her when she walked.

Her aunt and uncle looked nervous and followed behind her as she entered the room. When she saw me, her face lit up, her smile wide. Her eyes crinkled at the corners. I grinned back.

She slid into the desk next to me. "Hi."

Her aunt sat behind her, and her uncle behind her aunt. "Aunt Lydie, Uncle Roshaun—" She sort of waved her hand at me. "—you remember James."

I shook hands with her uncle. "Nice to see you again, sir." I smiled my best "you gotta love me" smile at her aunt, who looked like she was sucking on a lemon. It was hard not to laugh. Then I pointed at my parents. "These are my parents, Robbie and Annette Manarro." I turned to my parents. "Mom, Dad. This is Mr. and Mrs. Robinson. Shaniqua's aunt and uncle."

Mr. Robinson stood and shook hands with my dad. "Nice to meet you."

"If we could all take our seats, we can get started," Mr. Hansen said.

Everyone turned their attention to him.

After he'd been talking for a few minutes, Shaniqua leaned over to me. "I think that went well, don't you?" she whispered.

"Yeah, I guess," I whispered back. "Do you think they like me?"

She started to reach out to touch me, maybe brush the hair out of my eyes, then glanced at her aunt and stopped. "What's not to like?" She leaned in closer and glanced at her aunt again. "It's just…"

I didn't like the sound of that. "What? Did I do something wrong?"

"No, no. It's just that you didn't introduce me to your parents. My uncle won't care, but Aunt Lydie?"

"Oh, crap." I groaned and risked a peek at her folks. They both seemed entranced by whatever Mr. Hansen was saying and didn't seem to be paying attention to either of us.

Then I caught Mrs. Robinson giving me a dirty look.

At least, I thought so, but it all happened so quickly, I wasn't positive about what I'd seen. Not until the next day.

CHAPTER 6

Friday, September 18, 2015,
Nine Days to Full Moon:

S he said *what?*" Shaniqua, Watts, and I were hanging out in the Quad before school. I leaned against the wall and the girls sat on top of it. Shaniqua was drawing, as usual.

"Dude, that's just wrong." Watts shook her head and looked at me with what my mom calls puppy dog eyes.

Shaniqua sighed. "But it'll be okay. It's because you forgot to introduce me to your parents. She's real touchy about the racist thing."

"How can she think I'm racist, for Christ's sake? I introduced them to my parents and shook their hands. Would a racist do that?" It was incredible. Never in my entire sixteen years had anyone ever called me racist. "If I thought I was better than you, why would I even talk to you, much less go out with you?"

"I know, I know. Uncle Roshaun said we shouldn't worry, that he'll talk to her."

"But MORP is tomorrow. Are we still going to be able to go?"

A part of me actually hoped not, but mostly, I wanted to spend time with Shaniqua, and if she wanted to go, then that's what we'd do. As long as her folks let her.

The warning bell rang, and the girls hopped down from the wall. We all slung our backpacks over our shoulders. "Don't worry, James. Unless you hear otherwise, meet me here tomorrow night at eight. Okay?" She placed her hand on my arm and kissed me lightly on the cheek.

"Okay."

"I've got to use the ladies," she said. "Meet you in class."

"Okay." I headed toward the English building.

"Hey, James, wait up," Watts called after me.

"What's up?"

"Want to know how to get her aunt on your side?"

"Yeah," I said eagerly. "How?"

"Send her flowers."

I scratched my head. "Send her aunt flowers?"

"No, doofus. Shaniqua. Send Shaniqua flowers," she said with a chuckle. "Sending a girl flowers shows not only that you like her, but you respect her." She tapped my upper arm. "Old people love that. But not roses. Especially red ones. You don't want to send that message."

"What message?"

"That you want to get into her panties. Old folks…not so crazy about that."

"Thanks, Watts. Flowers but not roses. Got it."

I decided to do just that and, at Break, I ordered a dozen daisies to be delivered in the morning. Not the most romantic flower, but my mom said they were the friendliest. And they fit nicely into my budget, which was practically non-existent.

❑

Watts had to laugh. *Why are guys such morons?*

James was so panicked about Shaniqua's aunt. Didn't he realize that things like flowers and candy always went over with old people? It was a cliché for a reason, after all.

She thought about ditching but decided it was too early in the year for that. Best save it for later, when things got intense. Besides, she had friends now, and that alone might make this year tolerable.

She entered the Science building and headed down the hall to her Physics class. Some stupid freshman knocked into her and, without thinking about it, Watts growled. The look on the dude's zit-infested face would have made her laugh, but the skank next to him threw her arm around him and glared at her. "Don't worry about her, little bro. She's just an unhappy freak who growls at everybody."

Is that what I am? A growling freak? Well, at least I'm human.

She wondered where that thought had come from.

CHAPTER 7

Saturday, September 19, 2015,
MORP,
Eight Days to Full Moon:

Watts was right. The daisies swayed her aunt into letting us go out.

So here I was, getting ready to take Shaniqua to MORP, a kind of anti-prom for people who couldn't get dates to the real thing. Or so they said. We'd gone to lunch at PJs and spent the entire time trying to decide what to wear. It didn't matter to me. The whole point was to not dress up in tuxes and formals, so anything else was fine. I would have been okay with wearing regular school clothes, but Shaniqua wanted us to wear something similar. Matchey-matchey wasn't really my thing, but if it made her happy, then I would do it.

We finally decided we'd go Hawaiian. I figured my dad would let me borrow one of his tacky Hawaiian shirts, and she had one of those wrap-around sarong things she could wear with a tank top. It started at eight, so I needed to get going. We were meeting at school, and I didn't want to be late. I was just glad she was being allowed to go.

Getting there was easy. It was taking her home that

was the problem. The way the California laws worked, at sixteen, a driver could only drive with someone under the age of twenty-one if there was an adult in the car with them. You had to have your license for a year before you could drive your friends.

Made dating before seventeen really hard. I wondered if the lawmakers ever thought about that when they made that law. I knew they were trying to cut down on all the teen driving-related deaths over the past few years, but wasn't that like closing the gate after the puppy had already run away?

Good thing Shaniqua didn't seem to mind walking places.

I figured I'd drive to the dance, then maybe we'd walk to PJs and get a shake or share a banana split or something, then I'd walk her home and go back to school to get my car. Fortunately, it was still warm enough in the evenings that we wouldn't freeze.

When I pulled into the school parking lot, music blared from somewhere behind the school fences. *Oh, God. Please don't let her make me twerk.* I felt foolish enough just dancing, let alone twerking.

I parked the Le Mans and walked toward the Quad. As I passed a small green Toyota, the car door opened and Shaniqua climbed out. "Hi, there," she said, then leaned back inside the car. "Thanks, Uncle Roshaun. See you later."

"I'll pick you up right here. Ten thirty, Shaniqua. Not a minute later."

"I know. I won't be late."

"Hi, Mr. Robinson," I called.

He leaned across the console. "Hey, James. You kids have a good time."

"Thanks." I closed the door.

Mr. Robinson rolled down his window and called to

me. I looked questioningly at Shaniqua, who shrugged, and went to him.

"Nice touch, the daisies."

"Thanks."

"Do yourself a favor. Bring her out here a little early. And wait with her till she gets picked up."

I gave him a two-finger salute. "Will do."

He backed out of the parking space and drove off. Shaniqua and I headed to the Quad and into the dance.

▯

She didn't make me twerk, but we did Nae Nae and even danced Gangnam style, which cracked us up. Shaniqua was a really good dancer, which made my feeble attempt look even nerdier than usual. But she didn't seem to mind, so we danced almost every dance.

About half-way through, we went to stand in line for the photo booth. The background was painted like a freeway overpass that someone tagged. Everyone was laughing and having a good time.

And then Alexis, Nicole, Hannah, Destiny, and Cheyenne got in line behind us.

"Hey, look." Alexis shoved Shaniqua with her shoulder, knocking her into the people in front of us. "It's Ghetto Girl."

"Sorry," Shaniqua said to the girl she bumped into. The girl smiled and started to say something to her, then took one peek at Alexis and abruptly turned back around.

Hannah gave Shaniqua the once over, then did the same to me. "Hey, Ghetto Girl."

Shaniqua pursed her lips but didn't respond.

"Your bae there is *sooo* default Bale. Très boring," Hannah continued.

I didn't quite get what she meant, because as far as I

knew, Christian Bale wore black exclusively, and I almost never did. But you couldn't always tell with Alexis and her entourage.

"Thanks! I happen to like Christian Bale." Shaniqua took my hand and beamed at me, her eyes twinkling. "He made the hottest Batman, don't you think?"

Then she leaned into me, her body warm against mine, and kissed me. Surprised, it took me a second and then I kissed her back. Her tongue was super soft and tasted like peppermint.

Her feathers ruffled, for maybe the first time ever, Alexis snorted and studied her nail polish. "Come on, bitches. Let's bounce. It's a little basic here, don't you think?"

As they turned and strutted toward the dance floor, Shaniqua squeezed my hand and turned toward them. "At least I have a date tonight," she called.

"Uh oh," I said, shaking my head. "That's gonna cost you later, you know?"

She wrapped her arms around my neck. "I know. But it was so worth it."

Then she kissed me again.

☐

I'd done what Mr. Robinson told me and made sure we were waiting for him to take Shaniqua home, and wasn't all that surprised when Mrs. Robinson showed up five minutes early. After I said goodbye to both of them, I'd fired up the Le Mans and headed home. Sitting at a light, minding my own business, I thought about how much fun we'd had, and how much I was looking forward to seeing Shaniqua again. When the light changed, I started across the intersection and was barely half-way through when the car filled with blue and red flashing light. I didn't have to peer into the rear view to know who the Kojak light belonged to.

I pulled over and rolled down my window. Waited and watched Riggs climb slowly out of the cruiser, adjust his duty belt, check his reflection in the side mirror, and saunter over to me. I rolled my eyes and hoped I wouldn't burst out laughing, at least until Riggs was done with me.

"Riggs," I said when he reached me.

"Scum ball. What are you doing out of your cage?"

I gestured with my head. "Just on my way home."

"From?"

"School."

"It's a little late for school, freak. What were you, in detention?" He snickered like that was the funniest joke in the world.

I shook my head and tried to remain calm. "No, there was a dance."

"Who'd want to dance with you? Oh, wait, I know. That little ho I saw you with the other day."

"Shaniqua."

"What?"

"Her name," I said loudly, "is Shaniqua."

"Uh huh."

He stood there, glaring at me. I stared out the windshield.

"License and registration."

Every time. Every single time. Talk about holding a grudge. I sighed and pulled out my wallet and handed him my license, then grabbed my registration papers out of the glove compartment. As I handed them to him, he smirked.

"Proof of insurance."

That was new. I fished it out of my wallet and handed it to him. He glanced at it before heading back to the squad car to run my information. Just like he always did, and had every week for the three months I'd had my license.

Five minutes later, I was doing my best not to squirm and appear nervous whenever Riggs got around to giving me back my paperwork. The least little thing could set him off, and if I got into trouble, the state could take away my license until I was eighteen. And that would really suck. It was bad enough I couldn't drive Shaniqua home, or even on a date. But if I couldn't drive at all, especially during the full moon nights, I'd be screwed. If I had to, I guess I could just walk into the woods on those nights, but I'd be afraid I wouldn't be able to get far enough into them before the transformation hit.

And if anyone were around when that happened, well, talk about being screwed.

Riggs thrust my documents in front of my face, barely missing my nose. I must have flinched, because he snorted. "Scare ya?"

Taking them from him, I shook my head. "Nope."

He stared at his watch, and I prayed it wasn't past eleven yet. Provisional licensees in California couldn't drive between eleven at night and five in the morning, and even though I had an exception from the state, Riggs would love nothing more than to haul me in and make me sit in a cell until morning. A glance at my cell phone showed I still had about fifteen minutes.

"Get on home now," Riggs told me.

"I am." I waited until he returned to his vehicle before I blew the hair off my forehead. It wasn't that I was scared of Riggs, but the dude seemed to hate me so much that it made me nervous. I never knew what to expect, so I always expected the worst.

He drove slowly past me.

When his tail lights had disappeared into the night, I put away my papers and started the Le Mans. So far, I'd been lucky when it came to not being caught out after eleven on the nights when the moon was full. But I couldn't help wondering how long that luck would last.

And what would happen when it ended.

CHAPTER 8

Sunday, September 20, 2015,
Seven Days to Full Moon:

So we're agreed, then," Logan said.

They all nodded, although after that thing at the vending machines at school, when he lost control and grabbed James by the throat, Chase was pretty much over it. If he were to admit it, even to himself, he'd have to say that this bullying thing—because ultimately, that was what this was—was boring, stupid, and just plain wrong.

Logan had it all. Babes thought he was hot and fell all over themselves to give him their panties. He was a star athlete who also happened to be smart enough to take honors classes, and he was probably going to Berkeley or some Ivy League college, so why did he have to be such a douche? Sure, Chase was one of the few who knew about his stepfather, but wasn't he old enough to put a stop to it if he really wanted to? He was certainly strong enough. But Chase went along with it anyway. Because he *wasn't* strong enough to say no. He wasn't sure why he'd grabbed James around the throat that day. That wasn't like him. But there was no way he was going to actually beat on the freak. That was going too far.

"As soon as we can get Manarro alone in the locker room, we're going to pound him good. Right?"

Again, the guys nodded.

"Right," Liam mumbled.

"Sure thing," Boy-O agreed enthusiastically.

Mickey cackled hysterically. Chase shook his head. That dude was warped. Like he didn't even have a mind of his own, just went along with anything anyone else suggested.

They were hanging out in front of the new coffee place in town, Cuppa Joe. Logan might be an idiot, but he was generous with his money, and bought them all drinks. Chase sipped on his iced mocha while the others all ordered hazelnut lattes, Logan's favorite. How he could drink something hot in this heat, Chase had no clue. The others only did it because they were followers.

Chase was just about done with the whole thing.

He made a show of looking at his watch. It was way before his curfew, but he was bored and wanted to leave. All Logan and them ever talked about any more was Manarro this, and Manarro that, and Chase was beginning to wonder if Logan had a thing for the dude. Personally, Chase couldn't care less, but Logan would never admit it, even to himself.

"I got to bolt," he said.

"Fine," Logan said. "Let's meet back here in the morning. Seven fifteen. You can buy your own coffee."

Chase smiled thinly. *Whatever.* "Later, dude."

He pushed off on his board and headed home. When he rolled past the park that led into the woods where all those people were killed back in 2013, he skated a little faster. That place gave him the creeps. Just thinking about what it must have been like to have been hunted and killed by some maniac made him shudder. He was as much of a fan of horror movies as the next guy, but to think something like that could actually happen here in Wolf Creek made him want to puke.

What was that?

Chase stopped and stood with one foot on his board. For a second there, he thought he'd heard some weird sound. The wind picked up. Maybe that was it. He pushed off and continued slowly down the street. After a block or two, he had to laugh. *You're such an idiot, letting what happened two years ago still freak you out. It's over and done with. Ding, dong, the psycho's gone.*

Even so, when he got to the electrical easement that went up the hill and down into the elementary school, the place where that kid had been ripped apart by what the media ultimately called the Wolf Creek Shredder, Chase hesitated. It had been blocked off shortly after Riff was killed, but a few months after James shot the killer when she broke into his house and the town realized the nightmare was finally over, someone cut a hole in the fence and no one had bothered to fix it. It was an easy thing to pull the chain link away from the post and slip through. This was another place that Chase didn't like, but if he went the long way, that would add another mile or so, and all he wanted to do was go home, throw on his headphones, and put on *RuPaul's Drag Race,* his own personal guilty pleasure.

He'd never admit it to anyone, least of all Logan or them, but that show cracked him up. Watching all those dudes strutting down the runway in makeup and prom dresses was hilarious.

But even more than hilarity, it made him feel a little closer to Jake, his older brother. Jake had left home five years ago, when he was seventeen and Chase was almost thirteen, when their mother walked in on Jake in drag. She'd been horrified and kicked him out. They hadn't seen him since. Jake, who went by the drag name of Pantie Raid, had moved to San Francisco but texted Chase often.

Chase really missed him.

But if he couldn't sneak in an episode or two, then maybe he'd Netflix a movie. *The Purge,* or maybe *The Strangers.* Something psychological. Just not straight horror, with vampires or werewolves or stuff like that.

Just suck it up, will ya? The Boogeyman is for babies.

He tugged on the chain link and slipped through the opening. For a second, he thought he heard something, and paused in a crouch on the other side of the fence. Wind gusted past him, propelling debris into his eyes.

"Ow! Dammit."

It felt like a Ninja star was gouging his eyeball, and he turned away from the wind in an effort to shield himself from further torment.

As he rubbed and tried to get the boulder out of his eye, he thought he heard someone again, and stiffened. It was crazy. There couldn't be someone following him.

Could there?

□

Autumn was the werewolf's favorite time of the year. The blazing sun warmed its bones while the wind riffled through its fur and cooled its skin. It got a big kick out of the humans' reaction to the Santa Anas, known for their extreme dry heat and gusts up to eighty miles per hour and more. They all seemed to go a little bit crazy during the devil winds, and the werewolf was amused by the increase in suicide and homicide during a major windstorm.

Timid little housewifeys would feel the edge of their favorite carving knives and grin while they studied their overbearing hubbys' necks. The number of bar fights increased. Wildfires spread quickly and burned thousands of acres every year. Destruction everywhere.

What fun!

The werewolf loped along, going nowhere in particular, when it sniffed the delicious aroma of man. And not just any man. More like a man-child.

One of the ones it was hunting for.

❑

Chase straightened up and peered over the "No Trespassing" sign, positive he'd heard someone this time. It was hard to see because he hadn't gotten all the crap out of his eyes, but he blinked several times and squinted past the sign again.

No one had ever accused him of having an overactive imagination. In fact, many of his teachers had given up on him in that regard and hardly ever required him to write papers that even remotely required anything but the most logical and rational thinking. It wasn't that he wasn't smart. He was. He'd aced the Critical Thinking parts of his classes. Give him facts and figures and he could solve any problem.

But this? He wasn't even sure what "this" was, much less how to handle it.

Was he losing it, somehow? He didn't really believe someone was following him. Why would they?

But what if? What if someone *was* following him?

What if it was the Wolf Creek Shredder, back from the dead?

He shook his head. No. No way. That was impossible. No way was she back, thirsty for blood.

"Come on, Chase," he said aloud. "Get a grip, will you? Stop being such a pussy."

Even though he talked himself out of being scared, he grabbed his board and headed up the hill a little bit faster than normal. For the first time, he noticed how narrow the path had become, how overgrown with weeds and vines. After what happened two years ago, parents had forbidden their children from using the shortcut. And then the city put up the gate to ensure there were no more deaths. But he'd figured that the killer was dead, so what would be the harm? Now he wished he'd just gone the long way around. It would have taken him a lot longer, but at least he'd end up safe and sound at home.

Another gust of wind blew and a huge tumbleweed shot past him, nearly knocking him over, but he managed to dodge it just in time.

"Where the hell did that thing come from?"

It careened down the hill and broke into a million pieces when it hit the fence, the remnants carried away by the wind. When he headed back up the hill, another blast hit him with such force that he was knocked back a step or two. He slipped on a plastic grocery bag that had been snagged on one of the bushes that lined the path and his feet went out from under him. His arms pinwheeled, causing him to lose hold of his board, and he nearly went down but managed to catch himself by grabbing onto the branch of a scrub oak on the other side of the trail.

This was insane. He had to get out of this wind. Brushing himself off, he squinted and searched for his board. When he didn't find it immediately, he frowned and took a couple of steps back down the hill. Going home without it was not an option. It cost him nearly a year's allowance, and unlike Logan, Chase couldn't just leave it. He actually cared about things, like the pride of having been able to set a goal, save his money until he could afford to build the board he wanted, and then assemble it himself. When Logan lost stuff, he either talked his way into another, better whatever it was he lost, or else he just set his sights on something else. Either way, it was no sweat off his balls.

Chase took another step and tripped over something. His board! He reached down to pick it up and froze. This time, he knew he heard something—or rather, someone—rustling through the bushes.

"Who's there?" he demanded, with more authority than he felt. "What do you want?"

That's when he heard the growling. Low and menacing. Grabbing his board, he backed quickly up the hill. He didn't know whether to turn and run, or keep backing up so he could see if whatever it was decided to attack. But when the growling came again, he bolted.

▯

Snorting at the kid's terror, the werewolf took its time getting up the hill, delighting in the fear that permeated off Chase. Humans were so foolish. Anything they couldn't see or explain frightened them.

Nothing frightened the wolf.

It slowed to a trot as it neared the boy, raising its snout and scenting the air. The wolf slowly licked first one side of its muzzle then the other as it watched its prey. When the boy tripped over his skateboard, the werewolf growled with amusement. Then growled again as the boy fled up the hill.

The wolf would bide its time. It had no plans to attack the boy.

Not tonight, anyway.

▯

"Help! Help, the psycho killer is back!" Chase shouted as he raced up the hill. He glanced over his shoulder several times until he lost track of where he was, veered off the path, tripped over some chaparral, and ran headfirst into a scratchy scrub oak.

"Ow! Crap."

He put his hand up to his forehead, which felt sticky, and when he pulled his hand away, there was blood on it. A huge goose egg was already forming, and he was getting dizzy. He looked around, suddenly unsure where he was.

Then he heard the growling again, and remembered.

"Oh, my God," he whispered, afraid to move for fear he would run into it—whatever *it* was. Afraid not to move for fear it would get him anyway.

"What do you want?" He nearly gave himself whiplash scanning the area in a vain attempt to find his stalker. His only answer was a rattling of the bushes behind him, followed by another growl. "Leave me alone!"

Chase was crying by now, but he couldn't help it. He'd never been so scared in all his life. He twisted around, searching the heavy brush for any sign of what was following him. The scrub brush quivered and seemed to part slightly.

That's when he saw it.

There, deep within the chaparral and scrub oak, sat a pair of glowing red eyes.

□

Fear increased the delicacy of human flesh, turning it into something succulent and mouthwatering.

The wolf found itself salivating at the thought of devouring human flesh. Oh, what a tasty morsel the boy would make, when his time came. It could hardly stand the wait.

But, in the meantime, scare tactics were the plan, so it must content itself with that.

The wolf saw its opportunity when the stupid boy ran into the tree head first. It simply stopped a few feet in front of him, burrowed into a tight bush, and waited.

☐

Chase blinked and took a second look, not trusting his blurry vision. But damn if those weren't the reddest eyes he'd ever seen. And not red like when Logan's stepfather went on a bender. There was no white at all, and the irises were as bright as one of those spotlights they used in Hollywood for things like the Oscars, but as red as the hourglass on a black widow spider's back. The pupils were enormous and as black as a raven's back.

Blood dripped off his forehead and he hastily wiped it out of his eyes. He squinted and his sobbing slowed. As his eyesight cleared, his lungs filled nearly to bursting, and he struggled to release the air before he passed out. His eyes went wide and he thought, for a moment, that they were going to jump right out of their sockets and bounce on down the hill. Shaking his head, unable to believe what he was seeing, he rubbed his eyes vigorously and looked again, this time spotting a long-ass snout with about a thousand deadly yellow teeth that looked sharper and nastier than an Uruk-Hai scimitar.

Chase screamed, a high-pitched wail that, even in his terror, sounded to him like that of a little girl. But he didn't care. All he could think about was that he should run. Because if he didn't, he was going to die.

CHAPTER 9

Tuesday, September 22, 2015,
Five Days to Full Moon:

When I woke up that day, I had no clue what was waiting for me. That it would be a nightmare day. It started out just like every other school day. I kept hitting the snooze alarm until my mom yelled at me to get up already. I couldn't help it. I felt like I'd been running all night long. But I finally managed to drag my carcass out of bed, bolt down a quick piece of toast, and head off to school.

Everything was fine until PE. After we'd finished running up and down the court, dribbling the dumb orange ball, aiming it at a hoop only a giant could reach, we all headed into the locker room. It didn't take long for the whole place to fill with steam and explosions of raucous laughter. Jocks lying to each other about the previous night's hook-ups. Slapping each other on the back in approval. Snapping us nerds on the butt with their towels. Typical high school stuff.

Only this day, when I was standing in front of my locker pulling on my tee shirt, I suddenly realized that things had gone quiet. Eerily quiet.

Something was wrong.

I peeked out the crew neck of my shirt and looked around. The place was empty. *Where was everyone?* Somehow, while I was getting dressed, the other guys had vanished. Slipped completely out of the locker room. How had I not noticed?

I was alone.

The door to the locker room opened abruptly, slamming against the wall. I shook my head at what was lumbering into the room. Logan and his cohorts. Great. I rolled my eyes and turned back to my locker. And waited. I was pretty sure I knew what was coming.

I was right.

Logan pushed me into the lockers. With my face smooshed against the cool metal, barely able to breathe, I refused to make a sound, not wanting to give them the satisfaction.

"Listen, douche bag." Logan whipped me around to face him. Boy-O, Mickey, and Liam stood next to and slightly behind him, smirking. Chase was somewhere behind them. I wondered what they were planning. I mean, it was obvious what they were planning. They were going to beat the crap out of me. But why? What had I ever done to Logan? To any of them? I couldn't figure it out.

I contemplated my feet. They hadn't given me time to put on my shoes, so running wasn't an option. Not that I'd ever run from a fight. It's just that what with the whole transformation thing, I needed to keep my temper in check so it didn't happen spontaneously. My dad told me about a similar time when he was in school, and it had ended badly.

I hoped this wouldn't turn out even worse.

My mind raced while my eyes darted around, trying to find some way to get out of this in one piece. But there was nowhere to go. Defeat descended on me, pushing against me, crushing my spirit like ice. There was nothing

I could do. If these guys wanted to trash me, I was going to get majorly trashed.

Logan poked me in the chest. Hard. "I want you to disappear."

I frowned. "What? Why?"

A huge fist flew toward my face and I flinched. At the last second, the fist veered off and smashed into the locker beside my head.

"Because I said so, that's why."

Before I could stop myself, I snorted. "You got to be kidding me."

That was enough to send his fist into my stomach. I fell to my knees, clutching my gut, and struggled to catch my breath. Before I could, Logan grabbed my shirt and lifted me up far enough so that I was standing on my tippy-toes. The crew swarmed angrily behind him.

"No joke, ass hat," he spat. I grabbed his hands and squeezed. The anger was starting to well up inside me, red hot and smoking. I hoped to get a handle on it while I still could.

Just relax, I thought. *You can't let him get to you. Focus.* Loosening my grip, I took some small satisfaction at the relief that flooded Logan's face.

"What is wrong with you?" I asked. "What have I ever done to you, anyway? Why do you hate me so much?"

"Because you're a whiny little bitch," Boy-O said.

When I shot him a look, his eyes got really wide and he took a couple of steps back. "Dafuq?"

The rage was building. Kept building and building until it felt like the top of my head was going to detonate like the atom bomb. My body was turning into liquid fire, burning so badly I was sure my skin would blister.

From the terror splattered across Chase's face I realized that my eyes had flashed red and gold. It was all I could do not to growl. I was seconds away from becoming the wolf.

❑

Shaniqua had trouble concentrating. Mr. Sanderson was wrapping up the day's lesson in safety around the arc welders. She was dying to learn how to use one so she could start creating Meilikki and Wolfsbayne sculptures of her graphic novel characters. But for some strange reason, the last ten minutes or so of class, she just couldn't sit still.

Something was wrong.

But what? An inkling of dread wormed its way into her veins, curdling her blood and sending fissures through her bones that threatened to split her apart.

"Shaniqua Robinson!"

"Huh?" Everyone in class stared at her. Her face, neck and the tops of her ears felt flushed and she knew she was blushing. She hated being caught not paying attention. "I'm sorry, what?"

"Welcome back, Shaniqua," Mr. Sanderson said. The class tittered, all except Watts, who regarded her curiously. "I asked if you could tell me at least three of the nine safety rules that must be implemented when using an arc welder."

"Oh, um…" She shifted uncomfortably on her stool, trying to remember what her teacher said earlier. "Let's see. Um, make sure there's adequate ventilation. Make sure the welder is grounded and installed properly. And…" Racking her brain, she noticed that Watts had written something on her notebook and discretely pushed it toward her. Shaniqua read it, looked up at her friend and grinned. "Keep a fully stocked first-aid kit handy."

"Well done," Mr. Sanderson said.

Thank you, she mouthed to Watts, who shrugged and shook her head slightly.

But Shaniqua still couldn't shake the feeling that *something* was wrong.

☐

Somehow, I managed to regain control. I closed my eyes and sucked in air, blowing it out as slowly as I could.

Logan cocked his head and stared at me. "What the hell are you doing?"

Chase backed into the lockers on the other side of the aisle and pointed an accusing finger at me. "Did you see that?" His voice rose an octave. Maybe more. "Did you see his eyes?"

"What are you talking about, you freak?" Logan looked at him over his shoulder. His grip on me loosened a little more.

"What are you?" Chase screamed. He took a step back. "Your eyes—They turned red." He looked at Boy-O. "His eyes turned red. Didn't you see them?"

Boy-O shrugged.

Logan turned back to me.

"You saw it, right?" Chase turned to Liam, who just shook his head.

"Nope."

"Come on." Chase was practically crying now. Dancing on the balls of his feet. He'd jammed his hands back into the pockets of his Letterman's jacket. "You know you saw them. They were—were—red. Glowing, like."

"Well, lookie here."

We all turned toward the voice. It was Mr. Sanderson.

My bloodlust wilted and died. Relief flooded through me. No matter what happened next, I knew I could handle it.

"So, Logan. Boy-O. Chase. Liam. Mickey." He nodded at each of them. "James. How you doing?"

"I'm good."

"I take it y'all are just saying 's'up to James again, right?" Mr. Sanderson said.

"That's right." Logan let go of my shirt and smoothed out the wrinkles he'd made around the neck.

"My, what a friendly lot you are." Mr. Sanderson crossed his arms and glared at them. "I suggest you try being a little less so from now on. Or next time you'll be making friends in Detention. Last warning, Logan. Now get out of here."

Chase practically knocked Liam over in his mad scramble to leave. Liam and Mickey sauntered after him. Boy-O stayed where he was. Logan leaned into me.

"We're not done here," he whispered.

"Yes, you are." Mr. Sanderson got right up in Logan's face. "If I so much as hear a rumor that you're even *thinking* about hassling James—or anyone else, for that matter—I'll see to it that you never play another football game as long as you're a student here." He leaned in even closer. "You feel me?"

Logan's nostrils flared and he got this look of total and complete determination on his face. If he thought he could intimidate Mr. Sanderson, he was wrong. The Shop teacher was used to hard-asses and bullies. It took forever, but when Logan finally realized it, you could see the resignation on his face. And also the anger. He wasn't used to being spoken to like that. To having someone stand up to him and not back down. To not getting his own way. It made me want to laugh.

"Yeah," he said begrudgingly. "I feel ya."

Mr. Sanderson and I watched as Logan smashed through the locker room door, Boy-O following behind him. Logan didn't seem to care that he nearly ran over Mr. Hansen, who was on the way in.

"Martin." He greeted Mr. Sanderson with a nod.

Mr. Sanderson responded in kind. "John."

"I heard there might be a problem." Mr. Hansen peered over the top of his glasses. "Everything okay here?"

"Fine," I said, without looking up.

"Seems Mr. O'Shaughnessy was up to his usual tactics with James, here. But I nipped it in the bud. Well." He glanced at his watch. "Better get to class, James."

"I will."

"See you later, Martin." Mr. Hansen watched him leave then turned to me as I was pulling my backpack out of my locker. "You okay, James?"

"Yeah."

"So how long's this been going on?"

I shrugged. "Forever." Mr. Hansen arched his eyebrow. I sighed. "I don't know. Third grade, I guess."

"What happened?"

"I have no idea. One day, he just decided he needed to pick on someone."

"And there you were."

"And there I was." I turned back to my locker, took out my kicks, and sat on the bench to put them on. As I shoved my left foot into my shoe, I could feel Mr. Hansen watching me. "What?" I asked, pausing to listen without looking up at him.

"I heard, you know."

I froze. "Heard what?"

"What Chase said. About your eyes."

Trying to appear nonchalant in spite of the volcano that threatened to erupt in my stomach, I slipped on the other shoe and attempted to still my trembling fingers enough to tie the laces. My father's warning about not telling anyone the family secret set off alarm bells in my brain. How much, if anything, did Mr. Hansen already know? Was he one of us? Or was he a hunter, killing every werewolf he encountered?

Even if it was just a dumb kid.

□

"So what's up with you, anyway, Robinson?"

They were headed to Trig. "Huh? What do you mean?"

Watts gestured over her shoulder. "Back there. What was that all about?"

"What do you mean?"

"What do you mean, what do I mean? The space cadet act you pulled back there."

"What?"

Watts stared at her friend and tried to figure out what was going on. She was pretty, but she wasn't stupid and vacuous like the Barbie doll set. Why was she pretending she was?

"Sorry, Watts." Shaniqua grinned sheepishly. "I just—" She pulled Watts over to the side of the hallway, away from the stream of student traffic rushing to class. She glanced over her shoulder, and Watts looked over it, too, puzzled. Shaniqua lowered her voice to just above a whisper. "I have this feeling that something's wrong. With James, you know?"

Watts nodded, even though she had no clue what Shaniqua was talking about.

"I don't know what it is, but all of a sudden, in class, this feeling, this sense of…I don't know…Foreboding? Came over me. And James sort of flashed into my brain.

Like he was in trouble or something. You ever had anything like that happen to you before?"

"Not really." They weren't close enough yet for
Watts to tell her friend *all* her secrets.

"Neither have I. Until today." Shaniqua grabbed
Watts by the jacket and leaned in until she was so close
Watts shifted uncomfortably. "What do you think it
means?"

"I have no idea."

□

I was just an ordinary dude. Oh, sure, there was the
whole werewolf thing, which was pretty extraordinary. I
got that. But other than that, there was nothing special
about me.

But I'd noticed that one of the worst-kept secrets of
all time was that there were those who were born under a
lucky star and those who weren't. Most kids learned this
early, in the schoolyard, if not before. By the age of five,
some kids were simply smarter, faster, stronger than everyone else. And by the time they were six, those lucky
few had already become the cool kids.

Unfortunately, most adults weren't equipped to deal
with this truth. Oh, sure, parents and teachers felt it was
their job to try and convince their kids that everyone was
special, but it never worked. Kids could see for themselves that some kids had it, and some didn't.

I didn't, but Chase Kennedy definitely did.

Girls thought he was hot, like Logan. But he had that
certain something that Logan lacked. For one thing, his
smile was genuine.

He was also smart. Paid attention in class, didn't
cause trouble, or talk back to the teachers, turned in his
homework on time. A straight-A student from Kindergar-

ten, he was headed to Princeton, last I heard.

For all of his gifts and talents, he was remarkably unpretentious and humble. Never acted stuck up or conceited. And talk about cool. That was something else he didn't have to work at. If you looked up the word "cool" in the dictionary, it would have his picture next to it.

He didn't seem to have any enemies because he treated people decently. In spite of his hanging out with Logan, I liked him well enough. You couldn't help but like him.

That was why it was so hard for me to understand why he'd grabbed my throat that day. Sure, he hung out with Logan and the other troglodytes, but he'd always hung back a bit and didn't really participate in their antics. Not fully, anyway.

But then when he started screaming about red eyes, I had to wonder if maybe his luck had run out.

CHAPTER 10

Wednesday, September 23, 2015,
Four Days to Full Moon:

"So."

"So."

"So, are we going to sit here all day, or are we going to talk about what happened in the locker room?" Mr. Hansen asked. He'd dismissed first period early, and asked me to stay after everyone left. Shaniqua gave me a perplexed look on her way out the door, and I'd shrugged. The less she knew at this point, the better.

"What's to tell?" I slouched down in the desk directly in front of the teacher's desk and doodled on the cover of my notebook. "Logan's a narcissistic prick who's made it his mission in life to pick on me and make me miserable since the third grade. The end."

"Are you happy with things the way they are?"

Anger flared, and I did my best to tamp it down to make sure it didn't turn into a raging brush fire. "No, of course not."

"So what are you going to do about it?"

I couldn't tell what he was thinking. "What can I do about it? He's always got his crew with him, and they always do whatever he tells them to do."

"Well." Mr. Hansen got up from behind his desk, walked around, and stood in front of me. Towered over me, actually. I never realized how tall he was until now. His red hair was styled in such a way that it must have added a good three inches to his height. He reminded me of Conan O'Brien. "I think you already know the answer to that." He leaned back against his desk, all casual like, and crossed his arms and ankles. "Don't you?"

Was he saying what I thought he was saying? It reminded me of the time, at the funeral for all the people PJ killed in the woods that night, when Donna Glass pulled me into the crypt and informed me that she knew the killer was a werewolf, and that she was determined to help me kill it.

There weren't very many of us left in Wolf Creek anymore. Most left after PJ was killed, scattered all across the country. I'd heard a few families had even left the country. Those of us who stayed weren't pack animals, except for our own families. It just didn't make sense, in this day and age, to get a bunch of werewolves together in one spot on a regular basis. Too risky. Too many crazy lunatics out there building homemade bombs, who were more than willing to blow people up. I could just imagine what they would do if they found out that werewolves were real.

There was no way I was going to say it first. I'd have to be insane. I might be a werewolf, but crazy I wasn't. So I just sat there and looked at Mr. Hansen, waiting for him to say it.

He stood there and said nothing.

The bell rang. I got up and slung my backpack over my shoulder. "There's the bell. I've got to get to class."

"Sit down, James."

"But—" I glanced at the clock on the wall.

"Just sit down." Mr. Hansen's body language was

the same, and he was still smiling, but there was something in his eyes that scared me. I wasn't sure what it was, or what he was thinking, but I sank slowly back into the chair without even bothering to take off my backpack. "If you're worried about being late to Geometry, I'll give you a note. Don't worry. We'll be done before lunch, so you'll still be able to be with Shaniqua."

"How did you—" I started, but he cut me off.

"Never mind. We have business to attend to." He sat down in the desk next to mine. "And the sooner we get to it, the better for everyone concerned—especially Shaniqua."

☐

Mr. Hansen had my attention. I didn't want anything bad to happen to anyone, but Shaniqua most of all. I sat up and turned toward him.

"What do you mean?"

Was that a smirk I saw on his face? It came and went so fast, I couldn't be sure.

"Okay," he said. "If that's the way you want it, fine." He leaned closer to me. "We have something very special in common." He leaned back. "You know what that is, don't you?"

I wasn't about to tell him my secret, even though I was kind of tired of carrying it around with me. You never knew how someone would react. It would be one thing if he was a werewolf too, but if he was human, he'd either think I was ready for the rubber room, off my meds, or be so scared he could really cause problems.

Unless he was a hunter. Then it would be really, really bad. But mostly I just wanted to tell him and be done with it.

Then his eyes turned red, and I knew.

Mr. Hansen was a werewolf, too.

□

It was hard to wrap my head around a teacher being one of us. According to my dad, we were everywhere, in nearly every profession. Even though there weren't many of us left in town, he told me that we had a lawyer, a grocer, a bookstore owner, even a cop. So I shouldn't have been surprised to find out there was a teacher werewolf, but even still, it was a little shocking. I wondered what kind of uproar parents would make if they ever found out. It would be worse than if Mr. Hansen was gay, that was for sure.

"You can say it, you know," Mr. Hansen said. "It's okay."

"You're a werewolf?"

He nodded. "Sometimes, I wish there was a pack in town, instead of a bunch of lone wolves."

"Yeah," I agreed. "Why is that?"

"Most of us came here because we realized the necessity of living in harmony with humans, and with the pack mentality, that's pretty difficult to do." He shifted uncomfortably. "It's like with Logan and his buddies. Individually, they aren't bad kids. A little troubled, maybe—"

"Pfft," I said.

"Okay, maybe they're not the sharpest tools in the shed, either. But the point is, without someone like Logan urging them on, telling them what to do and how to do it, they'd probably never bully you or anyone else."

I reluctantly agreed. "Yeah, maybe."

"And just like with them being bullies in a group setting but not so much when they're by themselves, it's a lot easier for us to handle the bloodlust and rage on an individual basis."

"Maybe so, but it's still hard to deal with. My dad says it gets easier as time goes on, but I just don't know."

He put his hand on my shoulder. "That's where I come in."

I frowned. "Where?"

"I'm going to help you learn how to control the wolf."

☐

"But *why* do you have to meet during lunch?" Shaniqua asked. "It's not like we get a ton of time together."

"I know," James said. "But that's when he wanted to meet. What could I say?"

"I know." Shaniqua sighed. "I'll miss you."

"Me, too."

"What is it, exactly, he wants you to do again?"

"Some sort of…video something or other." James paused. Shrugged. "For a contest he wants the Media Production students to enter."

She could tell he was lying by the way he wouldn't look her in the eye. But why? What was the big deal?

Her natural instinct was to take him at his word, but after what happened with William, she wasn't sure she could do that. Shaniqua mentally shook her head. No, she didn't think James was like William, and made a conscious decision to believe him. "So what do you get if you win this contest?"

James seemed startled by the question. His eyes went wide, and she giggled and pushed him playfully.

"Never mind. Let's just enjoy lunch today."

"Sounds good to me."

☐

I felt like I'd dodged a bullet after telling Shaniqua about missing lunches with her. But only partially. I could tell she didn't really believe me. And when she'd asked me about the contest? I had no answer because I hadn't thought it through.

Dumbass.

But at least the rest of the lunch went okay. Watts was mysteriously absent, and I wondered briefly if Shaniqua asked her to leave us alone, but it didn't really matter. In some ways, she reminded me of my cousin Beth, who should have annoyed me but somehow didn't, and that pretty much described how I felt about Watts. There was something about her that I felt I could count on to be my friend no matter what, and I wished I'd met her before now. I sure could have used a friend like her after Riff died.

I wasn't sure yet how often Mr. Hansen was going to want to meet, but hopefully it wouldn't be every day. Or maybe it should be. I didn't know. So I figured I'd just enjoy this one and hope for the best.

When the bell rang for afternoon classes, we tossed our trash away and headed for the Science building. I had Chem and Shaniqua had Bio. They were at opposite ends of the building but I wanted to walk Shaniqua to her class.

"Hey, guys!" Watts appeared from out of nowhere.

"Hey, Watts. Where you been?" I asked.

She gave me a sly smile. "Oh, here and there."

I'd swear she winked at Shaniqua. What were they up to?

❑

"I just love doing that to him." Watts and Shaniqua stood outside Shaniqua's Biology class. Watts held the door while a flood of students piled inside. She nodded at everyone as they passed, giggling at the confused expressions on many faces.

"Doing what?" Shaniqua asked.

"Making him think something's up when there's nothing going on. Did you see the look on his face when I winked at you?"

"Yeah, you totally freaked him out." Shaniqua cocked her head. "Where were you, anyway?"

Watts held up her hand. "Hey, high five!" she said to some random dude, who frowned but slowly high-fived her back. She and Shaniqua looked at each other then burst out laughing.

The tardy bell rang, and Watts let go of the door. "Shit! Gotta jet." She took off down the hall to her own class, which luckily was only four doors down.

"Watts!" Shaniqua called after her.

Watts turned but kept backing up toward her own class. "Subway. I went to Subway. Couldn't handle another school burrito." She grabbed the door handle and pulled open the door, then made an exaggerated show of rubbing her stomach. "IBS kills."

Shaniqua snorted. "Yeah." She disappeared into her classroom.

"Besides," Watts mumbled as she entered her class, "a girl's gotta have some secrets."

CHAPTER 11

Today was my first lesson in control. Mr. Hansen promised to meet with me once or twice a week during lunch, and he was going to teach me how to keep from transforming. I could barely sit through my classes, I was so excited. As soon as the bell that ended fourth period rang, I was the first one out the door. Mr. Hansen was waiting for me in the Media room. He shared an office with another teacher, so I figured that was why he wanted to meet there instead of in his office. The classroom was actually the more private of the two places, because all the students were at lunch and most wouldn't be caught dead inside a classroom when they didn't have to be, and in the office, we could be interrupted at any time.

I ran all the way, but when I started down the corridor of the Language Arts building, I hesitated. What if what he showed me didn't work? What if it made things worse, made the wolf stronger, somehow? What would I do then?

The Media room door was open, a beacon that shined into my concern, and I shook my head and chuckled. *Stop being such a diva.* I took a deep breath, let it out slowly, and went inside.

"Hey, Mr. Hansen," I said with a small wave.

"Hey, yourself, James." Two desks were facing each other on the far side of the room with all the others pushed against the walls. Mr. Hansen sat in one of the desks, a crumbled brown paper lunch sack in one corner, eating a ham and cheese sandwich. A bag of pretzels lay next to his Sprite. He gestured to the other desk. "Join me."

I sat down and pulled out my own lunch. Peering into the bag, I wondered what Mom packed for me today. I never knew what I would be eating. One day, a sandwich and a piece of fruit, maybe a couple of cookies or a bag of chips; the next, it would be yogurt, string cheese, carrot sticks, celery and a hard-boiled egg. Left-over pot roast, sushi or cold pizza were also definite possibilities. I hoped it wouldn't be something weird that I'd have to eat in front of Mr. Hansen. Luckily, it was just a PB&J. I peeled back the bread a bit and grinned.

"What's up?" Mr. Hansen asked.

The "J" was apricot, Beth's favorite. After I killed the werewolf, Aunt Judy'd gotten a job on a small weekly newspaper and they'd moved to Colorado. Even though Beth visited us for a month this past summer, I missed her. She could be a real bossy pain in the butt sometimes, but even still, most of the time she was lots of fun.

"Oh, nothing," I told him. "Just thinking about my cousin. She loves apricot jam." I took a big bite and chewed happily.

We talked about nothing in particular while we ate, but as soon as we finished, he tossed his garbage into the trash can and rubbed his hands together. "So, are you ready?" he asked.

I took a last swig of my A & W Root Beer, balled up

my trash, and tossed it and the can into the wastepaper basket beside Mr. Hansen's desk. He glanced into the basket, glared at me, and reached into it, pulling out the can. "Dude. Recycle." The can went into a plastic bag he pulled out of the bottom drawer of the desk. He tossed his Sprite can in after it. "So," he said pointedly. "Are you? Ready?"

"I guess so."

"The first thing you need to learn is to be positive. None of this "I guess so" shit."

I'd never heard a teacher swear before, and it made me smile.

"You think that's funny, do you?"

"Dude, I never heard a teacher say something like that before."

"Well, *dude*, better get used to it. No sense pussy-footing around, is there?"

I'd never heard the word "pussyfooting" either, but I was pretty sure it meant to stop screwing around. I shook my head.

"Good." He got up and moved to the middle of the room. "Let's get to it. Come over here and face me."

When I did, he put his hands on my shoulders and stared into my eyes. It felt like he was peering into my soul. "The eyes are the windows to the soul," my mom liked to say. Maybe she was right.

Maybe they were.

□

"You ever do any meditation, yoga, anything like that?" Mr. Hansen asked.

"Nope. Why?"

"Because breathing and focus are the keys to control-ling the wolf. And we can do that through various techniques common to both." He took a deep breath and held it with his eyes closed.

And held it.

And held it some more.

"Mr. Hansen?" If he held his breath much longer, I was sure he would pass out. "Mr. Hansen, you okay?"

He expelled what seemed like an impossible amount of air in a loud whoosh. "Calm yourself. That's the key. You have to remain calm and centered."

"Centered?"

"Self-aware. Like Hermann Hesse said, 'within you, there is a stillness and a sanctuary to which you can retreat at any time and be yourself.' If you want to control the wolf, you must learn how to find that place whenever you need to."

"Who's Hermann Hesse?"

"Who's…" Mr. Hansen shook his head. "What you kids these days don't know." He clucked his tongue. "No matter. Anyway, are you ready?"

I was, I just didn't know what to expect, and the fluttering in my stomach was temporarily stilled by the bile that flooded into the back of my throat as a sudden, overwhelming feeling of dread overtook me. Shaking it off, I rolled my neck and nodded.

"Let's do this."

"Okay, the first thing you need to do is try and relax both your mind and your body. So I want you to do this: close your eyes and inhale as deeply as you can, hold it to the count of three, and then exhale slowly for three counts. Ready?"

Standing there in the middle of the Media room, surrounded by digital video cameras, DVRs and various sound equipment, I felt dumb and hoped no one walked in on us.

But I did as he asked and, closing my eyes, drew in a deep breath and held it. Let it out slowly. Looked at my teacher.

"Again." He breathed with me, and we did that about ten times. When I opened my eyes, he was staring at me. "How do you feel?"

I pursed my lips and cocked my head. It was amazing how relaxed I felt. "Great."

"Good. This is a good exercise to start with. Then Friday, we'll move on to what we call 'Stop Sign Visualization.'"

"Sounds like I'm supposed to picture a stop sign," I said and chuckled. "How's that supposed to help?"

Mr. Hansen put his hands on his hips and scowled at me. "Look, if you're not going to take this seriously, there's no point in continuing."

"I'm sorry," I said in a rush. The last thing I wanted to do was alienate the one person who wanted to help me. "I didn't mean anything."

He grabbed my shoulder and got right up in my face. "This is serious business, James, and you must take it seriously. Otherwise, you'll never control the wolf. And those who don't control the wolf will be controlled by it. Is that what you want?"

"No, of course not."

"Okay." He rubbed his hands together and looked at the clock. The bell was about to ring and people would be filing past the door and coming into the room for the start of afternoon classes. "That's all for today." He started putting the desks back in order. "You practice your breathing at home, and we'll meet back here tomorrow."

"Thanks, Mr. Hansen." I helped move the desks and had just grabbed my backpack when the door flew open and several kids came in, chattering away.

"You work on that extra homework I gave you,

James, and we'll see if we can bring up your grade." He winked at me, and I grinned back.

"Thanks, Mr. Hansen. I won't let you down."

As I headed out the door, I thought I heard him say, "We'll see."

What did he mean by that?

☐

It was after school and I was having a hard time keeping it from Shaniqua. The truth, I mean. I wanted to be honest with her, tell her who—and what—I was and why I had to meet with Mr. Hansen. But I'd given him my word that I wouldn't tell anyone.

I still didn't get what the big deal was, but a promise is a promise, so I was stuck.

"But why can't we have lunch together tomorrow?" Shaniqua asked. "I really missed you today. And it's Friday, the last day before the weekend." She didn't seem pissed, more like disappointed, but who could tell with girls?

"I told you," I said. I reached across the console of the Le Mans and took hold of her hand. "I can't tell you. Besides, I thought you liked a little mystery in your life." I smiled what I hoped was my most dazzling smile.

It didn't seem to work.

She pulled away and opened the door. "Fine. Whatever."

As she started to get out of the car, I grabbed her wrist. "Hey, don't be mad. I'd tell you if I could. Honest."

She seemed to scrutinize me forever. Like she was sizing me up or something.

"Swear?"

"I swear."

A faint smile played across her lips. "Pinkie swear?" She held up her hand, pinkie finger crooked at me.

I grinned back and grabbed her pinkie with mine. "Pinkie swear."

She tightened her grip on my finger and twisted hard enough to make me wince. But I knew where she was going with this, and that meant everything was all right. "Even if your mother goes to Hell if you're lying?"

"Even if my mother goes to Hell."

She shook my finger roughly and let go. We both giggled. We'd just reenacted a scene from *Stand by Me,* one of her favorite movies.

"Okay, then." She leaned over and kissed me. Her lips were soft and tasted like raspberry. I could have kissed her forever.

There was a loud tapping on the window. "So what do we have here?"

Shaniqua jumped like she'd been zapped with a taser.

"What the—" I started, then stopped, covered my eyes with my hand and shook my head. "Frickin' Riggs," I muttered. What was he doing here?

Riggs had banged on the window with his billy club and was peering in at us. "You weren't planning on doing anything naughty to this little girl, were you, punk?"

"We were just talking."

"Didn't look like that to me. Looked like you were getting ready to take advantage of her."

"No, really," Shaniqua said. "I was just telling him goodbye." She pushed open the door and got out of the car. "I kissed him first."

"Uh huh." Riggs oogled her, and I thought I saw her shudder. What was he up to? "You weren't planning on giving her a ride…home?"

I didn't like the innuendo, but thought it best to let it

slide. "Now you know I'm not allowed to drive her any-where. Not until June, anyway."

"See to it that you don't."

"Well, anyway, I'll see you tomorrow." Shaniqua closed the door and slung her backpack over her shoulder. Gave a small nod to Riggs. "Sherriff."

We both watched her walk away. When she disappeared down the street, Riggs turned back to me. He pointed two fingers at his eyes, then one at me. "I'm watching you, Manarro. Take one step out of line, and I'll see to it that you're locked up and never get to see your little girlfriend again." He tapped his baton on the windshield again, tipped his hat and left.

I wondered what happened in his life to make him such an asshole, or if he'd been born that way.

CHAPTER 12

Friday, September 25, 2015,
Two Days to Full Moon:

Our second session, Mr. Hansen was late, and when I got to the classroom, it was locked. I knocked. Knocked again. I frowned. *I thought we were supposed to meet today. Did I get it wrong?* It was the last chance we'd have to practice together before the next full moon, which was Monday. Even though it wouldn't rise until the evening, I wasn't sure how the lessons would go on full moon days. My heart raced and I had a hard time catching my breath. I wasn't ready to do this on my own yet. Not so soon.

"Mr. Manarro, what are you doing in here?"

"Huh?" I turned to find Mr. Petrellis striding down the hall toward me, like he was jet propelled. He came to a screeching halt in front of me.

"I asked you what you were doing. No students allowed in the buildings during lunchtime."

"I know, I—" What could I say? I couldn't tell him the truth.

"It's okay, Bob," Mr. Hansen said, seemingly coming out of nowhere. "I asked James to meet with me." He patted my shoulder. "I have a special project I need his help on." He turned to Mr. Petrellis. "A video I want him to help me make for our Language Arts class. He's in Media Production, you know." He turned back to me. "Isn't that right, James?"

"Um, yeah. A special project."

Mr. Petrellis narrowed his eyes and studied our faces, like he knew we were lying. But how would he know? Was he a werewolf, too? Finally, he took a step back. "Well, I don't like it, having students in the buildings when they aren't supposed to be. I don't like it at all." He gave us one last angry look and marched down the hall as quickly as he'd come.

We watched him go. Once he disappeared out the door, Mr. Hansen turned to me and grinned. "That was a close one."

"Yeah." *Too close.*

"Don't worry." He unlocked the door. "I'll see to it he doesn't bother us anymore."

We rushed through our lunch and I found myself looking forward to our session. I was actually learning something useful, something I'd be able to use all my life instead of the crap they made you take in school, like Algebra and PE. What a waste of time they were. Unless you were going to be some sort of professional mathlete or Olympic medalist, there was no real point to them. Or most of the other classes they forced on us.

"Did you practice your breathing since last time?" Mr. Hansen asked.

"Yep."

"Let's do about thirty seconds of it."

We closed our eyes and breathed, inhaling, holding and exhaling. At the end of thirty seconds, Mr. Hansen continued.

"Today we'll do some visualization." He glanced at me, and I avoided looking at him. "This exercise is called

Stop Sign Visualization." He cleared his throat. "You're what, sixteen, right?"

"Right."

"So you started transforming about six, seven months ago?"

"About that, yeah."

"Okay, I want you to close your eyes and think about how it feels when the Moon starts to rise. Think about the pull it has, that feeling of great power that comes over you."

To a werewolf, especially a young one like me, it was like nothing we'd ever felt before. The power of the gravitational pull on not only our bodies but our minds was incredible. Your blood boiled. Your skin itched so much it nearly drove you mad until the hair sprouted. After that, your bones crackled and snapped, growing longer and changing shape until you became the wolf. But it was what it did to the psyche that was the worst. It gave you a feeling of dominance over everything and everyone, like you were invincible. Impervious to pain. Superiority over human morals and ethics.

And the scariest part was that you lost your humanity.

"Maintain control, James. You must not let the wolf hold any sway over you."

"How do I do that?"

"As soon as the wolf threatens, you have to shut it down. That's where the stop sign comes in. Recognize each feeling separate and apart from every other feeling. The bloodlust. The rage. The heat. The pain. All of it. And with each one, visualize the biggest, reddest stop sign you can. They may be tiny at first, but will get bigger with practice. And once they are big enough to stop the feeling entirely, you will maintain dominion over the wolf. You will have sovereignty."

"But how do I do it when the Moon isn't full so I know what I'm doing when it is?"

"The way I learned was to name each feeling or sensation. Once I named it, I tried to feel it, even if just a little bit. As soon as I felt something, I would think of the stop sign."

I stood with my eyes closed, and tried to summon—something. Anything—but couldn't. I shook my head. "Nothing's coming."

"Try again. What's the first thing you usually feel?"

"I get hot and my skin starts to itch."

"Good. Feel the heat. Let it flood through your body."

I regarded him with one eye. This just wasn't working.

"You can do it. It takes a little getting used to, that's all. Go on." He gestured with his head. "You can do it."

Five minutes of struggling later, my temperature went up. I could feel the heat rushing through my blood. Bouncing on the balls of my feet, sweat dripping off my forehead and stinging my eyes, I pictured a stop sign. Squeezed my eyes shut. "Stop. Stop. Stop," I whispered.

And still I kept sweating. Then the strangest thing happened. The stop sign in my mind shimmered like a heat wave on the horizon, flickered a few times, and grew. Not only got bigger, but the color intensified as well. Became blood red.

"I did it!" I exclaimed, wiping the sweat out of my eyes as my body temp went down. "I actually did it."

Mr. Hansen beamed. "You certainly did."

I jumped around the room like a nuthouse inmate. "Woo hoo!"

"Don't get too excited, my friend." Mr. Hansen's words brought me back down to earth. "There's still plenty of work ahead."

"I know, I know. But I can't believe I did it!"

"With practice, you'll be able to do it without much thought. But until then, you need to work on these techniques as much as you can. Just don't let anyone know what you're doing. Not even your parents."

That made me pause. "Why not? They don't turn." I shrugged. "They'd get it."

"Just trust me on this. Tell no one what we do here, do you understand?"

"Fine. If that's what you want." I didn't understand it, but I wasn't in a position to argue. Not if I ever wanted to control the wolf.

CHAPTER 13

Saturday, September 26, 2015,
One Day to Full Moon:

Shaniqua sat at the kitchen table, working on her sketches. Last night she'd dreamed about Meilikki and how she became Wolfsbayne, and she thought it would make a perfect beginning for her graphic novel. She wasn't really much for writing, though, and she'd called James to come over so she could talk to him about helping her out.

Before long, he knocked on the door, and she got up to answer it. He stood on the stoop, his hair a little shaggy around the ears, and smiled at her when she opened the door.

"Hi!"

"Hey," he said.

She stepped toward him, placed a hand on his chest, and kissed him lightly. Then she took him by the wrist and pulled him inside, shutting the door behind him. As she guided him through the entryway, her aunt appeared as if out of thin air.

"Oh!" Shaniqua came to an abrupt stop when she saw her, and James bumped into her. "You scared me, Auntie."

James stepped out from behind Shaniqua. "Hey, Mrs. Robinson. How you doing?"

"Hello, James," Aunt Lydie said coolly. "Shaniqua, remember what I told you."

Shaniqua sighed heavily. "I know. I will."

"See to it you don't forget. James, can I get you anything to drink?"

"No, thank you."

"Okay. I'll be in the living room if you need me."

"We won't." Shaniqua turned to James, and when he started to say something, she shook her head slightly and put her index finger to her lips. She led him into the kitchen and they sat down at the table.

Shaniqua leaned around him to see if her aunt had really gone into the living room. The TV was on low, and she heard the pop of the recliner foot rest being raised. Blowing out the breath she hadn't realized she'd been holding, she turned back to James.

He was frowning. "Dafuq was that all about?" he whispered.

"She's just over-protective, is all." She held up one of her drawings for him to see. "What do you think?"

□

Shaniqua had to be one of the most talented artists I'd ever seen. Her drawings were fantastic. "Dude," I said when she showed them to me. "Did you really do all these?"

She nodded. "Do you like them?"

"Like them? They're amazing. You could do this for a living."

She giggled.

I held up the one I liked the best. "What's her name?"

"Wolfsbayne."

That freaked me out. Just what was going on here? "Wolfsbayne? What's her story?"

"During the day, she's known as Meilikki. But at night, she transforms into Wolfsbayne, a strong female werewolf hunter."

I didn't hear anything else she was saying because I felt like I might hurl. Who was this girl, and what was she doing here? Had she been sent here—Riggs flashed into my brain—to somehow trick me?

"So what do you think?" Shaniqua's voice finally broke through.

"Huh?"

"What do you think?"

"About what?"

"About doing a graphic novel together, silly."

Dozens of pairs of eyes stared up at me from Shaniqua's sketches. A comic book? That's what this was all about? A dumb comic book? "Um, sure. I guess."

"Um, sure, you guess? Don't sound so enthusiastic. Geez, never mind. Sorry I asked."

She sat back in her chair so hard I thought she might fall over backward, savagely crossed her arms, and pouted. Actually pouted, sticking her lower lip out so far it was a wonder it didn't scrape the floor. It reminded me of Beth, and I had to laugh.

"What's so damn funny?"

"Sorry, you just remind me of someone when you do that."

"Do what?"

"Pout like that."

"I'm not pouting." She turned her head away, and in profile she looked so much like someone who'd had an allergic reaction to a Botox injection in her lips that I chuckled again.

"You are so damn cute," I told her.

"I am *not* cute." She still wasn't looking at me, but the beginnings of a smile formed at the corners of her mouth. "I'm dark and mysterious."

I leaned across the table and pulled her arms apart, taking hold of her hands. "Sure you are."

She glanced at me and quickly looked away then peeked back and giggled. "I am. Seriously. I do have a few secrets, you know."

"Oh, I know."

There was something about the way she said it that made me wonder if she was hiding something.

This is the time when farmers and Native Americans harvest their crops of corn, pumpkins, squash, beans, and wild rice. The Harvest Moon occurs closest to the autumnal equinox, when night and day are almost the same length. Occasionally comes in October. Moonlight during the Harvest Moon is bright enough for farmers to harvest their crops late into the night.

CHAPTER 14

It was only the first month of school, and Boy-O already hated it. He'd never tell Logan and them, but he usually liked school, at least until the end of the first semester. He'd been looking forward to this year. Senior year was supposed to be a piece of cake, full of parties and good times. His only worry should have been whose panties he was going to get into, and when. Instead, he'd flunked two of his classes last year and was having to repeat them. The homework was already intense. It really pissed him off.

That was why, when his buddy Logan said they were going to pound that tool Manarro just for the hell of it, Boy-O didn't hesitate to agree. He sometimes wondered why he let Logan make decisions like that for him. Would he be a different person without Logan around? Maybe so, but he liked who he was and didn't intend to change, so what good did it do to think about things like that?

A sudden gust of hot wind blasted across his face and made him sneeze. *Great. So now my stupid allergies are going to start up.* How he hated those Santa Ana winds. He shoved his hands in the pockets of his jeans and watched a small dust devil whirl up some dirt and twigs off the sidewalk in front of him. Then the streetlights went on and that's when he noticed that it was nearly dark.

He frowned. *How did it get so late?* A glance at his watch showed that it was after seven-thirty. Coach had called a special Sunday practice, which ran late because he made them all run extra laps, just because he could. Supposedly for some stupid reason or other. Boy-O hadn't been paying attention. He'd been checking out the cheerleader babes. *Fresh meat.* Some of them wore shorts that barely covered their butt cheeks. It drove him bug-shit, just thinking about it. Apparently, most of the team had watched them, too, because that was when Coach slapped them with ten more laps around the field. He'd already been working them super hard because they'd lost the first game of the season. And then to have to run more laps on top of it. Crap, he was so tired. And he still had to study for tomorrow's test on Hamlet. God, how he hated Shakespeare. But at least it wasn't that lame Romeo and Juliet. His ma Netflixed the ancient nineties version with Leonardo DiCaprio and Clare Danes last year, after his father ran off with his assistant, and forced Boy-O to watch it with her.

Boy-O sneezed a second time and then stopped. He frowned again and looked over his shoulder. There was nothing there, of course, and he shook his head. He crossed the street and headed up the dirt path that led to the electrical easement. A kid was murdered here two years ago, his body torn apart. They'd found pieces of him all over the trail, hanging from the trees and stuffed under some scrub brush. There'd been rumors that it was a werewolf, but that was just plain dumb. There were no such things. Someone must have been smoking the funny stuff when they thought that one up.

He'd promised his ma that he wouldn't take the short cut to and from school, especially when he was alone, but he was late for dinner and she would be mad if he got there and it was cold. Besides, she was making meat loaf. His favorite. *I'll bet she made an apple pie, too. Gonna smother that sucker with tons of—*

A twig broke behind him and Boy-O spun around. It was the third time he'd thought he'd heard something. "Logan? Chase? That you guys?"

Only the howl of the wind blasting him in the face answered him. He thought for sure someone was following him, but it must be the wind. As if in agreement, another gust whipped his too-long hair into his face, and he angrily brushed it away.

It was too freaky. He had to be hearing things.

He took his smartphone out of his back pocket and continued his climb up the hill. *Might as well see what Clarissa's up to.* The year's first hook up. As he thumbed his way to a new text message, another dust twister swirled around him, engulfing him, and he tried to swat the dirt out of his face.

That's when he heard it. Growling, low and menacing. He whirled around, searching everywhere, but he couldn't find the source. Too many shadows. The bushes that lined the dirt path seemed to swell and reach out for him. He backed up a step. It suddenly occurred to him that it was dark here. Very dark. The closest street light was on the corner at the bottom of the hill, a good half-football field away.

He backed up another step.

The growling came again, this time louder.

Deeper.

Scarier.

Yes, Boy-O was scared. Something was wrong, seriously wrong. He had to get away, get home to safety. No way was the murderer back. No way. That freak Manarro shot her.

Hadn't he?

But what if he hadn't? What if that whole thing had been some sort of joke? What if the killer was still running around free, and hungry for blood? His blood.

The light from the street seemed so far away. *But how far is it to the top of the hill?*

The dust devil died, and everything went still. Silent.

Then the bushes around him quivered. His throat went dry. Sweat beaded up on his forehead and between his balls, which seemed to have crawled their way back inside his body. He had to get away.

Just then, the wind burst through the leaves on the trees above him and they blew down into his face. He batted them away. Took another step backward. Tripped on a tree root and nearly fell down. The wind screamed like an old woman, the way it usually did during the yearly Santa Ana Devil Winds.

Then he realized he was the one screaming.

Just about the same time, Boy-O saw the huge silver claws slicing through the air. *Oh, crap.* Then blood filled his throat and gushed out the side of his neck.

Wolf Creek's nightmare had returned.

CHAPTER 15

Tuesday, September 29, 2015,
Twenty-Eight Days to Full Moon:

It was always hard to remember what happens after the wolf takes over. My dad said it got easier as you got a better handle on the transformation, and that, with practice, you could control it so well that it no longer even tried to take you over with every full moon.

He told me that, first, I had to learn how to be comfortable with the knowledge of what I was. I was close, but not quite there yet. Hopefully it wouldn't take too much longer.

Not being able to remember what I did after transforming sucked big time.

This time, though, flickers of individual memories, like the pictures I used to make in school that Mom insisted on hanging on the refrigerator, came to me in bits and pieces. I remembered racing through the woods north of town. Of the joy it brought me. Of the ecstasy I felt every time I glimpsed the full moon.

It was almost like I was high.

And I remember loving the feeling.

I tried to make sense of it all. Even though I knew it wasn't a dream, I sometimes wished it was. Especially when I thought about how much I liked it. The control it gave me, basically a powerless teenager, over my own life. The freedom I felt as the wolf. But mostly, I enjoyed the feeling of dominance it gave me.

It made me wish I wasn't learning how to restrain it.

"What are you thinking about, Son?"

"Huh?"

"I've been standing here for the past few minutes calling to you, and you seem to be in a sort of a daze," my dad said. "So I was just wondering what you were thinking about."

I sat up and swung my legs over the side of the bed. "Oh, uh—"

"You're what, sixteen now, right?"

"Uh huh."

"So it's a safe bet that it's one of two things. Either it's that girl—" He shook his head. "No, you don't have that goofy love-struck look on your face. So it's got to be transforming. Am I right?"

I nodded. "You're right."

He sat down next to me. "What do you want to know?"

I told him what happened in the locker room, avoiding his gaze. I'd never squealed on Logan and them, even when it first started in third grade.

"So how do I control it, Dad?" I asked. "Those tips you gave me before, when I first began to transform? They don't really help all that much." I probably should have told him right then and there about Mr. Hansen giving me lessons, but I didn't.

"Well, that's a tough one. It's kind of like teaching someone how to pray."

"Huh?"

"You can tell someone how to go through the motions. Kneel, put your hands together, talk to God, that sort of thing. Teach them all the right words, help them memorize standard prayers. But what you can't do is teach someone how to *believe* in prayer. "Give it to God," people say. But I don't know how to do that. Do you?"

I shook my head.

"It's something that they have to figure out on their own."

"Like us?"

Dad put his hand on top of my shoulder. "Like us."

I sighed. "Well, that sucks."

Dad chuckled. "Sorry, kiddo. But that's why I haven't given you very many pointers. What works for me may not work for you. You just have to find your own way."

"Robbie!" Mom called.

"Coming." Dad turned to me. "You okay?"

"I guess."

"Well, you'd better get off to school. Sorry I couldn't be more help." He went to the door before turning back to me. "But you'll figure it out."

"Sure, Dad."

The question was, when?

◻

Shaniqua's aunt had a morning meeting and dropped her off at school earlier than usual. She sat in the Quad, on the retaining wall that surrounded what passed for a flower garden in the fourth year of a severe, state-wide drought, and went over her Trig notes for the three hundredth time. The first test was today, and she wanted to do well. She had a good feeling about it.

"Let's see." She held her notes to her chest and closed her eyes. "The Law of Cosines, for any triangle ABC is A squared equals B squared plus C squared—"

A pair of hands wrapped around her eyes from behind.

"And a partridge in a pear tree."

She laughed and patted James's hands. "Morning," she said, turning to kiss him.

"Morning," he mumbled into her kiss.

"You're late."

"Sorry," he said, looking sheepish. "Overslept."

She licked her fingers and patted down his cowlick. "I can tell."

First bell rang. They gathered their things and headed to class. Girls stood in small groups, jostling each other and maneuvering into position as they took selfie after selfie. Even with the threat of confiscation, several unauthorized Selfie Sticks were being used. The jocks who weren't trying to stuff an entire season's worth of sports gear into a locker originally built to hold two text books and a sandwich leaned against the various buildings saying intelligent things like "Hey, baby, you're the next contestant in the game of love," and "Hi, there. Check out my big…feet."

She and James were almost to the Language Arts building when two kids rocketed past them, clutching their backpacks to their chests. The tall, gangly one tripped over his untied shoelaces and went down, bouncing right back up as if made of rubber. The other one, a pimply-faced kid in an *Alice in Chains* sweatshirt—*as if*—two sizes too big, zig-zagged from one side of the hall to the other like some sort of crazy human pinball.

"What's their hurry?" Shaniqua said. "Someone light them on fire, or what?"

James laughed. "No, not today, anyway. You know nerds. If they aren't standing outside class before the warning bell rings, they think they're late."

He pulled her around the corner where, amazingly,

the hallway was empty, and pushed her gently against the wall. He placed his hands on either side of her head. She loved the way his hair fell down his forehead and across his eyes as he leaned forward, lifted her chin, and kissed her softly. The kiss built in intensity as his tongue darted quickly into her mouth before retreating again. When they broke apart, she was a little light-headed and breathing heavily.

"Wha—what was that for?"

He grinned, that silly grin that she'd so quickly grown to love. "Just because."

She smiled back at him. God, it was great to feel like a normal person again. She sighed and took his hand. "Guess we better get to class."

She wished they could stay here forever. But real life had a habit of getting in the way.

It wouldn't be long before she'd realize just how much.

☐

Sometime during second period, word came that Thomas Charles Campbell III, known to friends and family as Boy-O, had been murdered. The whole school observed a moment of silence for him. But for someone like me, who was neither friend nor family and, in fact, considered Boy-O a nasty, purple, pus-filled pimple on my butt that I couldn't quite reach but really wanted to pop, there was no way I would willingly stay silent to "honor" him. Instead, I wondered if PJ had somehow come back to life for vengeance and couldn't help chuckling to myself. *Yeah, right. A dead werewolf has come back to life to...what? Kill people who love to give you a hard time?* That didn't make any sense.

But even still, I couldn't completely dismiss the feeling that Wolf Creek was in for another shockwave of terror.

And that I was once again going to be front and center in it.

Until or unless that happened, though, I was going to make sure life went on as usual. And that included spending time with Shaniqua. I checked for her at Break and found her and Watts in the Quad, sharing a bag of baby carrots.

"Fine." Watts reached into the baggie Shaniqua was holding out to her and snagged one. "But I'm telling you, they'd be even sweeter if they were dipped in chocolate."

Shaniqua just shook her head.

I kissed Shaniqua and punched Watts lightly on the shoulder. "Hi, guys."

Watts rolled her eyes at me. "Can you believe it?" she asked and grabbed another carrot. "I mean, he was a creep, but murdered? Wow."

"I know, right?" I said.

"Do you think, maybe, I mean—"

"What?"

"It's not happening again, is it? What happened two years ago?"

"What happened two years ago?" Shaniqua asked.

Watts reached for another carrot. "A serial killer. They called her The Wolf Creek Shredder. She tore her victims apart."

"Eew, gross."

"It was pretty scary, all right." I tried to think of something to say to change the subject. It was hitting a little too close to home. Dad's warnings about learning to control the wolf loped through my brain, and I shook my head to clear it.

"Didn't she get your best friend, James? What was his name?"

"Riff. Yeah."

"Oh, James." Shaniqua put her hand gently on my arm. "I'm so sorry. That must have been awful."

I looked down at her hand then into her beautiful green eyes. They were the exact same color as a green M&M, ringed with gold flecks. The sympathy and kindness I saw there gave me a huge lump in my throat. I had to swallow twice to get it to release its hold on me. "Yeah, it was. I still miss him." I couldn't even play our old Gameboy video games anymore, because after Riff died, I sort of lost my taste for them. They just weren't fun anymore.

I cleared my throat just as the bell ending Break rang. Good thing, because talking about Riff still hurt. I hadn't gotten over feeling like I should never have let him walk home that day of the eclipse, his last day on Earth. No matter how much he wanted to.

"Well, guess we'd better get to class. See you at lunch."

CHAPTER 16

Friday, October 9, 2015,
Eighteen Days to Full Moon:

It was lunch time, and Shaniqua and Watts were at their usual table. James was at one of his mysterious "meetings" with Mr. Hansen that he wouldn't tell her about, no matter how much she pestered him. It was really getting old. *What's the big deal, anyway?*

Out of the corner of her eye, Shaniqua caught sight of Alexis and her entourage and groaned. She closed her drawing pad and shoved it into her backpack. It had many of her drawings of Meilikki and Wolfsbayne, and the last thing she needed was for Alexis to take it and parade it around school. Or worse, destroy them.

"What?" Watts asked. She peeled back her burrito's tortilla, exposing the gray beans and flecks of something orange that could have been cheese, and wrinkled her nose. "God, I hate these stupid hot lunches."

Shaniqua knew better than to make eye contact with the Beautiful People, as Watts called them, preferring to avoid any confrontation, and studied the wrinkles in her lunch sack instead. She gestured with her head, and Watts turned to see.

"Don't look at her!" Shaniqua hissed.

"Oh, you mean Buzzard Breath and the Old Crows?"

Shaniqua couldn't help herself and giggled. Leaning toward Watts, she whispered, "Gawd, they hang off her like dangly earrings, don't they?"

"More like the prickly hairs on my granny's double chin."

Alexis slinked up beside them, and Shaniqua squared herself for whatever Alexis was going to shovel her way, trying to keep in mind that without a clique behind her, a Mean Girl was nothing more than an angry little kid lashing out at the world and should be pitied. Not always the easiest thing to remember.

"Hey, Alexis," Watts quipped. "Your keeper leave the cage door open again?"

"Shut up, maggot." Alexis turned to Shaniqua. "Hey, Shana."

Shana? Really? "It's Shaniqua."

"Whatever." Alexis attempted a smile that never even thought about chatting with her eyes. Shaniqua tilted her head and wondered if she slept with tooth whitening strips on her gleaming white, perfectly spaced teeth every night. Kind of like the head gear Shaniqua had slept with in middle school to correct her own Bugs Bunny teeth. Only not. She stifled a giggle.

"So, I, like, totally had a nightmare last night," Alexis continued. "It was horrible."

"O-M-G, Alexis," Hannah said, right on cue. "What happened?"

"It was the most horrible, terrible, awful thing that you could ever imagine." She paused dramatically.

Shaniqua glanced at Watts, who rolled her eyes.

"I'm in shock," Alexis continued. "I still can't believe it."

"What? What?" her posse chorused.

"I dreamed I was you." Alexis laughed, a malicious

cackle that echoed through the mob behind her.

Watts looked at Shaniqua and shook her head. "You know what's scary? People like her parents being allowed to breed."

"Scumball," Alexis retorted.

"Good one. I'm, like, so impressed," Watts said in a thick, Valley-girl accent. "You think that up all by yourself, or did you have help?" Shaniqua kicked her under the table. "Ow. What?"

Alexis ignored her, glaring instead at Shaniqua. "You like that guy, James, right?" She didn't wait for a response. "Yeah, he's a great kisser."

Shaniqua's heart fluttered and not in a good way. *No way. Was there?*

"That's it," Watts said, getting to her feet and pushing up her sleeves. "Bite me, Alexis."

Alexis curled her fingers, brought her hand up to her face, and studied her nails. "You hear that?" She cocked her head. "It's the sound of no one caring."

She and her legion marched across the Quad in a perfectly choreographed procession. All heads but Shaniqua's and Watts's turned to watch them go.

"Don't pay any attention to her," Watts said, perching on her bench again. "She's superfluous. Pointless. Pathetic, even. And the rest of them are…are…well, they're just plain old smelly duties."

"Duties?"

"Yeah. You heard me." Watts sniffed and wiped under her nose, taking up a boxing stance while a barely suppressed smile played across her lips. "Want to make something of it?"

Shaniqua shook her head and tried to smile. But deep down, she was afraid Alexis was right. No one at school, except Watts, of course, gave a rat's ass about her.

Her own parents certainly didn't. Maybe not even

her aunt and uncle. *Not even James will care about me. Not after he finds out what I did.*

CHAPTER 17

Monday, October 26, 2015,
One Day to Full Moon:

Shaniqua spun the combination lock and thought for the millionth time about trying to have her locker changed, but she doubted it was possible. Every single one seemed to be in use. To the left of her was Alexis, who strangely enough was not clinging to Logan this morning like Saran Wrap. To her right were Hannah and Nicole. Farther down, in the next group of lockers, was Cheyenne and the rest of Alexis's posse. Or whatever they called themselves.

"Remember when that James kid supposedly killed that werewolf?" Alexis called to Hannah and Nicole.

Hannah snorted. "Yeah, right. That little twerp? Doubtful."

"Well." Alexis slammed her locker shut, spun the lock, and strolled past Shaniqua to stand next to Hannah, her back to Shaniqua. She lowered her voice to a stage whisper, but since they were about four feet away, she had to know Shaniqua could hear them. "I heard that he's a werewolf, and he killed that lady because she was going to tell the whole town."

Shaniqua noticed Nicole's eyes going wide and hid

her smile behind her locker door. Some people would believe anything.

"I think he and that new girl—what's her name?"

Shaniqua rolled her eyes at how transparent Alexis was.

"You mean the one who's so boring, she's like a password that's "password"?"

"Yeah, that one."

"Shanney Q? Shanney kwa? Something like that."

"I think they deserve each other. Boring as hell and…"

Shaniqua had had enough. She slammed her locker door and faced them.

They all turned and gaped at her. "Oh, sorry." Alexis sneered. "Didn't see you there."

It was times like these that Shaniqua wished Watts was around. She could always come up with a snappy retort. "It's okay. I have to go change my password to 'ur-a-skanky-ho.'" It was the best she could come up with on such short notice.

Alexis's mouth hung open like the large-mouth bass Shaniqua'd caught the last time she went fishing with her uncle, and even though she figured she'd pay for that later, she headed off to class with a huge grin on her face.

She was still grinning when she met up with Watts at lunch. "Hey, girlfriend," Watts said, greeting her.

"Hey." Shaniqua pulled out her lunch and groaned. Tuna. Again. She turned to her friend. "How are you always able to beat me here?"

"Talent, chick-a-dee."

Shaniqua bit into her sandwich and raised an eyebrow at her. "Chick-a-dee?"

Watts gave her a one-shoulder shrug. "I have an uncle who's Canadian."

"Huh?"

"Never mind. So where's the golden-haired beast?"

James ran his palm across the spikes of her Mohawk. "Miss me?" He straddled the bench next to Shaniqua and kissed her on the cheek.

"Not on your life, freakazoid."

It made Shaniqua so happy that she'd found such good friends. In all the time she'd been in Chicago, she'd never felt as close to anyone as she did these two.

When she'd finished her lunch, Watts tossed everything in the trash. "Gotta run," she told them.

"Where you off to?" Shaniqua asked.

"Girl's gotta have some secrets." She winked at Shaniqua. "Don't do anything I wouldn't do."

"Is there anything you won't do?" James asked.

"Ha, ha, very funny." Watts punched his shoulder and headed off across the Quad.

"I thought she'd never leave." James leaned over and kissed Shaniqua's earlobe, twirling a strand of her hair between his fingers.

Shaniqua leaned away from him. "And why would you want her to?"

He grinned at her. "Why do you think?"

She made a big show out of tapping her chin with her finger while gazing up at the sky. "Because…you're scared of purple hair?"

He smiled and shook his head. "Uhn uh."

"Because…the light from her smile is so brilliant you want to hide from it?"

"Nope." He kissed her neck.

"Because…you love me?"

"Yep."

She pushed him gently away. "You…love…me?"

He brushed his hair off his forehead. "Yeah, I guess I do. Is that okay?"

She grabbed him around the neck and squeezed so

hard, he coughed. "I love you, too!" She pulled back just enough to search his eyes. "I just didn't want to say it first." The last time she'd said it to someone, it ended up being the exact wrong thing to say. "So do you want to take me out tonight to celebrate?"

"Sure. Where did you want to…" He stopped and looked away, but not before she saw…something in his eyes. Fear? Regret? Guilt? She couldn't be sure. When he turned back to her, whatever it was, was gone. "Oh, wait. Tonight? I can't tonight."

"Why not?"

"I…just can't. I promised my mom I'd…watch this thing on Lifetime with her."

Mrs. Manarro loved Lifetime movies, but Shaniqua was pretty sure James was lying. "What thing?"

"I don't know." He stuffed his trash into his lunch sack and stood up. "Gawd, why the inquisition? Don't you believe me?"

She sighed. "Sure. I believe you. If you say so." Not only did she not believe him, she couldn't even look at him. First she'd heard rumors about who—or what—he was, and now he claimed he'd promised his mom that he'd watch a Lifetime movie with her? It wasn't so much his promising his mom he'd do that, it was more the way he'd changed his mind so abruptly about getting together with her.

Something was off.

He was lying.

Plus, there was his weird reaction when she'd suggested they write a graphic novel about a werewolf hunter. What was up with that?

She intended to find out.

No matter what.

□

Shaniqua was still wondering what was up with James as she sat in her room, trying to work on her Trig homework. Finding the hypotenuse of the triangle should have been easy, and normally, it would have been, but today, with her thoughts drifting to James, it was impossible. Finally, she shoved her Trig textbook off the bed and pulled her laptop to her.

And looked up when the next full moon was.

It happened to be just after five, tomorrow morning.

What did that mean, exactly? If he really was a werewolf, like Alexis suggested, would he turn tonight, or did the moon actually have to rise before he changed? Or would it happen earlier, say about ten or eleven? It would be much easier for her to get out of the house early in the morning, but it would also be easier for her aunt to discover she wasn't in bed when the alarm went off at six-thirty. She'd have to be home no later than six, just to be sure, and that would only give her about an hour or so, most of which she'd probably spend searching for James.

"Girl, what are you thinking?" she muttered. "Werewolves aren't real. Alexis and them were just messing with you. Trying to freak you out." Mean Girls were good at that.

But still, something nagged at her. Her uncle would call it feminine intuition. Her aunt would call it Spidey sense. They could call it whatever they wanted, but something was up with James, and she was going to find out what it was.

She tapped her chin with her pencil and started to formulate a plan.

❏

Something was up with Shaniqua. Watts could feel it. She'd been texting Shaniqua for the past two hours, and she had yet to answer. Watts glanced at her watch and couldn't help but smile, just like she did every time she looked at it. It had been her father's and featured Goofy peeking over the edge of the face. She treasured it.

It was only a few minutes after eight. Where could Shaniqua be? She'd told Watts after school that she wasn't going out with James, that she had to finish the monster Trig homework the troll had given them, but it was really easy and Watts finished it in less than an hour. She couldn't believe it would take Shaniqua much longer than that, even though Terwilliger had happily announced that it would take at least four hours.

Showed how much the old fart knew.

If Shaniqua wouldn't text her back, maybe James would. She picked up her cell phone. Couldn't hurt to ask.

~ What's up, dawg?

He hated that expression. She didn't know why, exactly, but she remembered a time when she'd passed him in the hall last year, and one of Logan's lackeys, either Mickey or Liam—she couldn't remember which. They were practically interchangeable—had called him that and not only had his hackles risen but she thought she heard him actually growl.

It had been well after he'd killed that diner lady and the rumors about him being a werewolf started.

Maybe the rumors were true. She didn't know. Didn't even care. He was a nice enough dude. Seemed more like the werewolf from that old movie, *Teen Wolf,* than the ones that ate people.

But why wasn't he texting her back?

Her cell chirped and she grabbed it and swiped it on.

~ Don't call me dawg.

~ Fine U w/ S?

~ Yeah. & we don't want 2 b disturbed.

She tossed her cell onto the bed. Why was he lying to her? What's going on? It didn't make any sense. Since when would their being together mean they didn't want to send a simple text or two? Or even three?

Why were they avoiding her?

Shrugging, Watts picked up her dog-eared copy of Anne Rice's *Queen of the Damned,* her favorite book, and began reading. Although she'd never particularly liked History classes, one of the things she loved about the book was that it was fraught with historical images. The relationship between Armand and Daniel intrigued her, as did how the first vampire came to be.

No wonder everyone—including her family—thought she was a freak. But ask her if she cared.

□

Two hours later, she laid the book down on the bed next to her and picked up her phone. A quick check showed that she hadn't missed a text from James or Shaniqua. What was up with that girl?

~ Where u @? U ok?

As she waited for Shaniqua to text her back, she picked up her book, but kept reading the same sentence over and over so she gave up.

By the time there was a knock on her door a few minutes later, she had worked herself up into what her mom would call "a tizzy." Her stomach fluttered and her throat burned.

Something was wrong. She could feel it. Shaniqua was in trouble.

"Barbie?"

Watts cringed when her mother walked in. She hated her real name, but couldn't get her mother to call her anything else. Probably because Watts was the nickname

Daddy gave her, and Ma hated her ex-husband. Daddy once told her that he hated the name "Barbara" but her mother had gone ballistic when he told her he wanted to name her Frankie, after him, so she'd been stuck with Barbara. Until the day she smiled for the first time, and Daddy decided to call her Watts.

"Barbara, are you listening to me?"

Sighing, Watts sat up and swung her legs over the side of her bed. "Sorry, Ma. What's up?"

She snuck a peek at her cell. Still no text.

"Can you stop at the market on the way home tomorrow? We need a few things."

Even though she didn't get along with her mother, Watts did respect her. She worked hard, never missing a day, even though cleaning other people's houses during the day and performing the same janitorial services around town at night wore her out, so Watts never minded doing chores for her, like marketing or picking up the dry cleaning.

Watts was careful with money so she and her mother had opened up a joint checking account so they could both access the funds and Watts could run the errands her mother couldn't.

Her father was supposed to pay child support to her mother but always made the checks out to Watts. Probably to piss off his ex-wife. Watts shook her head. The games adults played.

So Watts simply deposited the checks into their account and kept her mouth shut about it. Her mother said it was easier for everyone that way, but Watts knew she just didn't want the hassle of confronting him.

"Sure, Ma," she said. She'd pick up some cookies while she was at it and hide them in her room if she had to. "No problem."

"Thanks, hun." She took a step toward Watts, reaching out her hand, but stopped short of touching her. "You seem…worried. Is everything all right?"

For a split second, Watts nearly spilled everything. But at the last second, she thought better of it. Sharing had never been their thing. They didn't really have a thing. "Yeah, I'm fine, Ma."

"You sure?"

"Yep."

"Well, okay, then. I've got to get to work. See you tomorrow?"

"Have a good day—er—night, Ma."

As soon as Ma left, Watts picked up her cell again. Nothing. Might as well get back to Lestat and Akasha. Even though they basically became enemies, she bet *they'd* answer each other's texts.

□

I hated to lie to Watts, but how could I tell her the truth? If I couldn't bring myself to tell Shaniqua my secret, I sure couldn't confide in Watts. Besides, she might turn around and blab to Shaniqua before I had a chance to tell her myself.

Dad poked his head in my door "'Bout that time, kiddo."

"I know." I put my cell into my backpack, the one I used specifically for full moon nights, and slung it over my shoulder. "Just getting ready."

Dad tapped on the door frame. "Okay. Good luck."

"Thanks."

I grabbed my keys off the dresser and headed out, pausing on the front step to peer up at the sky.

"Plenty of time," Dad said. "It rises in the morning, about…" He glanced at his watch. "…five-oh-five. Ish." He grinned at me, and I wondered again if I would ever be as at ease as he was with the whole werewolf thing.

"Ish. Right." I sighed heavily and Dad put his arm around my shoulder.

"You'll be fine. Just let it happen naturally. After a while, you'll figure out for yourself how to keep the wolf at bay."

A pang of regret hit me, and I wished again that I could tell him about Mr. Hansen giving me lessons.

"If you say so."

"Hey." Dad turned me around to face him, peering into my eyes as if searching for something. "It will be okay. I promise."

"Okay, Dad. I believe you. It's just…hard, you know?"

Dad nodded. "I know, James. But you'll get through it." He glanced at his watch again. "You'd better get going now."

"See you in the morning."

"See you. Be careful. Pay attention to your surroundings."

"I will." I climbed into the Le Mans, started it up, and drove off.

□

The plan had been to tell Aunt Lydie that she needed some air and wanted to go for a short walk. What she'd actually be doing was going over to James's house to try and peek in the window and see if he really was watching TV with his mom. It made her feel like a peeper, or worse, a stalker, and she didn't really want to do it, but she didn't see any other option. She wanted to trust James, and she did, but she had to know the truth.

Had to know if she was in danger.

She grabbed her hoodie and wriggled into it.

"Where do you think you're going?" Aunt Lydie asked. When had she become so angry? Seemed like she was always mad about something.

"Nowhere in particular, Auntie," Shaniqua assured her. "Just feel a little claustrophobic tonight, for some reason. Thought I'd take a little walk around the block. Clear my head."

"You're sixteen. Your head is fine."

Shaniqua plucked her purse off the hook in the entryway where she hung it when she was home. "Oh, come on, Aunt Lydie. I won't be long."

Aunt Lydie crossed her arms and scowled at her. "I think you should stay home. It's late."

"Seriously? It's not that late."

"It's after ten thirty, Shaniqua. And a school night."

"But—"

"I said no."

Shaniqua turned to walk away, but the anger and frustration she'd felt ever since being sent here finally boiled over. She turned back to her aunt. "God, it's like I'm an F'n prisoner here. I can't do anything without you breathing down my neck." She could hear herself yelling but was unable to stop. "I made a mistake. I did a stupid, reckless, irresponsible thing. I get that. Believe me, I know how foolish it was. But I'm only human. People make mistakes." By this time, she was so pissed off, tears welled up, threatening to spill. "Why do you always have to remind me how stupid I am?"

Aunt Lydie took a step toward her. "Shaniqua, I—"

"Just leave me alone!" Shaniqua brushed past her aunt and raced out the front door.

What my dad really meant when he told me to be

careful was to be as far away from civilization as I could get before transforming, yes, but also, to keep on the lookout for Riggs. The last thing I needed was to have him catch me out driving past eleven. I wouldn't be the only one screwed if that were to happen. State exception or not, he would jump at the chance to make my life miserable.

So I kept looking around, making sure Riggs wasn't lurking anywhere. The plan was to head to Cailleach Canyon and the adjacent woods by the back roads. But I ended up taking a different route. Shaniqua hadn't bought my lame *Lifetime* excuse, and I was worried that she was angry at me.

That's why I did something I never should have done. I drove by her house.

I couldn't help myself. Didn't know what I expected to find, or see, but it was like I was compelled to do it, a force nearly as strong as the pull of the moon.

As I got close, I slowed way down. Inside, everything was all lit up, and I could see Shaniqua and her aunt through the living room window. They seemed to be in a heated discussion, Shaniqua waving her arms around like she did when she was excited or upset, and I wondered what was going on.

Without thinking, I braked to a complete stop and watched. I wanted to go to her, to comfort her if I could, but the moon was calling to me, and even though it wouldn't fully rise until morning, it wouldn't be long before the wolf would be scratching to come out.

I couldn't risk it. A glance at my phone told me it was nearly eleven. Shaniqua's aunt stood at the window, hands on her hips. Shaniqua was obviously yelling at her. You could tell by the way she was leaning forward, her mouth twisted angrily, and by the purple color of her face.

Wondering what they were fighting about and what had pissed Shaniqua off so much, I was startled when she burst through the front door, slamming it behind her with so much force I could actually see the windows rattle. She marched down the walkway, then stopped suddenly when she saw me.

She cocked her head and frowned. "James?"

Not knowing what to do, I froze for a second.

Shaniqua took a step toward me. "What are you doing here?"

Still frozen, I could feel my lips moving, but no sound came out.

She took another step closer. "James? James, what's wrong?"

Finally, I regained my senses. "Sorry. Gotta go." I stepped on the gas and sped away. When I glanced in the rearview mirror, Shaniqua was standing in the middle of the street, watching me go.

Dad was right. I was going to have to tell her my secret.

Probably sooner rather than later.

□

"Oh, my God," Shaniqua whispered. She'd run out into the middle of the street and followed James until he disappeared. Was it true? Was everything people said really the truth? He'd looked exactly the same, but not. Different, somehow.

His hair was longer, down past his shoulders, and a lot shaggier. But it was his face, his beautiful face, that had changed. His nose seemed longer, his teeth pointier.

She shook her head. It had to be her imagination at work.

Didn't it?

"'Niqui? Honey?" Uncle Roshaun approached her cautiously, concern etching deep lines into his face. "What are you doing out here?"

It took her a minute to realize that she was almost a mile away from home. Had she really followed James that far? Why hadn't he stopped? Better yet, why had he sped away when he realized that she'd seen him?

Because he really was a werewolf. That was the only explanation.

"Shaniqua?"

"Uncle Roshaun?"

"Yeah, baby."

"I—" What could she tell him that would make sense and not make her seem like a total loser? Or worse, delusional?

He put his arm around her. "Sweetie, did you and James have a fight?"

"What?" She pushed him away. "No!"

"Then what are you doing out here at eleven o'clock at night, chasing after him as he drove away from you?"

"I—It's complicated."

Uncle Roshaun scratched his head. "Does that mean it's complex, or is that some new slang term I haven't heard yet?"

Despite herself, she laughed. "No, Uncle. It isn't slang."

"So, you want to talk about it?"

She shook her head and screwed up one side of her mouth. "Not really."

"Well, then I suggest we get on home before your auntie sends out a search party."

She suddenly realized how much her uncle and James were alike. Except for the whole werewolf thing. They both always seemed to know the exact right thing to say to make her feel better.

She looped her arm through Uncle Roshaun's. "Okay, Uncle. And thanks."

He looked at her quizzically. "For what?"

"Just…thanks."

They talked about nothing in particular all the way home.

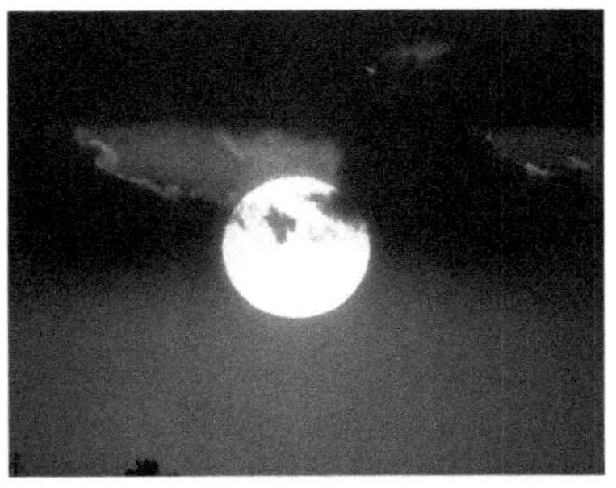

Tuesday, October 27, 2015
Blood Moon
Moon rises at 5:05 a.m.

The fields have been reaped. Hogs were fat after eating all summer, and farmers would slaughter them for meat while Native Americans would hunt for the fattest game to carry them through the winter. With winter knocking at their door, the Hunter's Moon was accorded special honor, serving as an important feast day.

CHAPTER 18

Hannah wiped the sweat off her forehead with the crook of her elbow. Her brother was late. Again. She hated when he was supposed to pick her up from these early morning soccer practices because he never got there on time. Loser always overslept. It was like he made her wait on purpose. He had no life and loved to screw with hers.

"Bye, Hannah," one of her teammates called. "Sure you don't need a ride?"

Hannah shook her head. "No, thanks. My brother will be here soon." And if he wasn't, he was going to hear about it. She still needed to shower and get ready for school. Where was he, *already*?

"Okay. See you at school."

"See you." Hannah waved as her friend's mom drove off.

She dug around in her sports bag and pulled out her smartphone. After dialing her brother's number, she realized that she was the only one left in the sports park. There was a slight breeze that made her shiver, even though it was a warm morning.

"Come on, come on," she said as the phone rang and rang. When it went to voice mail, she swore under her breath. When she heard the beep that indicated the recorded message was done, she walked over to the nearest light post. "Where the hell are you, Michael? I've been waiting for, like, ever. Did you forget you were supposed to pick me up after practice? I've got to get to school, loser. Call me as soon as you get this. You better not have forgotten."

She disconnected the call and accessed a new text message. She had just started typing when an old car pulled into the parking lot and drove over to her.

The window rolled down, and she walked over to it, peering inside.

"Hey, do you need a ride?" the driver asked.

Relief flooded her. "Yeah, my stupid brother must have forgotten to pick me up."

"Get in."

Hannah grabbed her sports bag, trotted around the car to the passenger side, and slid inside. "Thanks. Thanks a lot."

The driver steered the car out of the parking lot and headed east. "You live in Wolf Creek Estates, don't you?"

"Yeah. How did you know?"

"Where else would someone like you live?"

Someone like me?

Warning bells went off in Hannah's head.

□

The werewolf couldn't believe how easy this one was going to be. How fun it would be to watch as it dawned on her that she was about to die. That was the best part about being a werewolf. None of this stupid "control the wolf" bullshit.

Where was the fun in that?

It sniffed slightly, enjoying the girl's scent: poise and

self-confidence mixed with a touch of sweat and disquiet. Soon her scent would be riddled with the acrid odor of fear.

And the werewolf became excited.

☐

"So," Hannah said, scooting as close to the door and as far away from the driver as she could, her hand inching toward the handle. "What kind of car is this?"

The driver looked at her for a brief moment before returning his gaze to the road. "You interested in cars, Hannah?"

She shook her head. "No, not really."

"Didn't think so." The driver drummed his fingers on the steering wheel. "I'm not into them, either. I just like the way this one looks. It's a Le Mans. A 1969."

"Oh," Hannah said. They were coming up to the monument declaring the entrance to Wolf Creek Estates, one of the priciest patches of real estate in town. Hannah was very proud of the fact that her family lived there. She glanced at the driver and wondered where he lived.

She waved her hand towards it. "Turn here."

The driver made no attempt to slow down for a turn.

"Slow down! You're going to miss it."

The car accelerated, and Hannah watched as they shot past her turnoff. "Hey!"

The driver flipped a switch on his door, and the lock on her side clicked. She grabbed the handle and jiggled it, but it didn't move.

She was locked in.

☐

The werewolf, in its human form, licked its lips and flicked the switch that locked the vehicle's doors. Turned to the woman-child and grinned.

□

When she got to school, Shaniqua noticed that the flag was flying at half-mast, but it didn't really register.

Kids roamed about the Quad and were lined up against the lockers. "Did you hear about Hannah Avery?" one of them asked her friend as Shaniqua walked by.

"I know. Can you believe it?" the friend replied.

Shaniqua turned to them. "What happened to her?"

"Dude," the first one exclaimed. "You live under a bridge or something? She was murdered this morning. Her father practically tripped over her body when he left for work."

The other one leaned over to the first one. "Lives under a bridge. Good one!" She laughed, and continued in a stage-whisper. "Think she's a troll?"

"Ripped apart, they say," the other one continued with a sideways glance at her friend. "The cops have no suspects. But we know better, don't we?" She winked at her friend. Actually winked.

Shaniqua couldn't believe it. "What does that mean?"

"Oh, nothing." They both slammed their locker doors shut and walked away, not even bothering to hide their laughter.

Shaniqua stood at her locker while kids streamed past, spreading rumors about Hannah and the murder. Apparently, her body had been found within minutes of her being killed, and the story made the morning news. Everybody was talking about it. Fear seized her and she felt like she was going to drown. The full moon was still up, even though it was now low in the sky. Had James transformed and killed Hannah? She'd been part of the Mean Girl posse that took such delight in trying to humiliate Shaniqua.

Did James kill her for me?

Bile rose in her throat and she struggled not to vomit.

A loud crash to her right startled her. Watts was banging on the locker next to hers to get her attention.

"Hello, earth to Shaniqua," she said. Today she was dressed in a red and green Tartan plaid skirt over ripped purple leggings and a tank top with the shark from the *Jaws* movie poster on it. "What's up, Buttercup? I sent you, like, a bazillion texts last night."

"Sorry," Shaniqua said. "I went to bed early."

Watts narrowed her eyes and studied Shaniqua's face. Shaniqua couldn't hold her gaze. "No, you didn't," Watts demanded. "Why are you lying?"

"I have to tell you something," Shaniqua confessed, looking over her shoulder to make sure no one was close enough to hear them.

"Shaniqua?" Watts asked. "Are you okay?"

"No." She shook her head violently, tears welling up behind her eyes. "It's James. I—I just love him so much."

"Oh, I know. I totally understand," Watts said. "The first time I was in love, I was eight, and I knew my life was never going to be the same."

"No, it's not that. It's not that I've changed, it's something about James that's changed." She could feel herself breaking out in a cold sweat. *Should I just blurt it out? Will James forgive me if I tell his secret? But what if I'm wrong? What if I'm imagining things?*

She didn't know what to do.

Maybe she should do nothing. At least until she could figure it out, maybe talk to James about it. "I got to go." She shoved past Watts as the bell rang. And tried not to notice the expression on her friend's face.

Going to class would be the right thing to do. She knew that. She felt good about the fact that, even though she'd been in that really uncomfortable predicament that got her exiled to this crappy little town in the first place, she'd never lied about it. That wasn't her style. She also never stole anything, except that one time when she was three and tried to take a piece of candy out of the open bin and been caught by her mother and forced to apologize to the store manager. Her feelings of guilt and humiliation, not to mention fear of punishment, made a lasting impression on her.

Another thing she'd never done was cut class. That was practically inconceivable. She was a teacher's wet dream, or had been until...the incident. But desperate times called for desperate measures. And this was definitely a desperate time. Besides, she wasn't ready to face James, and he would be waiting for her outside Language Arts. She'd managed to successfully avoid him so far this morning, texting him that she was running late and would meet him in class, but once she got there, he'd be able to tell something was wrong. Even Watts noticed it right off, and while the girl had great instincts, she wasn't the most observant person in the world.

So instead of going to Language Arts, she turned away from the English building and headed for the library, head down, hoping she could hide out there for a while and figure out what she was going to do.

"Shaniqua?" Mr. Petrellis appeared in front of her. "Shouldn't you be in class?" He smiled at her, obviously not expecting her to be cutting class.

"Um..." Never having cut class before, she wasn't prepared to give an excuse. One suddenly sprang to mind, one she was positive would give her a pass. "Cramps. Ms. Garcia said I could go to the library instead of dressing out."

She prayed he wouldn't remember that she didn't actually have PE until second period.

"Oh." Mr. Petrellis turned green, and it was all she could do not to laugh out loud. "Of course. By all means." He waved her on.

Even though she'd known it would work, she couldn't believe it *worked*. Was it really that easy? To fool people? To be someone she wasn't? She hurried on to the library as quickly as she dared. She didn't want to attract any more attention. The next adult might not be so easily fooled.

When she got to the library, she headed straight to the back, as far away from the librarian and anyone else who might be in there as she could get. Sitting at a table in the Biography section, she dumped her backpack onto the table, folded her arms across it, and used it as a pillow. She thought about how, when you found out that your boyfriend was not even of your species, much less a creature you'd grown up believing was a monster found only in horror movies, other things seemed to pale in comparison. It really didn't matter that you got a C on your last Biology quiz, or that you have to walk everywhere because your parents wouldn't let you get your driver's license until you graduated high school.

The only things that mattered were how James was handling the situation, whether or not he would ever trust her with his secret, and what she was going to do with the knowledge.

At some point, she must have dozed off, because the next thing she knew, someone was shaking her shoulder. She looked up, blinking against the bright overhead lights.

The librarian frowned at her. "Break's over. You need to go to class."

"Oh," Shaniqua said, gathering her things. She'd actually slept through two classes *and* Break? Well, she tossed and turned most of the night, so who could blame her? "Okay. Sorry." She slung her backpack over her shoulder. What had James thought when she hadn't shown up for class and was still gone at Break?

With a heavy sigh, she headed off to Shop. She wondered if Watts would cover for her then chuckled. Of course, she would. What were best friends for?

□

She'd totally forgotten it was their day to weld. Using the dangerous equipment and wearing the cumbersome welder's masks would prevent a lot of chatter. Maybe she could even start a first sculpture of Meilikki. Or maybe Wolfsbayne would suit her better today.

She dumped her things on their table and headed toward the corner of the shop where the heavy equipment was kept. "Hey," she said.

"Hey, Robinson," Watts said. She'd already gotten into her coveralls, and tossed a pair to Shaniqua without looking directly at her. "Where were you at Break? James and I looked all over for you."

"Yeah, me too." Shaniqua wriggled into her coveralls, still distracted by what she'd seen last night.

"Uh huh," Watts said. "See, this is how a conversation works. One person says something or asks a question, in this case me. Then the other person, you, says something back in response. Something that actually relates to what the first person, me, was talking about. Kind of like the second person, you..." She raised her voice loud enough for others to turn and look at them. "Actually. Cared. About. It."

Two boys gawked at them.

"What?" Watts demanded.

They quickly went back to cutting a piece of sheet metal.

"Huh? I'm sorry, what?" Shaniqua watched Watts pull on her welding gloves and thought about how cool she was. The gloves were her own, which no one could mistake for belonging to the school. School gloves were gold leather and about a hundred years old. Watts's were bright blue and lined with Kevlar. She'd also drawn small skeletal cross bones on them. A rattler had been burned into the leather and wrapped around the left wrist while a bracelet of dandelions decorated the right.

Watts was definitely fierce. She unwrapped a piece of Juicy Fruit, folded it into thirds and popped it into her mouth before offering Shaniqua one. "Man, you're really out of it today. What's up? Your aunt all up in your grille again?"

Shaniqua so wanted to tell her friend the truth about what she'd seen and what she suspected. After all, if anyone would be willing to hear her out without judgment or calling her a freak, it would be Watts. But she wanted to see for herself first. *Because if Watts believes it too, then I'm not crazy.* "Did you ever wonder how legends and myths get started?"

Watts stopped chewing. "What? Where'd that come from?"

Shaniqua glanced at the two Shop geeks across from them who'd looked panicked when Watts raised her voice, but they were completely immersed in their own project. So was everyone else. Mr. Sanderson was bent over a table clear across the room, explaining something to a couple of kids. She and Watts might as well be on Pluto, as far as anyone else was concerned. Good.

"I need to tell you something," she said. "But not here."

"Okay." Watts put on her helmet, leaving the eye guard up. "Where?"

"I'll call you tonight, okay?"

"Tonight? You're really going to make me wait till then? Fine. Be that way." Watts struck the arc. "Long as you're not going to tell me you've been sniffing my Doc Martens again."

Shaniqua wrinkled her nose. "Eew, gross. Those nasty things? I'm not crazy, you know."

At least, she hoped not.

◻

Shaniqua wasn't in class this morning, and I hadn't been able to find her at Break, either. Even Watts said she didn't know where she was. It wasn't like Shaniqua to be absent. We hadn't known each other very long, but of that I was sure.

So where was she?

"She must have recognized you last night," I muttered. I was such an idiot.

Shaniqua suddenly appeared next to me as if out of thin air. "So that *was* you."

I'd never been so happy to see anyone in my whole life. I ignored her comment. "There you are." I leaned over and kissed her cheek. "We were worried about you. Where've you been?"

"We?"

"Yeah, we. Me and Watts. I looked for you before school, and Watts and I both looked at Break." I tilted my head and frowned. "So, where were you?"

"That's not important. Let's just say I needed some time by myself. What is important is—" She reached over and tugged something out of my hair. Harder than I thought was really necessary, but whatever. "—this." She tilted her head in an imitation of me and frowned back, but her eyes were twinkling. "Don't you brush your hair in the morning?"

My stomach clenched, and I was afraid I might lose my breakfast. Swallowing with great difficulty, I snatched the twig out of her hand and broke it into tiny bits, letting the pieces fall discreetly to the ground. "Oh, you know me. Bird watcher extraordinaire."

She giggled and patted my shoulder. "Yeah. Right." She hefted her backpack onto the other shoulder. "What do you say we go grab some lunch."

And just like that, everything was okay. I felt like I'd dodged a bullet. I only hoped it wouldn't turn around on me.

And be made out of silver.

□

She'd been talking to Watts now for over an hour and a half, and still hadn't worked up the nerve to tell her what she suspected about James. She'd managed to avoid it for quite a while, but if she didn't say something soon, she wasn't sure what would happen.

"Hey," she said, interrupting whatever it was Watts was prattling on about. She hadn't been listening, so she had no idea. "Do you believe in…monsters?"

"Monsters? You mean like the boogeyman? Frankenstein? That kind of monster?"

"Not exactly. Have you heard anything about there being…something here, in Wolf Creek?"

Watts was silent for a few moments, and Shaniqua was afraid her friend now thought she was nuts. "Watts?"

"We—ell," she started slowly, drawing it out. "There was that thing a couple of years ago. People were murdered, and some thought the killer was a werewolf. Is that what you mean?"

"A werewolf. Yeah. Do you believe in them?"

"I don't know. I've never seen one—"

"That you know of."

"What do mean, that I know of?"

"Well, aren't they human most of the time? Only change during a full moon?"

"So they say."

"So do you believe in them?"

"Do you?"

Shaniqua nodded and covered her mouth with her hand so that if anyone came in right then, they wouldn't hear what she was going to say. She thought about the leaf she'd taken out of James's hair this morning and how he hadn't even realized it was there. "Yes, I do. I do believe in werewolves. And I think I know one."

"Shaniqua, it's after eleven."

She was so startled, she dropped her phone on the floor. Her aunt stood there in the doorway, looking worried. And maybe a little pissed.

"Oh, is it?" Shaniqua faked innocence. "I'm sorry. I didn't know."

"Tell Watts good night."

Shaniqua bent to retrieve her cell. "I gotta go."

"Yeah," Watts said. "So I heard. Later."

"Bye." Shaniqua ended the call and plugged her phone into the charger on her nightstand.

Aunt Lydie stepped inside the room. "You know, I heard what you were talking about."

Shaniqua frowned. "You were eavesdropping on me?"

"Sweetheart." Aunt Lydie sat down on the bed and patted Shaniqua's knee. "I think maybe you need to talk to someone."

"What do you mean? I talk to James and Watts every day."

"No, I mean—" Aunt Lydie hesitated, and Shaniqua felt a weird sense of portent come over her.

"Aunt Lydie?"

"A professional, Shaniqua. Uncle Roshaun and I think you need to talk to a professional. We think you're depressed."

"A professional? You mean a shrink?"

Aunt Lydie held up her hand to stop her. "Honey, I know what depression looks like. And what it feels like. It's no wonder, what with everything you've gone through lately. Everything that happened back home."

"But I'm not depressed. I'm not!"

"You make a good show of it, Shaniqua. You do. You follow the rules. You're pleasant enough to your uncle and me. You do things with your friends. You're doing well in school. But when you're home, you hide here in your room. You used to sit out with your uncle and me and chat. Or you would spend hours drawing your cartoons. But now you think werewolves are roaming the streets, and your only girlfriend looks like a vampire."

"What ever happened to not judging a book by its cover?" Shaniqua argued. *How come I'm the only one who can see how amazing Watts is?* "And I was only kidding about there being werewolves. Just pulling Watts's leg. Really." She took her aunt's hand in hers. That usually went a long way with her. "I'm fine," she said steadily. "Seriously."

Aunt Lydie pulled her hand away. "Tomorrow, I'm going to call a doctor friend of mine. See if I can get you an appointment."

There was no point in arguing, so Shaniqua accepted defeat. She'd just have to convince the shrink that her aunt was overreacting, and that she wasn't depressed.

"Fine. Whatever."

"Good girl." Aunt Lydie patted Shaniqua's knee again and stood up. "Thank you for not fighting me on this."

Shaniqua propelled her body down across the bed, her legs dangling over the side, her hands under her head, and stared at the ceiling. *Like I have a choice.*

Aunt Lydie stroked her forehead. "Well," she said. "Goodnight, then."

"Night," Shaniqua grunted.

Her aunt hovered over her for a few moments before finally leaving her room, closing the door quietly behind her.

"That's just great," Shaniqua muttered. "Now what am I going to do?"

CHAPTER 19

Thursday, October 29, 2015,
Twenty-Seven Days to Full Moon:

What was all that stuff about last night?" Watts asked.

She and Shaniqua were sitting in Trig, waiting for Terwilliger to pass out their tests from last week. Neither girl was especially worried about their grade. Both found the class fairly easy, and more than a little boring. Watts had been right about the troll.

"What do you mean?"

Watts stared at her with something like amazement on her face. "What do you mean, what do I mean? All that stuff about legends and myths. Monsters. Werewolves."

Terwilliger handed out the class's tests individually. He wasn't allowed by school rules to announce individual scores, but that didn't stop him from making snarky comments.

"Well, congratulations, Mr. Evans," he told one student. "Your percentage finally topped your IQ."

"Unfortunately, Miss Cramer," he said to another. "Your age is greater than your score."

Shaniqua pretended to listen for Terwilliger to call

her name in the hopes that Watts would stop her inquisi-tion. It had been a mistake to tell her about her fears and suspicions. Unfortunately, Watts was having none of that. She poked Shaniqua in the side.

"Hey. What's going on? Talk to me."

"Nothing's going on," Shaniqua snapped.

"Why you lying to me again?"

"I'm not lying. Now can we just drop it, please?"

Watts sat back in her seat dramatically, crossed her arms, and shook her head. "Whatever," she mumbled.

Shaniqua earned a smile—if that was what you could call the toothy grin a badger made right before it tore into a ground squirrel—as the teacher handed over her test: ninety-four percent.

When Terwilliger got to Watt's test, on which she'd received a ninety eight, he simply handed it to her with no comment, other than to glare at her. People could be so judgmental about the most insignificant things. Sha-niqua thought it was probably because of Watts's offbeat wardrobe and weirdly colored hair styles. She was a great person, kind, sensitive, smart, and cute. Or she would be if she ever gave that thick black mascara and eyeliner she wore like a shield a rest.

She glanced at Watts, who was studying the floor and obviously ignoring her, and sighed. She'd just have to make it up to her later, once she figured everything out.

If *I can figure it out, that is.*

CHAPTER 20

Monday, November 16, 2015,
Nine Days to Full Moon:

When Shaniqua was a little girl, her father used to take her ice skating. He'd take her tiny hands in his oversized ones then push off, skating backward so she could balance. It wasn't long before he was able to let go and she glided forward on her own. She remembered putting one foot in front of the other, faster and faster, until she felt like she was flying. He taught her to skate backward and to pirouette like a ballerina. He wanted her to be a figure skater, but she felt awkward in those sparkly outfits and preferred the rough and tumble of hockey.

She woke up shivering and realized she'd been dreaming of happier times. She missed her parents. Loneliness settled in around her, squeezing her heart like Chef Anne Burrell squeezed the limes she used to marinate fish for her fish tacos.

Shaniqua stared up at the ceiling as the feeling washed over her. A single tear escaped from the corner of her eye and settled in the hollow next to her collarbone. She laid there for several minutes before finally rolling onto her stomach and reaching for her phone.

"Hey," she said.

"What's wrong?" Watts asked sleepily. "Boogeyman hiding under your bed?"

"No." Shaniqua attempted a tiny chuckle. "Nothing's wrong."

"It's five o'clock in the morning, and I can tell you've been crying. Don't tell me nothing's wrong."

Shaniqua rolled over on her back and sighed. "I had a dream about my dad."

"You did? How come?"

"I don't know. I guess I just miss him. Them. I miss my parents."

"That must suck."

Shaniqua sniffed. "First I get exiled to this crappy little town."

"Hey!"

"Where I meet the amazing and unique Watts."

"Thank you very much."

"And then, my aunt and uncle decide I'm crazy and want to send me to a shrink," she blurted out without meaning to.

"What? Why?"

"Well, um…" A picture of James, snarling at her viciously after turning into a werewolf, flashed into her mind. She just couldn't believe he would ever hurt anyone, werewolf or not.

"Hey, Robinson," Watts said. "Where'd you go?"

Shaniqua blinked several times. "What? Oh, sorry."

"What's up with you these days, anyway? You've been acting like a space cadet for, like, ever." Watts paused. "This have anything to do with that conversation you wouldn't finish? That one about monsters and stuff?"

If she wanted to keep Watts as her friend, Shaniqua was going to have to put on her big-girl panties and quit hiding the biggest thing ever from her. "Tell you what.

Meet me at Cuppa Joe's about seven fifteen. I'll buy you a scone and tell you everything. Promise."

"Make it a donut," Watts replied. Shaniqua could almost hear her grin. "And you got a deal."

"See you then."

Watts just might believe me after all.

◻

Two hours later, at seven-twenty that morning, Shaniqua ordered coffee and a blueberry scone for herself and chocolate milk and a chocolate cream-filled donut for Watts.

They took their breakfast to a small round table in the corner.

"Aren't you afraid all that sugar will give you pimples?" Shaniqua asked her friend.

Watts took a huge bite of her donut, and the filling spilled out all over her chin. She shoveled the cream into her mouth and licked her fingers. "And spoil the gorgeousness that is me?" She waved her hands up and down the side of her face, mimicking a spokesmodel showing off a shiny new product. "Not a chance." She wiped off her chin with a napkin and took another, smaller bite. "Now, spill it, Shaniqua. What's going on?"

Shaniqua looked over her shoulder at some of the other customers. While she couldn't really tell what they were saying, she did catch little snippets of their conversations.

"Did you hear—"

"…happening again?"

She thought she even heard someone say werewolf, but she shook it off as just her imagination. She turned back to Watts. "You won't believe me. No one will."

"Hey," Watts said sharply. "What the hell? Did we

not just establish that I'm your best friend? If you believe it, I'll believe it."

Shaniqua owed it to Watts, she guessed, so she took a deep breath and plunged ahead. "Okay. What I'm going to tell you stays just between us. You can't tell anyone else. Okay?"

"Got it."

Shaniqua picked up her coffee and set it down without taking a sip. "Now, it's not going to make sense. You're going to think I've totally lost it. But I need you to hear me out and not judge me, okay?"

Watts snickered. "Look at me," she said. "Look at my hair." She'd combed it down over one eye, Emo style, and colored it orange. She gave it a good tug. "What I'm dressed in." Today's ensemble included a Gilmore Girls tee shirt, leggings dotted with skulls-and-cross-bones sporting glittery pink bows, and a sparkly purple plastic belt fastened loosely around her hips. She looked over at Shaniqua. "Do I look like I should be judging anyone?"

"Good point. But you're going to want to at first. That's all I'm saying."

Watts nodded. "'Kay."

Shaniqua started at the very beginning, and told Watts about the broken dates, the not answering texts or calls, the adamant refusal to work on a graphic novel about a pack of superhero werewolves. The preoccupation with the full moon. How James killed that woman and the rumors that she'd been a werewolf. Her suspicion that James was one, too.

When she was finished, Watts was quiet for what seemed like forever. She didn't even finish her donut, just sat there with a blank expression on her face.

Shaniqua sipped her coffee and nibbled on her scone until she couldn't stand it any longer. "Watts?"

"Hmm?" Watts wouldn't look at her.

"What do you think?"

Watts shrugged. "That's a lot to take in."

Shaniqua sat back in her seat. "You think I've lost it, don't you."

Watts shook her head. "No."

"So do you believe me?"

"Well," she said slowly. "I believe *you* believe it."

"That's just great." Shaniqua crossed her arms angrily. Tears welled up behind her eyes. Maybe she should forget about everything, go crawl under a rock somewhere. Make friends with the bugs who lived under them.

"Hold on a minute there, spanky. I didn't say I wouldn't still help you."

"You will?"

"I am your best friend, aren't I?"

Shaniqua nodded, the tears changing instantly from those of anger to those of relief.

"In the meantime, let me give you a few tips about the shrink. He'll constantly try to trip you up, so be careful what you say. Stick to the truth as much as possible. Too hard to keep track of lies. But don't go overboard."

Shaniqua sipped at her coffee. "What do you mean?"

"If you feel bad about something, it's okay to tell him, but don't get all wiggy and start crying and stuff."

"Right. No crying."

"And most important. Do not, I repeat, do not, fall for the silent thing."

Shaniqua frowned. "What's that?"

Watts shook her head. "You never heard of that? It's when the adult looks at you but never says anything. It's a trick to get you to say things you don't want to, just to fill up the silence."

"Got it." Shaniqua popped the last of her scone into her mouth and brushed the crumbs off her fingers. "Thanks." She cocked her head and tried to appear casual. "So, how come you know so much about this stuff anyway?"

Watts shrugged. "Been going to various shrinks since, oh, I don't know. I was ten, maybe?" She jammed the rest of her donut in her mouth. "They're all the same. Totally useless."

Studying her friend's face, Shaniqua decided not to question Watts about why she'd been in therapy. Maybe someday, she'd share it with Shaniqua.

Watts downed the last of her chocolate milk, wiped her mouth on the back of her hand, and burped softly. "So there you go. Speaking of which, we'd better get a move on. Don't want to be late, or Señorita Humphries will make me wear her stupid sombrero for the whole class." Watts held her hands above her head as far apart as she could reach. "Dude, thing's about the size of a hundred-pound burrito."

Shaniqua giggled, and they both grabbed their packs and tossed out their trash.

"Seriously," Watts said. "Why you laughing?"

CHAPTER 21

Tuesday, November 17, 2015,
Eight Days to Full Moon:

Shaniqua hated Biology, no question about it. And the teacher, Mr. Romanio, didn't make it any easier. Pale, overweight, with a scraggly soul patch and severe comb-over, he looked nothing like the hipster he thought he was. Plus he so obviously favored the Beautiful People, it was ridiculous.

And today was no exception.

Class started out innocuously enough. She walked in and went directly to her table, not really minding that it was Frog Day. Dissect a frog, that was. There was an amphibian lying on a metal tray on every table, one per pair of lab partners.

Except her table.

"Everyone have a frog?" Mr. Romanio said as soon as the bell rang.

Shaniqua raised her hand. "Mr. Romanio?"

"What is it, Shaniqua?" Yep, she definitely wasn't one of the popular students.

"I don't."

"You don't what?"

"Have a frog."

"Oh. Well." He surveyed the room—for what, she couldn't say. "Ah. We seem to have handed out all the frogs. You and your partner—"

"My partner's not here today." *Remember?* She was getting frustrated. Was this guy being purposely obtuse, or did it come naturally? Up until now, her lab partner had been Harold Gunderson, but he was adamantly opposed to hacking up another living thing—even if it *was* already dead—and his parents had gotten him out of it. Instead of the dissection, he was allowed to write a paper on the use and dangers of antibiotics in chickens.

She thought it was a lousy topic. Everyone knew Harold was a vegan. But that was just the kind of guy Mr. Romanio was.

"Hmm." He glared at Shaniqua like it was her fault. "You can pair up with Alexis."

"Gah! You've *got* to be kidding me," Alexis whined.

Mr. Romanio—the *teacher*—actually looked sheepishly at Alexis. "Sorry, kiddo," he said. "You're the only other one without a partner today. Shaniqua, get your stuff and move over with Alexis."

Shaniqua did as she was told, trying to dodge the daggers Alexis was shooting out of her eyes. She sat down on the stool next to Alexis and glanced down at the poor, dead amphibian. Alexis moved as far away from her as she could and still be in the same zip code. Then she leaned toward Shaniqua. "Touch me," she whispered, "and you will regret this."

"Now, class," Mr. Romanio said, holding up his own frog. Shaniqua wondered why she couldn't have used that one. "I want you to pick up your frog and measure from the tip of the head to the end of the frog's backbone, on the dorsal side, like this."

Shaniqua picked up the ruler. "Do you want to go first?"

Alexis shot her another dirty look. "I'd rather have zits."

Shaniqua touched her cheek, where a new crop of pimples had sprung up overnight, and envied Alexis's perfectly flawless skin. "Okay, then," she said, picking up the frog and stretching its leg.

Mickey loudly dragged his stool over to their lab table, sticking it right in between the two of them, and straddled it with his back to Shaniqua. Apparently, he was now the third lab partner, since Mr. Romanio pretended not to notice. Of course.

"Hey, good-lookin'." He grinned at Alexis. "How's about you and I take in a movie tonight?"

Apparently, Logan was no longer her octopus of choice, and Shaniqua wondered briefly what had happened. Not that she cared, but she hadn't heard anything about them breaking up.

"I'm not in the mood," she said. "I have to go home and take a shower." She looked pointedly at Shaniqua. "With a loofa and some heavy duty exfoliant."

"So is that your secret?" he asked.

Alexis twined a strand of perfect hair around her fingers. "Secret to what?"

"Your royal hotness."

Shaniqua rolled her eyes. *More like royal fungus.*

"Okay," Mr. Romanio said. He'd finished measuring the frog's length. He laid it on the table, clapping his hands loudly and then rubbing them together. "Now comes the fun part." He picked up the frog and a scalpel. "I want you to cut—gently—down the middle of the stomach from here—" He indicated a spot right below the chin, or where the chin would be if frogs had chins. "—to here, just above where the legs are attached."

He walked around the class, demonstrating how to cut open the frog, completely ignoring the fact that there were three people at Shaniqua's table. "Okay, now, what's the first thing you see?"

Shaniqua waited for Alexis to examine the frog. She didn't even pretend to be interested. "You want a turn?" Shaniqua asked her.

Alexis blew a bubble in her gum and popped it.

"Gotcha," Shaniqua said. She picked up a pencil and poked at the frog. Something was off, and she frowned. She jabbed at some goop that looked like jelly, and picked some of it up with the point of the pencil. After inspecting it closely, she realized what it was.

"What should we get to eat tonight?" Mickey asked, not taking no for an answer.

"Eggs," Shaniqua said, wrinkling her nose.

Mickey and Alexis contemplated her with disgust. "Who asked you?" Alexis asked.

"No, I mean the frog. It has eggs."

Alexis flipped her hair. "Who cares?"

"Hey, cool!" Mickey said, surprising Shaniqua by actually seeming interested in something other than himself and Alexis. He poked his finger into the frog's belly and pulled out the eggs. Brought them up to his nose and sniffed. Held them out to Shaniqua.

"Look, Shani…Shana…whatever your name is. They finally found someone who wants to have your babies."

He flicked the frog's eggs at her. They splattered the front of her shirt, startling her so badly that she reeled back and fell off her stool, which clattered to the floor. Somehow, she must have flailed her arms on her way down, because the frog, remaining eggs and all, came crashing down on top of her.

And a whole three eggs splattered onto Alexis's cheek. At first, she simply sat there, her eyes wide, her perfect mouth a perfect "O" of surprise. Then, as it slowly dawned on her what had happened—what Shaniqua had done—a wail started within her. Softly at first, then growing in scale into an earsplitting scream, about the same decibel level as a tornado warning siren.

Of course, everyone turned to see what all the racket was about. When they saw her lying on the ground, and the splatter pattern on Alexis, everyone started to laugh. Shaniqua was positive that even Mr. Romanio was laughing at her.

"What's going on here?" he asked, striding toward them.

"Oops," Mickey said. "My bad."

He didn't even bother to help me up. Asshole.

"All right, everyone," Mr. Romanio said. "That's enough."

The laughter died down, but didn't stop completely. A few snickers lingered.

Shaniqua picked herself up and tried to brush off the egg goo, but only succeeded in smearing them into the fabric of her shirt. The stain reminded her of a Rorschach ink blot. She looked from Mickey, who stood there grinning at her, to Alexis, who was busy texting something, to Mr. Romanio, who shook his head and glared at her like this was all somehow *her* fault.

That was it. She couldn't take it anymore. It was even worse here than back home. At least there, she'd been mostly invisible. Until she wasn't, that is. But here, in Wolf Creek, it seemed impossible to fly under the radar.

She grabbed her backpack and fled.

☐

Shaniqua raced down the hall, not knowing where she was going. All she could think of was finding somewhere to hide from the world. If she could clean herself up, too, that would be a perk. But she just had to be alone for at least a few minutes. It was that or burst into a million pieces right here in the hall.

The closest place to hide turned out to be the faculty restroom. She almost raced past it before she realized where she was. She wasn't in the habit of sneaking into places she wasn't supposed to be in, like a faculty bathroom, and she never had before, but she'd done several things recently that weren't something she'd ever thought about doing, so she supposed one more thing wouldn't matter.

Not only could she clean the gunk off, but faculty bathrooms had locks on the outside doors. She wouldn't have to worry about being hassled by Mean Girls, or having to deal with either gossips who would further spread the word about what happened and what she was doing hiding out in the bathroom, or nerds who would run to the office and rat her out.

It was the perfect place.

She rushed inside and quickly checked under all the stall doors, relieved to find it empty. She locked the door, dumped her backpack on the floor, and stood in front of the mirror, then clasped the edge of the sink. She leaned forward and closed her eyes. *Just count to ten. It'll be all right.* Opening her eyes, she turned on the water and splashed her face. With water dripping off her chin, she examined herself in the mirror.

Liar. It was not going to be all right. By tomorrow, what happened would be all over school, the subject of endless conversations. She grabbed several paper towels, dampened them and started scrubbing her shirt, but it only seemed to make things worse. She grabbed more paper towels and repeated the process. It was no use. The stain was not going to come out. And the smell. Formaldehyde and death. Yuck.

There was no question about it. No way was she going back to class. She'd just tell Mr. Romanio that she'd been so traumatized by what happened that she'd had a panic attack and needed to find a quiet place to calm down. It wasn't far from the truth, and with all the school shootings going on all over the country these days, she was sure that her claims would be taken seriously. They might even offer to provide some sort of counseling.

A loud knock on the door startled her. "Just a sec," she said.

She finished cleaning up, and fished in her backpack for her hairbrush. After rummaging through crumpled bits of paper, the cap to a ball point pen long gone, cookie crumbs, bits of lint and thirty-seven cents, she finally found it and ran it through her hair, but gave up after a few passes. Sighing heavily, she put the brush back in her backpack and headed for the library to hide for the rest of the day.

□

"How's your cartoon class going?" Aunt Lydie asked as soon as Shaniqua slid into the passenger seat of her car. "Still like it?"

"It's called "Animation Projects," and I'm quitting. Drawing. High school. You know, life in general."

Aunt Lydia glanced at her and gripped the steering wheel so tightly her knuckles were white. "Alright," she said with a sigh, clearly expecting the worst. "What happened?"

Shaniqua crossed her arms tightly and stared out the window. "I don't want to talk about it." Her phone chirped, so she pulled it out of her pocket.

~ *Where'd u go?*

Watts. She'd forgotten they were supposed to meet

up after school. After what happened in Biology, Shaniqua didn't feel like talking to anyone, even Watts. She
was sure her bestie would commiserate with her, but she
just couldn't bring herself to talk about this latest catas-
trophe. Besides, there was no way she wouldn't notice
Shaniqua's becoming an even bigger social outcast than
she already was.

She put her cell back in her pocket.

"You going to answer that?" Aunt Lydia asked.

Shaniqua shook her head and went back to studying
the mailboxes as they passed each house. Some were
square black, ugly things. Others were fancy white with
filigreed edges. One was painted like a fire engine and
appeared homemade. They didn't have mailboxes back in
Chicago, at least not in her neighborhood, which was all
apartments. Unless you counted the wall of locked boxes
in the lobby where the mail was deposited.

"Well," her aunt commented, "whatever happened,
it's nothing a nice cheeseburger and some chili-cheese
fries can't fix. How about we go to PJs for dinner? I can
call Uncle Roshaun to meet us."

Even though both her aunt and her uncle had full-
time jobs, they couldn't afford to go out to eat except on
special occasions, so Shaniqua knew what a big deal it
was for particularly her aunt to offer. She was touched,
she really was.

"Thanks, Auntie." She pasted on a weak smile. "I
appreciate it. I do. But I just want to go home."

Her aunt scrutinized her for a long moment then
turned her attention back to the road. "Shaniqua, are you
sure you're okay?"

"I'm fine, Aunt Lydie. I just have…a headache. And
a ton of homework."

"Uh huh. Well, you know you can talk to me about
anything, don't you?" Aunt Lydie paused and looked

over at Shaniqua. "Even your werewolf…thing."

"I know. Thanks." *Werewolf thing? Really? They must think I'm totally mental.*

She managed to successfully avoid conversation for the rest of the ride home. They'd hardly pulled into the driveway when she bolted into the house, barely making it all the way down the hall to her room before bursting into tears. She threw herself onto her bed and buried her face in her pillow.

In the middle of her meltdown, her phone blasted *Animals* by Maroon 5, and she couldn't help but smile through her tears. James. Even though she didn't want to talk to anyone, James wasn't just anyone.

She picked it up and accepted the call. "Hi," she said as brightly as she was able.

"You okay?"

Warmth flooded through her, from her belly to her fingertips and toes. It amazed her how well he was able to read her, even over the phone. "Sorry," she said, sniffling. "I had a really rotten afternoon."

"So I heard," James said.

Shaniqua sat up. "What did you hear?"

"That a certain frog in a certain Biology lab gave a certain Beautiful Person a lap dance." James snickered. "God, I wish I could have seen it. I'll bet it was great!"

Shaniqua groaned. "Great? Do you realize what I've done? Tomorrow, when I show up at school, everybody's going to hate me. Those who don't already, that is."

"So what? I won't hate you. Watts won't hate you. None of the geeks and nerds will hate you. Or anyone else she's ever been cruel to." He chuckled. "I'll bet even most of Alexis's friends secretly cheered when they heard."

She wiped her eyes on her sleeve. "You think so?"

"Sure."

"You think Nicole and Destiny and them actually cheered when they heard?"

"I heard Logan even laughed when he heard. That's what I heard, anyway."

While she realized that was probably a lie, she pictured Logan, with his perfect hair, charismatic magnetism, and insanely white teeth guffawing it up at Alexis's expense. God, what a sight that would have been. Almost made her own humiliation worth it.

Almost.

"Shaniqua, who are you talking to? I thought you didn't want to talk to anyone." Her aunt stood in the doorway with a plate in one hand and a bowl in the other.

Shaniqua jumped off the bed and shoved her phone into her pocket. "I'm not."

"I brought you some comfort food." Aunt Lydie raised the plate a little bit. "Grilled cheese and some tomato soup. I remembered how it used to be your favorite meal when you were a little girl." She handed Shaniqua the food. "I know all about cell phones, you know. They have speaker-phone capabilities, don't they." It wasn't a question.

"I'm sorry, Auntie," Shaniqua said. She put the food down on her desk and pulled her phone out of her pocket, flipping it to Speaker mode. "I'm talking to James. I wasn't sure you'd approve."

Aunt Lydie scowled at her. "Hello, James."

"Hi, Mrs. Robinson."

Aunt Lydie shook her head. "I like James. You know that," she mouthed silently.

"Sorry," Shaniqua mouthed back.

"Well, don't let your food get cold. Bye, James."

"Bye, Mrs. Robinson."

When she left, Shaniqua closed the door and flounced back down on the bed. "That's not good."

"Why? What do you mean?"

"Don't get me wrong." She threw her arm across her eyes. "My aunt is a great person, and I love her. But she gets her feelings hurt easily and then tends to pout for days."

"Maybe I should come over there. Help you eat your grilled cheese and all."

"All?"

"Well, we could always find something else to do, you know."

A shiver ran down her spine. Just the thought of being near him made the skin on her arms break out in goose bumps. The thought of him kissing her again made her lips tingle, and she rubbed them gently with her fingers. She may never get used to being his girlfriend. She kind of hoped she didn't, because the feelings he aroused in her were new and wonderful, and she wanted them to last forever.

"After all," he continued. "We make a pretty nice couple. What with me being so rakishly handsome and all."

Shaniqua snorted, glad she hadn't taken a bite out of her sandwich yet, since it would have been launched across the room. "Rakishly handsome?"

"You don't agree? I'm hurt. I'm really and truly hurt. Now I'm gonna go pout."

Shaniqua grinned. "You're such a dork."

"Isn't that why you love me?"

"Shut up and tell me about Alexis again."

Maybe things weren't so bad after all.

CHAPTER 22

Wednesday, November 18, 2015,
Seven Days to Full Moon:

Two years ago, today, my best friend was ripped to shreds by a werewolf. The cover story was that he was a victim of the Wolf Creek Shredder, a crazed serial killer that had been stalking the town. Riff was a cool dude, and I missed him like crazy. I still thought about him all the time. About all the things we were supposed to do together. Get our driver's licenses. Go to Prom. Start our first job together.

But none of that would ever happen now.

I'd tried to make friends, but no one ever measured up to Riff. No one knew me like he did, accepted me and all my weirdness, quite like that butt munch. Or maybe I just never gave anyone else a chance. I don't know.

At least, not until I met Shaniqua. She didn't seem to care that I was a nerd. She was a bit of one herself, and while not as out there as Watts, she wasn't like everybody else.

But even so, she wasn't Riff. A dude needs another dude in his life so he can be completely himself, let him call them a butt munch without getting all offended, or talk about cute chicks in general or even a specific one without asking if the dude thinks the chick is cuter than he is, like girls sometimes do.

All the things best buds were for.

I was thinking about all this as I locked the Le Mans and headed in to school. It'd been all I could do to crawl out of bed and get ready this morning, and if I didn't get a move on, I was going to be late. Last year, Mom let me stay home and veg, but this year she insisted that I get over it and get to school.

How was a dude supposed to get over the murder of his best friend?

"Hey, James, wait up, will you?" Shaniqua hurried up to me, panting slightly. If I hadn't been so distracted thinking about Riff, it would have turned me on.

"Oh, hey." I kept walking.

"Oh, hey?" She tugged on my arm to get me to stop. "Is that all you can say is 'oh, hey?' How 'bout a kiss?"

I stopped and shrugged. "Sorry." I kissed her briefly and jammed my hands in my pockets.

She cocked her head and narrowed her eyes. "What's wrong?"

"Nothing's wrong. We going to stand here squawking all day, or are we going to class?" I knew I was being snarky, but I couldn't seem to help myself, not even when I saw the hurt flash across her face.

I turned and headed on to class. I guess Shaniqua must have stood there for a few minutes, probably trying to figure out why I was being such an ass, because the tardy bell was ringing as she hurried through the classroom door and sat down heavily at her desk.

□

The whole Biology fiasco yesterday wasn't the worst thing that ever happened to Shaniqua—certainly not as bad as what happened back home—but it was still bad. In the age of cell phones and texting, the best she could hope for as she arrived at school the next morning was that word hadn't got around yet. But those hopes were dashed the minute she set foot on campus. It started with some of the Beautiful People pointing and whispering as she walked, head down and arms wrapped around her backpack as though it were a shield she could use to protect her in battle, through the Quad and around the Science Building to her locker.

It continued when the nerds, geeks, and the also-rans saw her and made comments like "way to go, girlfriend" and "nice one." There were more high fives and thumbs ups than she could count.

Maybe James was right. Maybe what happened really wasn't a big deal.

But she was realistic enough to know that it was a big deal. It was a big fat hairy deal to the Mean Girls. The only questions were, when would the retaliation come, and how bad would it be? She worried about it all day. And it didn't help that James was being so weird. Was he getting ready to break up with her?

When they met up at lunch, Watts took one look at her and shook her head. "You shouldn't have let it bother you, you know."

Shaniqua dropped her backpack on the table and sat down next to her. "What?"

"The frog thing." She took a bite of her sandwich and grimaced. She spat her mouthful into the baggie and wiped off her tongue with a napkin. "Liverwurst. Gross."

Shaniqua couldn't help but giggle. "It was pretty funny, the look on Alexis's face."

"Man, I wish I could have seen it. Must of been something."

"It was. It totally was." But then she started thinking

about James, and her smile vanished as quickly as it had appeared.

Watts stopped digging through her lunch sack and frowned. "So what's the prob, Bob?"

"It's James."

"Oh." She resumed her search, pulling out a bag of broken chips. "Yes!" She popped several into her mouth. "So, the werewolf thing again."

Shaniqua shook her head. "No, not that. He's acting really weird today. I—I think he's going to break up with me."

Watts scowled. "No way." She shook her head. "Not possible."

"Yes, way. When I saw him this morning, he barely spoke to me." She rubbed her eyes hard enough to see spots.

"He'd never—Wait, what's today?"

"It's Wednesday. What's that got to do with anything?"

"No, I mean the date."

"The date? It's the eighteenth. Why?"

"Well, there you go then." Watts munched on another mouthful of chips.

"There I go where?"

"The eighteenth. I think that's when his friend…that Riff guy…I think his name was. That's when he was supposedly eaten. By the werewolf."

Shaniqua nearly choked on her food. "By the what?"

"Serial killer. What did they call her?" Watts snapped her fingers. "Yeah, the Shredder. That's it. The Wolf Creek Shredder."

"See? You do believe in—Wait, what? His friend was killed—by a *werewolf*?"

"Well, that was the rumor, anyway."

"That's awful. No wonder he didn't want to talk. I wouldn't either."

They sat there for a few minutes, eating their lunch. Shaniqua was thinking about James and what he must have gone through when Watts turned to her.

"So what type of shindig do y'all have for Thanksgiving?"

Shaniqua stared at her. "Shindig? Y'all?"

Watts grinned. "Yeah. Shindig. As in party. A time to whoop it up. Eat lots of food. And pie. There must be pie."

"Pumpkin or apple?"

"Girl, please. Those are for amateurs. I make the most amazing Harvest Pie known to man. Pumpkin, apples, cranberries, pecans, cherries all mixed together in a buttery crust that flakes like you've never seen. Nom, nom, nom. My favorite part of Thanksgiving."

"Wow, that does sound amazing." Especially the part about Watts baking. No matter how hard she tried, Shaniqua couldn't picture Watts wearing an apron and covered in flour.

"Maybe, if you're really nice to me, I might save you a piece. Maybe."

Thanks to Watts, by the time the bell rang, Shaniqua felt a little better. Even still, she hid in the library again. No way could she face going to Biology. She'd just have to make up some excuse, like she had terminal humiliation syndrome or something. There was a table in the back corner, and she sat there with her Trig homework in front of her. For all the good that did. Concentration was impossible, so she just waited for the bell to ring so she could go to Animation Projects, her last class of the day. With any luck, she'd be able to lose herself in her favorite class. After Shop, that is.

But as much as she liked Ms. Van der Haven and,

even though she was really interested in animation—she wanted to write and illustrate a graphic novel, after all—she barely made it through the longest fifty-one minutes of her life, glancing at the clock on the wall every few minutes. Her mother's voice came to her: '*A watched pot never boils.*' But she couldn't help it. She so wanted this day to end.

She should have known it would only get worse.

▯

Really, it was her own fault her day got worse. But she couldn't help it. Shaniqua needed to talk to her guardians. Her secret past was burning a hole in her soul, and now that she understood why James had been acting so weird, between that and what she suspected—no, what she *knew*—about him, she didn't know how much longer she could take it. She was pretty sure they wouldn't agree, and would probably insist she keep quiet. That was impossible, but she felt she should at least talk to them first. Let them know what she was thinking. After all, keeping her feelings to herself was what got her into trouble in the first place.

She waited until they finished dinner. Her uncle was washing the dishes while Shaniqua dried and handed them over to Aunt Lydie, who put them away. It was kind of nice how they seemed to enjoy doing everything together. Her parents hardly even spoke to each other anymore, and things had only gotten worse after what happened.

"Aunt Lydie, Uncle Roshaun?"

"What's up, baby?" Aunt Lydie finished drying the last fork and stuck it in the drawer.

Shaniqua glanced from her aunt to her uncle and back. Aunt Lydie immediately came to her. She seemed to have a sixth sense about these things. "Are you okay?"

"Not really," Shaniqua answered. "Can I talk to you guys?"

"Of course," Uncle Roshaun said. "Let's go into the living room where we can be comfortable."

"Do you mind if we just sit in here?" Somehow, she felt safer with a table between them. Not that they would ever hurt her, not in a million years. They certainly wouldn't slap her across the face and call her nasty names like slut and whore, like her mother had. And she didn't think they would give her the silent treatment like her father. Four months without a word. It was insane.

But still, having something between them gave her a sense of security.

They all sat down at the table.

Her aunt and uncle looked at her expectantly.

And waited.

Waited some more.

Uncle Roshaun cleared his throat. Aunt Lydie raised an eyebrow and watched her questioningly.

"We going to sit here all night, or what?" her uncle asked. "Because Project Runway is on pretty soon, and I'd rather watch that than sit here and stare at each other all night. That Tim Gunn is *hot*."

This made Shaniqua smile and shake her head. Her uncle hated that show. Said it was nothing but a bunch of angry divas running around screaming and crying all the time and stabbing each other in the back with a pair of rhinestone-studded scissors. Not to mention it was on on Thursdays, and this was Wednesday. And it wasn't even the right season. Or so she thought. She never watched the show either. She took a deep breath and let it out slowly. "Okay, here's the thing. The thing is…"

Her aunt and uncle exchanged glances. Her uncle shrugged. "What's the thing?" he asked.

"The thing is…"

She wasn't sure she could say it. What would they think of her? It was one thing for the kids at her old school to pass judgment and say mean things to and about her, and she'd gotten over her parents' reactions, more or less, but if she lost the love of her aunt and uncle, what would happen then?

Where would she go?

"Honey," Aunt Lydie said gently. "Just spit it out. Whatever it is can't be that bad." She turned to her husband. "Can it, Roshaun?"

"Nope. Spill it, girl."

"I know. You're right. The thing is, I want to tell James." She suddenly found a crumb on the tablecloth extremely interesting.

"Tell him what?" Uncle Roshaun asked.

"Tell him about…before."

Aunt Lydie shook her head vehemently. "No. No way. It's in the past. Let's leave it there."

"But—"

"No!" Aunt Lydie pushed her chair back from the table so hard it banged against the wall. "Absolutely not. I forbid it." She stormed out of the room.

Shaniqua watched her go and struggled to keep the tears from falling. She'd known her aunt wouldn't approve, but she'd thought she'd at least listen to her before getting mad.

"Well, that went well." Uncle Roshaun smiled. "Don't look so shocked," he told her. "I was young once myself, you know."

"I know." She smiled, a happy one this time. "I can't picture you as a little boy. Or even a teenager."

"I'll have you know, I was quite the pip."

"Pip? What's a pip?"

"Pip. You know, like Gladys Knight and the—oh,

never mind." He sat back and slung an arm over the back of Aunt Lydie's empty chair. "Let's talk about you."

"O…kay."

"So, you want to tell James what happened."

She nodded. "Yeah," she mumbled.

"Why?"

"Why?"

"It's an easy question, 'Niqui."

"I know, I just…" She shrugged. Tapped her fingers on the table. Sniffed and wiped her nose on the back of her hand.

"You're in love with him, aren't you?"

"Yeah. Yeah, I guess I am."

Uncle Roshaun got up and walked over to the fridge. "This sounds like a two-scoop chat." He pulled out the carton of Rocky Road. "You want to grab us some bowls?"

"Sure." Shaniqua handed her uncle the bowls and got out the spoons while he scooped up the ice cream. She didn't feel like something sweet right now, but it gave her time to go over what she wanted to say.

And what she had to keep hidden.

❑

Shaniqua pushed her ice cream around and around the bowl. Her uncle had practically finished his. He raised his eyebrows at her, but didn't say anything. When he was done, he picked up his bowl.

"Uhn?" He gestured at her with it. Then stuck his face into it and started licking. When he came up for air, his nose and chin were covered in ice cream. A tiny piece of marshmallow clung to his eyebrow.

Shaniqua giggled.

"Uhn?" he repeated, and stuck his head in his bowl

again.

"Okay, okay." Shaniqua grinned and handed him a napkin. "I get it. It's an easy question. Just not so easy to answer."

Uncle Roshaun wiped off his face. "Let me ask you this. How did you feel when you realized what happened with…what was his name?"

"William," she mumbled.

"William. So how did you feel?"

"Awful. Hurt. Betrayed."

"Are you willing to risk that pain again?"

"See, that's the thing. I don't think James would ever do something like that."

"But didn't you think that about William?"

Shaniqua lowered her head. Before she could stop herself, she reverted back to her childhood habit of chewing on her thumbnail.

Uncle Roshaun reached across the table and gently lifted her chin so she couldn't help but see him. "I'm not trying to make you feel worse, 'Niqui."

"I know."

"I'm just trying to get you to see that you can't let your heart rule over common sense."

He didn't understand her. Or James. Or their relationship. And she didn't know how to make him.

"But if you really think James will be okay with it, then I guess we can't stop you."

"What about Aunt Lydie? She'll hate me."

"Don't worry about your Aunt Lydie," Uncle Roshaun told her. "I'll take care of her. Just promise me one thing."

"What?"

"Promise me you'll think on it some more. Think about how it will inevitably change your relationship. You know that it can't help but change things. James will no doubt look at you differently."

She sighed. "I know."

"You also need to think about what happens if he can't handle it. If he leaves you. Or worse, if he tells everyone about it."

"James would never do that."

"I know you think that now. But humor me for a second. If people here find out, what will you do then? Will you be able to handle it? I mean, that's the whole reason you came here, isn't it?"

Well, that and the fact that my parents said even worse things about me than anyone at school.

"You know you're welcome to stay here as long as you want to. No matter what." He patted her arm. "You know that, don't you?"

Shaniqua nodded.

Uncle Roshaun sat back. "So just think about it, really think about it, before you tell him, okay?"

"Okay, Uncle Roshaun. I'll think about it some more."

But she'd already made up her mind. She was going to tell James her secret. And hope that he would tell her his.

CHAPTER 23

Friday, November 20, 2015,
Five Days to Full Moon:

She'd pretty much decided she would tell James her secret, and probably Watts, too. But every time she tried, she chickened out. Kept telling herself that she was waiting for the right time. But really, there was something she needed to check on before she could do that.

She was thinking about how best to figure out if James really was a werewolf when the bell rang. Grabbing her things, she scurried off-campus, hoping to miss both her friends so she could have one more day to think about it.

To her surprise, she found her uncle waiting for her in the parent pick-up line.

She leaned into the open passenger window. "Hi, Uncle Roshaun. What are you doing here?"

"Just thought I'd give you a ride."

Frowning, she climbed into the car, strapped in and smiled weakly at her uncle. "Thanks." She couldn't help but wonder what he was really doing here. He would have had to take off work early. Something was up.

"So how was your day?" He glanced in his side view

mirror and pulled away from the curb, heading out into traffic.

"Fine."

"You need to work on your poker face if you're going to lie, Shaniqua."

"What do you mean?" she asked. "Did you hear something?"

"No. But I can tell just by looking at you that something's wrong."

She sighed and shook her head. "Just another day in paradise, Uncle Roshaun."

He glanced at her but didn't say anything. They drove in silence for several minutes before he pulled over and parked. "Shaniqua." He shifted in his seat to look at her.

"What?"

"Honey, see, this is why your auntie and I want you to talk to someone."

"God. I told Aunt Lydia that I'm not depressed. Why don't you guys believe me?"

"It's not that we don't believe you. It's just…"

"Just what?"

Uncle Roshaun shifted uncomfortably. "Let's see what Dr. Sizemore says, okay?"

"Fine." She crossed her arms and counted the trees that lined the street.

Uncle Roshaun rubbed the top of her shoulder. "Just humor me, okay? If he doesn't think you're depressed, you don't have to keep going. Deal?"

When she didn't respond, Uncle Roshaun sighed and started up the car. "We should be there in about ten minutes. Your appointment is for three thirty."

"What, now? You didn't say it was today."

"There's no shame in seeing a psychiatrist, Shaniqua."

Oh yeah? Try telling that to the kids at school. What if they find out? I'll be labeled a psycho on top of everything else. "Easy for you to say. You're not the one being forced to go."

"He's only going to chew the fat with you for a little bit. Talk about what happened back in Chicago. See if that's what's making you…make up these stories about werewolves."

"I'm not sad. I told you that. And I'm not making up stories, either."

It was all too much. First, the thing with Alexis in Bio, then worrying if Watts was going to stop being her friend. And if James was a monster. Then him acting all weird, like he was over her. It was all she could do not to cry. She was so pissed she wasn't sure she could hold back the tears. But if she didn't, they'd take it as more proof of her supposed depression. Sure, she was sad about what happened back home. Who wouldn't be? But there were things going on now that she needed to figure out. And it had nothing to do with being sad. Besides, who liked being told what you were supposed to be feeling—and why?

"We just want to make sure you're okay. That's all. That and that you know the difference between reality and make-believe."

"Oh. My. God. You have *got* to be kidding me!" Shaniqua shouted. "You think I'm some psycho who runs around making up stories about people because I've lost my grip on reality? On *reality?*" She crossed her arms so hard she almost knocked the wind out of her lungs. "You have no idea how real my life is."

"Honey…"

"Just stop." She held up her hand in an effort to end the conversation. "Please. Just leave me alone."

They rode the rest of the way in silence, Uncle

Roshaun glancing over at her every few minutes. *Probably to make sure I'm not going to jump out onto the highway.*

❑

Aunt Lydie had gotten to the shrink's office before them, and she was sitting in the waiting room, nervously gnawing on a hangnail as she waited. Uncle Roshaun plopped down next to her and thumbed through an ancient *Arizona Highways* magazine.

"Hello, Shaniqua," Dr. Sizemore said when she entered his office.

She couldn't help but giggle. It was decorated with all things Harry Potter. *And this guy's supposed to help me get over what Aunt Lydie calls my "werewolf thing"? Seriously?*

"Have a seat." He gestured at a couple of comfy-looking La-Z-Boys, like her parents had back home. When she looked at him curiously, he chuckled. "You were expecting a couch, weren't you?"

Maybe this won't be so bad after all. "I kind of was," she said and sat.

"Everyone does," he said, and sat down in the other chair. "So, I'm guessing you'd rather be anywhere but here. Am I right?"

She nodded.

"Name three."

"What?"

"Name three places you'd rather be than here."

"Really?"

"Really."

She thought about it for a minute. Tapped her mouth with her index finger. Studied the doctor. "Getting a root canal, in rush-hour traffic with a bad case of diarrhea, and…at a Justin Bieber concert."

He leaned back and winced. "Justin Bieber? That bad, huh?"

"Yep." She felt her lips twitching and covered her mouth with her hand.

This guy wasn't so bad, not nearly as bad as she'd expected, and she relaxed. He had a nice smile and a way about him that put her at ease. She couldn't put her finger on it, but for some reason, he reminded her of James.

James. What was she going to do about him?

"Not really happy to be here, I take it."

"What?" She snapped her attention back to the doctor, hoping she could convince him that there was nothing wrong with her.

"You don't really want to be here, do you?"

"Not really." She frowned. "Hey, where's your tape recorder or your notebook, or whatever you use to take notes?"

"I never take notes during a session. I find it leads to clients not being totally honest with me because they're afraid people will read them."

"But you make notes afterward?"

He nodded.

"Hmm." She looked out the window again.

"Everything you say to me during our sessions is confidential."

Shaniqua turned back to him. "Everything?"

"Everything."

"Good to know." She went back to staring out the window. Not much chance she'd tell him what she actually-ly thought, but if it was true that he wouldn't reveal any-thing she said, then maybe…

"Your aunt and uncle are worried about you. They tell me you've made some pretty wild statements lately, and that you're depressed and spending too much time alone in your room."

"What's wrong with that?"

"Nothing, as long as it's not an indication that you're hiding from something." He leaned forward and lowered his voice. "They told me what happened in Chicago."

"Oh, great." Shaniqua got up and began to pace. "Why don't they just blog about it so the whole world knows?"

"I'm sure they felt it's all part of the problem," he said gently. "I did ask them why you were living with them, after all."

Tears sprang to her eyes and she wiped them away angrily. "Because my parents hate me, that's why!"

"Why do you say that?"

"Because they exiled me to this crappy little town that's full of…full of…oh, never mind!"

"What were you going to say, Shaniqua?" he asked quietly.

"Nothing."

"It's not nothing, Shaniqua."

She whirled around to face him. "No, it's not. But you won't believe me, anyway." She sniffed. "No one does."

"Try me."

She stood at the window and watched people walking down the street. Two kids about her age hung out in front of The Pizza Man, snickering and poking fun at anyone who passed by. It made her think of Watts and how much she regretted what happened between them. If they were really friends, she never should have ignored Watts' texts or blown her off when she wanted to finish talking about werewolves, and called her when she said she would.

Watts was pretty smart, and Shaniqua had known for a while now that her friend was growing more and more frustrated every time Shaniqua pulled back.

She didn't know what she would do if she lost Watts's friendship.

She turned back toward the doctor and shrugged. "What the hell. You ever heard of PJ, of PJs Diner?"

"Used to eat there all the time. What about her?"

"My boyfriend was the one who shot her."

"That must have been very traumatic for him."

Shaniqua snorted. "That wasn't even the worst thing."

"It wasn't?"

"No, it wasn't. Do you want to know what was?"

The doctor shrugged. "Only if you want to tell me."

"Why not?" She took a deep breath and blew it out slowly. Regarded the doctor. Smiled slyly.

"She was a werewolf."

☐

"Shaniqua," Dr. Sizemore said. "Sometimes it's easier to make things up than to deal with reality."

Shaniqua snorted. "Yeah, I figured you'd say something like that."

The doctor remained silent for a few minutes. When he spoke again, his voice sounded different. All gravelly, like. And deeper than it had been.

"Shaniqua," he growled. "I think we need to get something straight right now."

"Yeah?" she said, turning from the window. "And what's that?"

"Sometimes, the line between fantasy and reality blurs, and they can seem one and the same."

Shaniqua's eyes went wide. Her heart thundered in her chest. The air seemed thin and she couldn't breathe.

Dr. Sizemore was gone. In his place stood the biggest, most frightening creature she'd ever seen. None of her favorite horror movies had prepared her for this.

Dr. Sizemore was a werewolf.

□

Shaniqua felt like she'd been stuck for days on one of those carnival rides that spin you around and around so fast that you think you're going to be launched into the air. She moaned and opened her eyes, blinking in the bright light. "Where am I?" she asked.

"In Doctor Sizemore's office." Aunt Lydie hovered over her, heavy worry lines etched into her face.

"What happened?" She rubbed her forehead and tried to sit up. A large hand pushed her gently back to the floor.

"Don't try to get up just yet." The voice sounded familiar, but she couldn't place it. "You fainted."

Dr. Sizemore. Now she recognized the voice. And remembered everything. Her eyes widened, then narrowed into slits.

"We were talking about the difference between fantasy and reality, and it got pretty hairy there for a bit," Dr. Sizemore explained.

Yeah, you could say that again. She sat up slowly and winced.

"How do you feel?" Aunt Lydie asked.

She looked directly at Dr. Sizemore. "I've had better days, Auntie."

Her aunt smiled. "Yeah, I'll bet." She gently took hold of Shaniqua's arm and helped her stand. Shaniqua wobbled a bit, and Dr. Sizemore took her other arm and they both guided her over to the recliner.

"Here, sit down," Dr. Sizemore said. He turned to Aunt Lydie. "Lydie, why don't you go ask Jewels to get you a cool washcloth for Shaniqua's forehead? And Roshaun, she could probably use something to drink, don't you think?"

Uncle Roshaun nodded, and Aunt Lydie glanced at the doctor, then looked back at Shaniqua. "Will you be okay, honey?"

Shaniqua glanced at Dr. Sizemore. "Sure."

"Well, okay. We'll be right back." They hurried out to the receptionist to get the washcloth and some water.

"How long was I out?" Shaniqua asked.

"Not long."

"And?"

"And what?"

She regarded him suspiciously. "Seriously?"

"Seriously, what?"

She crossed her arms defiantly and looked out the window. "Fine. Whatever. I get it."

"Do you?"

"Look, I'm not in the mood to play twenty questions. I know what I saw." She turned back to him. "And I know what you are."

Dr. Sizemore studied her for a moment. Then he nodded. "It's true."

Shaniqua sat up a little straighter. "It is?"

He nodded again. "But you mustn't go around blabbing about werewolves any more. Your life could be in danger if the wrong people found out."

"What people?"

"Just trust me on this."

"Fine. I won't say anything to anyone." She looked at him slyly. "As long as you answer me one question."

"Okay. But just one."

"How can you change when it's not a full moon?"

"First of all," Dr. Sizemore said. He leaned forward in his chair and steepled his fingers. "We don't change.

We transform."

"Transform. Got it."

"Anyone who is born a werewolf can transform at any time. It's only those who are made that change because of the gravitational pull of the moon. They can't control it like we can."

She stared back at him, head cocked, while he played the shrink game of remaining silent that Watts warned her about. When it was obvious he wasn't going to say anything else, she gave in. "So how come you decided to tell me what you are?"

"Because I didn't want you to run all over town blabbing to anyone who would listen that there are werewolves living here. That would be very dangerous, not only for you but also for the werewolves. The rumors are bad enough, but if any sort of proof surfaced, it could be catastrophic for all of us."

"Oh." She nodded. "That makes sense."

Her guardians rushed back into the room. "Here we go." Uncle Roshaun handed her a glass of water, and she dutifully took a sip before handing it back. Aunt Lydie folded and unfolded a washcloth.

"Don't you think she should put her feet up?" she asked. "Relax a little bit?"

"I'm okay, Auntie."

"Oh, I think she's going to be just fine."

Dr. Sizemore winked at her. Like they were great friends or something. But weren't you supposed to be able to trust your friends? She wasn't sure she could trust him.

"But what do you say we humor your aunt and lie back for a few minutes?" He flipped the lever to bring up the footstool and pushed the back of the chair a little. Then he took the washcloth from her aunt and laid it across her forehead, covering her eyes.

What the heck. Might as well. If nothing else, it will give me time to think.

◻

Feeling the need to tell James about Dr. Sizemore to see what he thought, Shaniqua hid herself away in her room and pulled her phone out of her backpack. There was only a little battery life left, but she didn't want to risk her aunt or uncle barging in and hearing her still talking about werewolves, so she decided to plug it in after texting James.

~ *I've been shrunk.*

~ *Always wanted a tiny little woman.*

She giggled at his reply. He always knew the right thing to say.

~ *How'd it go? U ok?* he asked.

~ *Shrink's a little on the hairy side.* She chewed on her lip, waiting for his reply, and wondered if James knew Dr. Sizemore was a werewolf.

~ *Not sure what u mean.*

She sighed. ~ *Never mind.* She should have figured he wouldn't 'fess up. Not yet, anyway. But one day soon, she would confront him and see what he said then.

"Shaniqua!"

Shaniqua rolled her eyes. "Now?" she muttered. "Seriously?"

"Shaniqua?" Aunt Lydie called again. She was getting closer.

~ *Gotta go. Txt me L8r?*

~ *L8r,* he replied.

She shoved her phone under her pillow and grabbed her sketch pad and charcoal pencil.

Her aunt stuck her head in the door. "What are you doing?" Her eyes lit up when she saw Shaniqua drawing.

"Oh, hey, look at you."

"Yeah, I figured it was time to get back to my graphic novel. James has been bugging me to start up again."

"That's great!" Aunt Lydie said, obviously surprised. And pleased.

The look on her face made Shaniqua smile, relieved that since she was responsible for taking the sparkle out of her auntie's eyes, she could finally do something to put it back in. Even if it was a lie.

"I'm glad."

Shaniqua nodded. "Yeah, sorry about all that werewolf stuff. I don't know what I was thinking."

Aunt Lydie walked over and kissed her forehead, stroking the back of her head. "It's okay, sweetie. We all handle stress differently." She paused. "But I still want you to talk to Dr. Sizemore a few more times, okay?"

Shaniqua sighed dramatically. "Okay, Auntie. That's fine. Whatever." There was no use in arguing. When she thought about it, it was actually a little funny. They wanted her to talk to someone about her "werewolf thing," and the guy they picked was a werewolf. Talk about irony.

"Just wanted to let you know that Watts is here. Okay to let her in?"

The last thing Shaniqua wanted to do was hang out with Watts right now. She needed to finish up with James. But she couldn't very well send her friend away. Not if she wanted her aunt and uncle to believe her so they'd leave her alone. And besides, she was afraid if she did turn Watts away again, that would be the end of their friendship.

"Sure," she said with as much enthusiasm as she could muster. She turned on her iPod and stuck the ear buds into her ears.

Less than a minute later, Watts walked into her

room, sat down on the bed across from her, pulled out one of Shaniqua's ear buds, and stuck it into her own ear.

"What are you doing here?" Shaniqua asked.

"Dafuq?" Watts said. "Since when do I need to make an appointment to hang out with you?" Her brows knitted fiercely and she screwed up her mouth on one side. "Geez, Robinson. Maybe you do need to see a shrink." She yanked the ear bud out of her ear. "I could care less if you're cray-cray and ready for the rubber room. But if you keep listening to *Frozen*, I'm going to have to kill you."

Shaniqua laughed and turned off the music, putting her iPod on her nightstand next to her phone charger.

"So," Watts said, lying across the bed. "How did it go?"

"How did what go?"

Watts rolled her eyes. "Your chit-chat with the head shrinker. Duh."

"Oh, fine. No big deal."

"You sure?"

"I'm sure."

"Good." Watts got up and paced across the room. "'Cuz I need all your brain cells firing properly."

"Why? What's up?"

"I told you about my brother, right?"

"The one who lives on a farm in Kansas somewhere? Doesn't his wife smell like cabbage or something?"

"Oh, gawd," Watts moaned. "I totally forgot about that. Yeah, that's the one. Anyway, my ma's making me go there for the summer. Can you believe it? I swear to God, if I have to slop the pigs or reach under a chicken to steal an egg, I'm gonna puke."

"They have pigs and chickens?"

"Who knows? The point is, I have to go there for the whole summer. Can't you just see it? Me in East Nowheresville, wearing overalls and having to watch where I step for three whole months." Watts stopped pacing and turned to Shaniqua. "They don't even have cable." She went back to her pacing.

Shaniqua felt bad for Watts, but all she could think about was what she was going to do about James's secret. "Look at the bright side," she said.

"There's a bright side?"

"It's only three months. It could be worse. You could be exiled there forever." *Like me.*

Watts nodded. "Wow," she said slowly. "Thanks for the sympathy."

"Don't take it like that."

"How else should I take it? I thought you were my friend. I thought you might actually care." She headed for the door.

Shaniqua jumped up and blocked her way. "I do care, Watts. And I feel bad. But it's not the end of the world, you know."

Watts reached around Shaniqua and tried to grab the door knob. "Oh, but it is the end of the world. My world, anyway. Obviously not yours."

"Aren't you being a little melodramatic?" Shaniqua forced out a laugh, hoping Watts would see the humor in the situation. It was pretty funny, when you thought about it, to imagine someone like Watts, who thrived on fast food and nineties punk, on a farm somewhere in the middle of nowhere. And without cable.

"Thanks a lot, Shaniqua. I know you have a lot on your plate right now, what with your boyfriend being a werewolf and all, but I came over because I wanted my best friend to commiserate with me, to tell me that my summer's going to suck. To say that your summer will suck, too, because I won't be here. To show some sympathy. In other words, to take my side. Obviously, I was mistaken. Now move." Watts shoved Shaniqua aside and opened the door.

A California wildfire erupted in Shaniqua's stomach, and she realized she'd blown it. Again. Maybe she should tell Watts what was really going on. Maybe then they'd stop having all these stupid little fights.

She grabbed Watts's arm and held on. "It's just that there's so much going on in my life right now."

"Yeah," Watts said. "Right. But apparently that doesn't include me." A tear formed in the corner of Watts's left eye. Unlike Shaniqua, Watts wasn't one to cry easily.

"Don't say that. You're still my best friend."

Watts shook off Shaniqua's hand. "Well, guess what, honey pie? You don't get to decide that. It takes two to make a friendship. Two people who work hard at being friends. And these days, I seem to be the only one working at it."

"Oh, Watts," Shaniqua said. "Come on." She reached out for her, but Watts backed away.

"Just answer me one thing, okay? Who made it clear from the very beginning that I would always have your back? No matter what?"

Tears flowed down Shaniqua's face. "You did," she mumbled.

"And who stayed by your side when people were laughing at you because of that stupid frog egg incident?"

"You." Shaniqua wiped her nose with the back of her hand.

"Well, good luck finding another best friend who'll have your back like that, ever again." She walked out of the room, slamming the door behind her.

□

"Shaniqua?" Aunt Lydie said. "Honey?" She opened the door and peeked inside. "Everything okay?"

"Yeah."

"You sure? Watts didn't look very good when she left. She practically knocked your uncle down running out the door."

"Sorry."

"Honey—"

Shaniqua rolled over and faced the wall. "I don't want to talk about it."

Aunt Lydie sat down next to her and rubbed her arm. "Well, whenever you're ready to talk, *if* you want to talk, I'm here for you." She brushed the hair out of Shaniqua's eyes, stroking her head behind her ear. "I have an idea…"

Shaniqua wiped her tears and looked over her shoulder at her aunt.

"Want to watch a movie?"

Shaniqua turned back and looked at her aunt. "With cheesie poofs and soda?"

"Sure." Aunt Lydie smiled. "You pick the movie—" She held up her hand. "Before you even ask, yes, we can watch one of your B horror movies. I'll go get the snacks while you grab the DVD."

"Okay," Shaniqua said quietly. "Sounds good."

Not wanting to deal with any more of her aunt's worries about her, she figured she'd choose something about as far away from horror as she could get. She thought about watching *Stand by Me*, but that would only remind her of James, and then she'd never be able to turn off her brain and just enjoy the movie. *Sleepless in Seattle* was one of her auntie's favorites, so she grabbed it off the shelf instead.

As she headed down the hall to the living room, the thought of a quiet evening spent watching movies, like old times when Uncle Roshaun and Aunt Lydie lived in

Chicago, two blocks away, calmed her.

"Hey, Auntie," she called. "Got those cheesie poofs ready yet?"

☐

After the movie, Shaniqua told her aunt she felt a little tired, and excused herself to go lie down. "It's been a long day," she explained.

"That's a good idea," Aunt Lydie said. "You hungry?"

"Little bit."

"Then we'd better feed you. I'll make you a little something, okay?"

Shaniqua kissed her aunt on the cheek. "Thanks, Aunt Lydie. I really do feel better about…things."

Aunt Lydie beamed, relief flooding her face.

Shaniqua went to her room, shut the door, and immediately pulled out her phone. She sat down on her bed and started to text Watts. Worried that her aunt might barge in unexpectedly to check on her, she also pulled out her sketch pad and opened it to a half-finished drawing of James. Not James the werewolf, just James. She thought that might fool her, at least long enough for her to do what she needed to do.

She texted Watts. ~ *Im an idiot.*

Waited forever for the chirp that signaled an incoming message. All the way to the count of seventy-six.

~ *Tru story*, came the reply.

Shaniqua smiled. ~ *Ur bros wife is Pennywise in drag.*

~ *Xplains y she smells like a sewer.*

Shaniqua nearly laughed out loud.

There was a knock on her door, and she grabbed her pad and pencil and stuck the phone under her pillow.

"Come in."

Her aunt carried in her tray with a sandwich and a mug of soup. "Ham and cheese and beef barley soup," she said. "Sorry, I didn't have any regular bread for grilled cheese. Just a couple of Kaiser rolls. But just wait until the day after Thanksgiving. Lots of leftover turkey and cranberry sauce. I make a mean turkey sammie."

"Can't wait! But this looks great, too. Thanks." Shaniqua took a tiny bite out of the sandwich. Aunt Lydie moved toward her like she was planning on sitting with her while she ate. Maybe make sure she finished. "Um…Auntie?"

Aunt Lydie sat down beside her, just like Shaniqua expected. "What?"

Shaniqua shifted uncomfortably. "Is it okay…I mean…"

Aunt Lydie reached out to brush the hair off Shaniqua's forehead. "What is it, baby?"

"Would it be okay if I eat, you know, alone?"

That was the exact wrong thing to say. Her aunt reeled back as if slapped.

"It's not that I don't want to be around you and Uncle Roshaun or anything," Shaniqua rushed on. "It's just that I want to think about what Dr. Sizemore told me. And I'm really tired, so after I finish eating, I just want to go to sleep."

That seemed to pacify her aunt. "Oh, okay." She nodded. "Sure. I think that's a good idea. We can talk about…things…tomorrow."

Shaniqua tried to look like that was the only thing in the world she wanted to do, when, in fact, it was the last. "That would be great."

Aunt Lydie kissed her forehead and headed out the door.

"Auntie?"

She turned back to Shaniqua.

"Thanks. For everything." And that, she meant.

Wednesday, November 25, 2015
Hunter's Moon; Beaver Moon
Moon rises at 2:44 p.m.

Leaves begin to fall and game is fattened. This is the time for hunting and laying in a store of provisions for the long winter ahead. Beavers are busy preparing for winter, and Native Americans would set their beaver traps before the water froze to ensure they had enough warm pelts to last through the harsh winter. Farmers could expect the first snowfall.

CHAPTER 24

Lately, James was always busy with Mr. Hansen. Watts had been avoiding her for days, ever since she'd acted like such an idiot when Watts told her about Kansas.

Shaniqua didn't know how much longer she could stand it. The loneliness. The guilt. She might as well be back in Chicago.

Aunt Lydie had spent the afternoon complaining about having the sniffles so she and Uncle Roshaun had gone to bed early and left her on her own. She'd thrown together a dinner of Cocoa Puffs and an apple and taken them to her room.

She needed Watts's help, but she wasn't sure she could even get her to talk to her, much less help her out.

Shaniqua took a spoonful of cereal, but had a hard time swallowing it. What she was about to ask Watts was such a big deal. It was something she felt she had to do, for the sake of her own sanity, but she was terrified that if Watts didn't help her, she really would go crazy. With her own personal shrink, she wondered how easy it would be for her guardians to have her committed.

Not to mention what it could ultimately do to hers and Watts's friendship. If she agreed or if she didn't.

But she had to do it, so she took a deep breath, let it

out slowly, picked up her phone, and began to text. *~ I need ur help.*

~ That y u txtd me? Cuz i don't know if im available, Watts replied.

Shaniqua sighed. *~ I no i have no right to ask.*

~ No u don't.

~ Plz Watts. Ur the only 1 I trust.

Shaniqua waited anxiously for Watts to text her back. She tried to eat her dinner, but couldn't get any-thing down, so she ended up chewing on a hangnail in-stead. After nearly five minutes, her phone chirped, and she sat and contemplated it for a moment. What if Watts said no? What would she do then?

Finally, she opened the text.

~ Gimme 10 min. Ma pigging out on pizza & wine. Will b comatose soon.

~ U don't have a car, Shaniqua replied.

~ Ma does. Duh.

□

Shaniqua licked her lips and looked around her room. Tonight was the full moon, and she had to find out, once and for all, if her suspicions about James were right. If she'd really seen what she thought she'd seen last month, or if she'd just been imagining things.

But how to get out?

Too risky to just walk out the front door. She won-dered if she could make it out the window without break-ing something, like a leg. Or her neck. Then she scoffed at herself. *Get a grip, girl. You live on the ground floor. It's not like you're Spiderman climbing the Sears Tower or something.*

She opened the window, shivering at the blast of cold air that rushed in, and studied the screen. Her apartment in Chicago had storm windows but no screens, and she wasn't sure how to detach it. If nothing else, she figured she could take her scissors and cut her way out.

She was digging through her backpack for some notebook paper when Watts's head popped up outside her window.

"Boo!" she said, startling Shaniqua.

Shaniqua covered her heart with her hand. "Oh, God, you scared me."

Watts grinned. "Sorry."

"Yeah, sure you are." They giggled. "Shh," Shaniqua warned. "Not so loud."

"Come on, let's blow this popsicle stand," Watts said. She quickly pushed on the screen and lifted it out.

"Wait a sec. I want to leave a note so they don't worry."

"Must be nice," Watts mumbled.

"What?"

"Nothing. Hurry up."

Shaniqua ripped a piece of paper out of her binder and scribbled a note to her aunt and uncle, in case they checked in on her while she was gone.

> *There's something I have to do.*
> *Please don't worry. I'll be back soon.*
> *Thank you for understanding.*
> *I love you both.*
> *Shaniqua*

After looking it over, she added: ♥♥♥

Slipping into her coat and knit cap, she propped the note up on her pillow, took a last look around the room, and climbed out of the window.

"Come on. Hurry up!" Watts grabbed her hand once she was outside and they raced down the block to where

Watts had parked her mother's minivan. She aimed the key fob and unlocked it. "Get in," she said.

Shaniqua got inside and strapped on her seat belt then looked over at Watts.

"What?" Watts said after starting the car.

"Nothing." Shaniqua shook her head. "You just look…different behind the wheel."

"What, you expected me to fly over here?"

"Well, you did show me that one picture that time, that one of you dressed up like a flying monkey for Halloween."

"Ha ha, very funny." Watts started slowly down the street. "You owe me big time for this."

"I know."

They puttered along and Shaniqua couldn't help but squirm in her seat. Watts was driving like she was a hundred years old, and, at the rate they were going, the moon would be down before they even got there. Providing she could find the right spot.

"Think we could go a little faster, Watts?" she asked.

"You want to drive?"

"No, no. That's okay. You're doing fine."

Watts looked at her out of the corner of her eye. "Might help if I knew where we were going."

"Good question."

Watts shot her another look. "What does that mean?"

Shaniqua grinned at her sheepishly and scratched her head. "Well, I'm not exactly sure where we're going."

"Um…what?"

Shaniqua glanced up at the sky. The moon rose early, right about the time school ended, and she hoped she wouldn't be too late. It had been dark for several hours now, and she wasn't sure what kind of effect that would have on James.

If the moon rose during the day, did that mean he'd

transform during daylight hours, or would he be able to wait until dark?

So many questions—she just had to get answers. "Keep going this way," she told Watts. "You know how to get to the picnic area of the Cailleach Canyon park?"

Watts snorted. "Doesn't everyone?"

Shaniqua settled back in her seat. For the next fifteen minutes or so, they drove in companionable silence. Buildings and streetlights gave way to the woods and the bright illumination of the moon. Trees hugged the highway, and the air smelled of pine and must.

"This is about James, isn't it?" Watts suddenly asked.

Shaniqua thought about denying it, but one look at Watts and she knew it would be all over if she did. "Yeah," she admitted.

Watts nodded and kept driving.

When they reached the turnoff to Cailleach Canyon, Shaniqua told Watts to pull off the road and stop. Watts glided slowly to the shoulder and turned off the engine. She gazed up through the windshield at the full moon. "So," she said. "Now where?"

Shaniqua gestured up the turnoff. "I'm going up there a ways." She turned back to Watts. "You're going home."

"What?" Watts shook her head violently. "No way. I'm going with you."

"I can't let you do that, Watts. It's too dangerous."

"Exactly why you can't go alone."

"No, Watts. I need you to go home and wait for me to call. If anything happens to me, you're the only one who can tell my aunt and uncle what happened." Shaniqua opened the door and jumped out. "Besides, your mom will kill both of us if she finds out you stole her car."

Watts waved her hand. "That's the whole point. Grand theft auto. Even Juvie beats Kansas for the summer."

They laughed. Shaniqua stood there and hoped it wouldn't be the last time she saw her friend.

"Hey." Watts put on her seat belt again. "You sure you want to do this alone?"

"Positive. You okay to drive home by yourself?"

"Pfft. Piece of cake, Princess."

"Thanks, Watts. You don't know how much this means to me."

She shrugged. "What are best friends for?"

Shaniqua watched Watts's car as it disappeared back down the road. Hefting her backpack up on her shoulder, she turned and headed up the trail that led into the woods. Even with a full moon, she was surprised at how much darker it was than she thought it would be, once she got away from the parking lot and picnic areas. She reached into her pack and pulled out her flashlight.

Shining her light on the path ahead of her, she peered through the trees lining the trail. When she and James walked this trail one day when he brought her here for a picnic, they'd seemed perfectly normal, welcoming, even. Now, they were somehow creepy, silhouetted by the full moon behind them.

A slight breeze rustled what few leaves were left on the branches. At least, she thought it was the breeze. Shivering a little, she was overcome with a feeling of being watched. She shined the light back and forth across the trail, moving the beam up into the trees.

Nothing was there. She was alone.

Or was she?

She couldn't shake that feeling. It started in the very bottom of her stomach and spread outwards, tentacles of fear worming through her body. She walked backwards slowly, a step at a time. Her eyes followed the light as she ping-ponged it back and forth across the trail.

A wolf howled in the distance.

She whirled around, startled, unsure if that was really what she'd heard. A few years back, a lone grey wolf had been spotted crossing into California from Oregon, where he found a mate and had a litter before supposedly returning to the Oregon forest. But what if those wolves had actually stayed in California? Could they have gotten all the way from the Northern-most border clear across the state into Southern California? That was over eight hundred miles.

The wolf howled again, closer this time.

Run!

The rational part of her brain told her that she was imagining things. That was not a wolf. It was a dog, a lonely, probably hungry dog. Or maybe a coyote. There were lots of them up in the nearby mountains, after all, and they frequently came into town searching for food and water.

This time, when the wolf howled, it sounded like it was right behind her.

Run! Run NOW!

This was the primeval lizard-brain speaking. The collective unconscious, the voice of survival that the ancients always listened to.

The shadows beneath the trees moved. But how was that possible?

A dark shape seemed to pull itself out of the shadows, little more than darkness, and slithered across the dirt path towards her.

Her legs turned to jelly, preventing her from moving. Total fear invaded her mind, flooding it with a kaleidoscope of frightening images: a killer clown like Pennywise, a big ass spider the size of a Hummer, being torn limb from limb by a crazed wolf—or was it a *werewolf?*

Shaniqua's heart hammered so hard in her chest that every bone in her body seemed to shudder, except for her legs, which felt like they were liquefying. Sweat rained out of her pores. She whimpered.

The shadow before her rose up to its full height. A wolf! But like no wolf she'd ever seen. Its mouth was filled with dozens of razor-sharp teeth. Coarse hair covered every inch of its body. And its eyes. Its eyes were redder than the Blood Moon they'd had last month.

They terrified her, those eyes. They were unlike anything she'd ever seen before. And yet, there was something familiar about them. Something like…

Could it be?

"James?"

The werewolf cocked his head and seemed to be considering her. It was breathing heavily, practically grunting. It took a small step towards her and sniffed.

"James, it's me. Shaniqua." She held out her hand for the wolf to sniff like she would a friendly stray.

The werewolf went back down on all four paws and backed slowly away.

She took a step towards it.

The werewolf growled. It seemed to shake its head at her then turned and headed toward the trees, where it stopped and looked at her again. It lifted its head and howled—a low, mournful sound filled with sadness and melancholy.

Then it loped slowly away.

□

Logan O'Shaughnessy sauntered across the street without bothering to look. He was invincible, and nothing—or no one—would dare hurt him. *Except my stepfa-*

ther, the fat fuck. Logan frowned. He thought about the first time the dude hit him. Logan was six, and he'd forgotten to put his bike away. His stepfather went ballistic, came up behind him, and beat him with Logan's bike helmet.

Ever since then, he'd picked one dude to hassle as often as he could till the end of the school year. One year—it must have been about second or third grade—the target had been this ugly little girl. But she'd ratted him out and word had gotten back to his stepfather, who'd used it as just one more excuse to beat him. Not that he ever needed one. But this time, he'd burnt him on his arm with the cigarette that normally dangled out of the corner of his mouth. Logan still had the scars to prove it, and he rubbed them absently. He supposed he'd have to stop having fun with losers after he graduated this year, and that made him a little sad, but he'd be leaving home to go to college and getting away from the asshole, and that was a good thing.

As soon as he'd seen him at school, Logan decided on the spot that this year's target would be Manarro. He and his pack were going to have some fun this year. Seeing as how it was their last year and all.

But, in the meantime, he was stuck walking to the store for the canned yams his mom needed for Thanksgiving dinner. Walking. Him. Logan O'Shaughnessy. Son of Ian and Tilly. He couldn't believe it. He'd had a tiny little fender bender a couple of weeks ago, and his stupid stepfather not only kept the insurance money for himself, but refused to allow Logan to fix the car. His mother meekly agreed, and he couldn't really blame her for that. She was more afraid of her husband than Logan was.

He pounded his fist into his palm. "One of these days," he muttered.

"What?"

He'd finally gotten to the store, and the woman coming out of the door was staring at him.

"What, what?" he said angrily.

The woman hurried past him and he went inside.

Yams. I don't even like them. Why am I stuck getting them?

□

It was the middle of the afternoon, and, when the full moon rose on days like this, the werewolf was thankful the town had many dark hiding places.

The werewolf lifted its snout into the wind and sniffed. The redolent odor of human slammed into its face and filled its nostrils. It was nearly insane with hunger. Under normal circumstances, it would race toward the scent, ready to devour the human it belonged to. But not today. Today it was hunting for one particular human.

And when it found him, that's when the fun would begin.

□

Logan waited in the check-out line, bouncing up and down on his toes. The old bat in front of him was taking forever unloading her cart one item at a time. She should have let him go ahead. After all, he only had one big can. What would it have hurt?

When she was finally done, she backed the cart up, right over his foot.

"Ow! Watch it, you stupid cow," he said crossly.

"Oh, I'm terribly sorry, young man," she said. "I didn't see you there."

He jammed his hands in his pockets and glared at her. "Then maybe you should open your eyes, you old bitch."

When she finished paying, which she also seemed to do in slow motion—she had to be at least a hundred and twelve years old. Why do they let people that old out in public, anyway?—he took his place at the register.

The cashier scanned his yams and stuck the can in a plastic bag. "Four sixty nine," she said.

Logan pulled the five his mother had given him out of his pocket and handed it to her. She glared at him while she took it then turned, put it into the register, and counted out his change. When she handed it to him, she held her closed fist over his outstretched hand and waited.

"What?" he demanded.

"You didn't have to be so mean to Ms. Cunningham, you know."

"Who?"

"The lady in line in front of you. You were mean to her. She didn't run over your foot on purpose, you know? She doesn't see that well."

"Then maybe she shouldn't be out in public where she can hurt someone. Now give me my change and shut your piehole."

▢

Logan strode purposefully across the parking lot. His father, when they were still a family, had once told him that appearance was everything. He should draw himself up to his full height and never slouch. Stick out his chest to make himself look fierce. Strong, so people would think he was. Pretend he had all the answers and people would believe he did. If he acted like a leader, people would naturally follow him.

Just like Chase and Boy-O. Or it was until Boy-O got himself killed and Chase wimped out. What was wrong with that dude? He used to be right there, ready for any-thing and everything. But lately, ever since that day in the locker room, he hadn't been around much. He'd claimed he'd been chased by something with red eyes. Red eyes! Talk about a tool.

Logan thought about his crew. He'd been friends with Chase, not to mention Liam and Boy-O, for as long as he could remember, and Mickey came along in middle school. He'd immediately fit right into their gang. But lately, things were changing, and Logan blamed it all on James. Logan slammed his fist into his other palm a cou-ple of times, relishing the sound it made and wishing it were that queer boy James's face.

After what happened a couple of years ago, Logan was positive that James was somehow responsible for his man Boy-O's murder. And Chase's wimping out. Logan didn't know how, but he felt it deep in his bones. And Manarro was going to pay for it.

Oh, yeah, he was going to pay for it big time.

⬚

The wolf knew it must be patient and wait for its golden ticket, the opportunity to destroy the boy. It was difficult to wait, but it would have to. Normally, it would pacify its thirst for blood and hunger for human flesh with anyone unlucky enough to be caught out on the night of a full moon.

Not tonight. Tonight, it must be strong. It must wait.

But not for long.

Its chance would come soon enough.

⬚

The wind picked up a bit. Logan pulled up his Letterman's jacket and jammed his hands in his pockets. Damn, it was cold. Weren't the Santa Ana's supposed to be hot and dry? He hated being cold. And it was all his stepfather's fault that he was out here in the first place. Someday, he'd get even with the creep.

Someday soon.

But until then, he'd be forced to continue schlepping to the store for canned yams and whatever else his mother forgot.

Something rattled behind him, and he whirled around, nearly toppling himself over before he managed to pull his hands out of his jacket pockets and steady himself. A Coke can bounced along the gutter, occasionally hitting the curb.

Logan let out a sigh of relief. *Don't be an ass. Nothing scary about a soda can, right?* He turned back and continued on his way. Plotted ways to kill his stepfather. "Revenge is a dish best served cold," his father once told him.

He wasn't sure why he'd told Logan that, couldn't even remember what they'd been talking about, but Logan took it to heart.

He looked at his watch and groaned. He'd been gone forty minutes. His mom was going to have a shit fit for him being gone so long. Was it his fault every blue-hair in the county had been at the market?

What he wouldn't give to have his iPod back, but he'd lost it somewhere and his mother and stepfather had refused to replace it. Said he needed to learn to be more responsible, and they'd also suspended his allowance so he couldn't even buy another one.

No car, no iPad, forced to walk everywhere, playing fetch it for his mom every time she forgot something.

Yes, revenge would be served soon.

◻

The werewolf reveled in the fierce Santa Ana winds as they blasted through its fur. They called to the wolf with a kind of mad ferocity that made its bloodlust surge.

Fortune shined upon the werewolf this day, allowing it to find Logan all alone.

◻

The trees that lined the street had dropped most of their leaves. Logan enjoyed watching them turn from the lush green of spring and summer to the golden red of autumn, then fall completely off the branches and line the sidewalks underneath them. No one would ever believe he could be so…so…what was the word? Poetical. But he loved the transition from the dry season to the wet.

He also got a kick out of jumping from one pile of leaves to the other. Not only was it fun, reminding him of a time when his father was still around, but it also pissed off the adults because they'd have to sweep up after him.

Glancing over his shoulder to make sure no one was watching him, he ran across the street and leaped into the biggest leaf mountain he could find. Then jumped into the next one. And the next. And giggled like a little kid.

He scooped up a handful of dead leaves and tossed them into the air, ducking underneath them as they drifted down toward his head. But just before they reached him, a big blast of wind exploded through, sending the leaves darting away and pummeling him with several twigs that had gotten caught up in the gust.

The wind shrieked again and he whirled around. He thought he heard footsteps, but the street was empty. In fact, it was weird how there was no one around. It was early, a little past four in the afternoon. Where was everyone?

"Hey, kid." Mr. Taylor stood in the entrance to Anderson's Hardware, his legs crossed at the ankles, leaning casually against the doorjamb. That flaky Anderson fled town shortly after all those people got killed that night in the woods, abandoning the hardware store to the bank. The new guy bought it at auction for about a quarter of what it was worth. Logan wondered why the new owner hadn't bothered to change the name of the place.

"Hey, Mr. Taylor. Howzit hanging?" Logan looked up and down the street then turned his attention back to the old man.

"Slightly to the left," Mr. Taylor responded.

"Ha ha," Logan said. "Good one." He thought he heard something…was that growling?…underneath the wind, and peered down the street again.

"You ready for Thanksgiving?"

"I guess so."

Mr. Taylor cocked his head and frowned. "Something wrong, Logan?"

"Um, no, not really."

Then he heard growling again, low and barely perceived, but there, just under the whining of the wind.

"Did you hear that?"

"What? The wind? It sure is blowing hard, isn't it?"

"No, something else. Something…underneath the wind."

"Underneath? I'm not sure what you mean."

"Sounded like growling. Or something."

"Growling?" Mr. Taylor shook his head. "No, I don't hear anything like that. Are you sure you're not just hearing the wind?"

Logan shrugged. "Maybe."

Or maybe not.

□

The werewolf raced along on all fours, relishing the fear radiating off the boy in waves, and breathed deeply its intoxicating scent. The pumping of Logan's blood thundered in the beast's ears as though it were its own.

It loped past the boy and hid behind a thick bush, rattling the branches and snickering when Logan whimpered.

The werewolf licked its lips.

It wouldn't be long now.

□

Logan walked quickly down the street. He couldn't help himself. He was seriously freaked. There was something out there, he could feel it. Watching him. Waiting.

But for what?

He had no clue. All he knew was that he needed to stop being such a pussy, get home before his stepfather realized how long he'd been gone and gave him another ration of shit, and binge-watch *The Hundred,* his latest obsession. *That Clarke chick is* hot.

Another gust propelled the remains of someone's fast food lunch across his path hard enough to send everything, including a chicken nugget box, up into a twister of dust and debris. Logan watched as it all sailed away, noticing that the moon was high in the late afternoon sky, a full, bright white button against the fading twilight, and hurried on.

After only a few yards, he thought he heard that weird growling again, and stopped to listen. The growling stopped with him.

He shook his head and hurried on.

A few more yards, and the growling started up again, and with it, the quiet sounds of footsteps keeping pace with him.

"Who's there?" he demanded. Sweat beaded up on his upper lip, and he swiped at it with his finger. "What do you want?"

The street was empty.

He walked faster.

The sound of the footsteps became clearer, louder. Closer. Someone was definitely behind him. His skin crawled.

He began to run.

He was only four blocks from home. Okay, so the last block was up a steep hill, but still, he should be able to outrun anyone—or any*thing*—that was behind him. He was the school's fastest wide receiver, after all. Nearly made the all-state team last year.

The footsteps kept pace with him.

The growling got louder.

Another gust of wind blasted down the street from the east, hitting him in the face full force and knocking him back two unsteady steps.

The growling was right behind him.

□

The moon had risen early, waving to the sun as it headed off to bed. The werewolf growled low in its throat as it watched the boy. His breath came in short, hard bursts, and he took off running.

The boy thought he could run fast, but he would never be able to outrun the wolf.

□

Logan began to whimper. He was only three blocks from home and tried to run faster, but he was just about tapped out. It wasn't fair, his being out here, alone. Vulnerable. Whatever was back there was gaining on him. His lungs were on fire. His calves burned. For the first time in his life, Logan was truly afraid. Afraid he wouldn't succeed. Afraid he'd never eat another Thanksgiving dinner, no matter how crappy the food.

Afraid he'd be dead before he made it home.

Only two more blocks.

Sweat poured down his face, stinging his eyes, and he tried to wipe it off with the bottom of his shirt. Instead, he got tangled up and tripped.

He went down, hard. Hit his head on the cement sidewalk and saw stars for a few seconds. When he sat up, he felt nauseated, put his head in his hands, and moaned. He came close to hurling, but managed to push the gorge back down. Climbing slowly to his feet, he stood there, unsteady, and nearly toppled over again. He grabbed on to a tree limb to steady himself.

He was almost home. One more block, and he'd be Netflixing in no time. He almost forgot why he'd been running in the first place.

Almost.

Then the growling came again, much louder this time, and more insistent.

Logan's balls shrank to the size of peas and were trying to burrow back into his groin. His heart beat erratically, hammering against his sternum so hard that he could feel it in his forehead, his neck, even his fingertips.

He turned around slowly.

Rows and rows of fangs, dripping with hot saliva, greeted him. The creature before him slowly rose up from all fours, as if relishing Logan's terror. Its paws were the size of catcher's mitts, but the toes ended in four-inch long claws. Logan watched in horror as the creature...*was it actually a werewolf?*...towered over him, a good eight feet tall, broad at the chest and narrowing at the hips. A long pink tongue lolled over the side of its mouth, then slowly licked first one side of its muzzle, then the other. Logan tried to swallow, but he had no spit left. The worst part of it all were the red eyes, the huge eyes that were redder than anything he had ever seen before, staring at him hungrily.

He thought he heard a siren going off somewhere in town. Then he understood that it was him, screaming like a little girl, his cries growing in intensity as he realized that Chase had been right about James after all.

There was a werewolf loose on the town.

CHAPTER 25

Thursday, November 26, 2015,
Thanksgiving,
Thirty Days to Full Moon:

Unfortunately for Shaniqua, Watts knocked on her bedroom window at the butt crack of dawn.

"Hey," Watts said the very second Shaniqua opened the window. "What happened? You never texted me."

Shaniqua yawned and rubbed her eyes. "What time is it?"

"Six-fifteen. You gonna let me in, or what?"

Shaniqua moved aside so Watts could climb through the window.

"Nice look, by the way." Watts chuckled and shook her head. Shaniqua was wearing one of her uncle's oversized Chicago Bears tee shirts. She was pretty sure her hair looked like it always did when she first woke up—like something had made a nest in it.

"Yeah, well, I wasn't exactly expecting company at this ungodly hour, now, was I?" Shaniqua plopped down on the bed, drawing her legs up into a lotus position, and tried to dig the sleep from her eyes.

"So," Watts said, sitting down next to her. "What happened?"

"What happened when?" Shaniqua played dumb. She'd never been especially coherent when she first woke up.

Plus, she had too much on her mind and wasn't up to dealing with all Watts's questions. Or talking about how she believed her boyfriend was a werewolf.

"Last night. Where'd you go? What did you do?"

"Nothing." Shaniqua stumbled to her closet and pretended to rummage inside for something to wear, hoping it would give her time to think of a good excuse.

"Dude." Watts grabbed Shaniqua roughly and whirled her around. "What's up with you, anyway? Why you so pissed off at me these days? It's like you're always blowing me off. Did I do something to you? Kill your cat or something?"

"What are you talking about? I never blow you off."

"Yeah. Right. Just like you didn't beg me to drive you out to the Canyon because there was no one else to do it."

"That's not why I asked you. Honest!"

"Let's review." Watts counted off on her fingers. "One. I tell you I'm being sent to Kansas for the summer and you could care less. Two. You don't wait for me after school any more. Three. First you tell me werewolves are real and you think your boyfriend might even be one, then you deny you ever said it. What's up with that, anyway?" She shook her head and sighed heavily. "Four. I steal a car for you and you can't even be bothered to send me a simple text letting me know you were okay. Even after you promised you'd call."

Shaniqua started to respond, but Watts held up her hand to stop her. "And five, and best of all, yesterday at lunch, when I told you I farted out a leprechaun and his pot of gold at the end of the rainbow, you said, and I quote, 'Good to know.'"

"Well," Shaniqua said, grinning at Watts. "It *is* good to know. I always said you were unique."

Watts did not see the humor in that.

"Sorry," Shaniqua said. "I've just been a little…distracted lately."

"You know what?" Watts turned on her. "I don't care anymore. I've stood by you, stood *up* for you, since day one. Remember? When Boy-O called you a dyke, who deflected his attention away from you onto herself?"

"You did, Watts."

"Damn straight. And who told Alexis off the day after you gave her a facial with fish eggs?"

"They were frog eggs."

"What?"

"Frog eggs. Not fish eggs."

"Whatever. Who told her off?"

"You did."

"And who listened to your fears about werewolves being real, and living in Wolf Creek?"

"You, Watts. You've been a good friend to me."

"So, you really going to stand there and tell me you're being totally honest with me? That you're not hiding something from me? Everything's fine. Is that your story?"

"Look, Watts," Shaniqua said. "I'm not hiding anything. Honest." Another lie. Who was she turning into these days? "Things are really crazy at home right now. Aunt Lydie wants me to keep seeing that shrink."

"Big deal. You know how many times I've had to go to one? Since I was seven. Seven. That's nine years of head trips. Just agree with everything the shrink says, and you'll be fine. But don't agree too soon." A malicious grin spread across her face. "Make the sucker work for it."

"Work for it. Right. Anything else, Obie Gone Cray-Cray?"

Watts stared at her, stone-faced, for exactly five seconds before busting out in raucous laughter. Shaniqua joined in, and they laughed until tears streamed down their faces.

And just like that, they were BFFs again. Which was a good thing. Shaniqua was going to need her friendship now more than ever, since she'd decided today was the day she was going to tell James her secret.

No matter what.

CHAPTER 26

Friday, November 27, 2015,
Twenty-Nine Days to Full Moon:

Logan's death made the eleven o'clock news that night and was the lead story all the next week. The whole town was on edge. I wondered why another curfew hadn't been put into effect the moment what happened to Logan was made public, but then I realized that Sheriff Brazelton was no longer in charge. He'd been recalled by public vote after the last set of attacks. Even though it had been two years since then, I had a hard time remembering that Riggs was now the sheriff. It didn't make sense to me. Riggs was a judgmental moron who couldn't tell the difference between his butt and a whale's blowhole. But surely even he couldn't deny what was happening to the town. Even though most people were simply burrowing down, pretending everything was okay, that it wasn't happening again, I wondered if Riggs would eventually be fired.

I sincerely hoped he would, but tried not to think about the rest of it.

Instead, I thought about how glad I was that my room was finally back to normal. When my cousin Beth and her mom moved in with us two years ago, Mom made me give Beth my room and insisted that I take down all my posters so it would be more "girl-friendly." What I didn't know at the time was that she had thrown all of them in the trash. It really pissed me off, especially since I loved the one of the Kardashians in the white bikinis. The others I could live without, but that one? How could she just throw it out like that?

I hadn't been able to find another one like it, but that was okay. I'd moved on. Now I was into Nicki Minaj. I didn't like her music—never been a fan of hip hop or rap. My taste in music was a little eclectic. I like Muse and Paramore, but I also listen to Queen, Skillet and Travis Tritt. Plus, I listen to NPR—but, dude, was Nicki ever hot. I was using her Pink Friday poster as my focal point and had been spending a lot of time practicing the techniques Mr. Hansen had given me.

At first, they seemed silly. I mean, formulating a mental image of a stop sign while telling the emerging wolf to stop? Visualizing myself as a tree? Seriously? But the more I tried his techniques, the easier they became and the more sense they made.

In addition to the three-count breathing, core rooting, and stop-sign visualization, he'd given me a phrase to repeat to myself. Called it a mantra. I was to close my eyes after finding my center and say, "I am not the wolf. The wolf is not me." This was what I was doing when there was a knock on my door.

Before I could respond, the door opened and Shaniqua poked her head inside. "You busy?" she asked.

"No." I hoped she hadn't heard anything. It was embarrassing. Plus how would I explain it? I couldn't exactly blurt out the truth. "Come on in. I was just..." I felt like an idiot. What was I just?

Shaniqua plopped down on my bed, and I sat at my desk. She scowled at something over my shoulder. I turned to see what she was looking at and stifled a smile. Was she jealous about my Nicki Minaj poster?

"How was your Thanksgiving?" she asked me.

"Good." I rubbed my stomach. "I think I'm still stuffed, I ate so much."

But then I took a closer look at Shaniqua. She seemed…funny. Something was off. She ran her fingers along a crease in my sheet. Sat on the very edge of the mattress, about as far away from me as she could be and still be on the bed.

"Shaniqua, what's wrong?"

"I—nothing." She shook her head, but I could see a tear beginning in the corner of her eye.

"Then how come you won't look at me?"

Her eyes flashed up at me for a split second before returning to the crease.

I inched closer to her. Reached out with my index finger and touched her knee. "Sweetie?"

That's when the tears started to flow. I tried hard not to squirm. What was I supposed to do with a crying girl? Hug her? Tell her everything was going to be okay? Ignore the tears? What I really wanted to do was run away, but that would only make things worse. Instead, I scooted over and wrapped my arms around her. At first, she tensed up, and I was about to let go until I felt her relax and melt into me. I held her for a good five minutes, stroking her hair, which smelled like coconut, and murmuring into her ear before she finally pulled back.

"Sorry about that," she whispered.

"It's okay."

She seemed so sad. I rubbed her upper arms and bent my head down so that I could look into her eyes. With a little sigh, she sat up and tucked a strand of hair behind her ear. "I have something to tell you."

"Okay," I said weakly, my mouth going dry. "You know you can tell me anything."

Her lower lip trembled, and I could tell the waterworks were about to start again. I shifted a little and wished she'd just rip the Band-Aid off already.

"I love you, James, you know? I really love you a lot."

"I love you, too. So what's the problem?"

"Once I tell you my secret, you might…you might…oh, you'll hate me!"

"I could never hate you, Shaniqua." I took her hands in mine, rubbing my thumb across the back of her hand. It was an old trick my mom used to comfort me when I was little. "No matter what."

"Promise?"

"Promise. On my big fat tookus." I patted my butt.

Shaniqua giggled and leaned over to see it. "But it's such a nice tookus."

We sat there grinning at each other a few moments. Then she took a deep breath and told me her secret.

"I had to leave my old school," Shaniqua said.

"Why? What happened?"

She kept fiddling with the crease in my sheet. "I did something incredibly stupid…and illegal."

"You did?" I wondered if she'd done something like TP a teacher's house or tag a building or a bridge or something. I could see her doing that. Her artwork was amazing. But would that be enough for her parents to send her so far away? My parents had been pissed at me that time I broke into Riggs's Mustang, but they'd just made me confess to him and take the community service hours. They never would have sent me away.

Shaniqua nodded. "Yeah." She inhaled sharply. "I sent my boyfriend a text."

"So? How is that illegal?" I was confused. There had to be more to it than that.

"I was naked in it. It was a sext."

I just stared at her. She'd never mentioned anything about having a boyfriend before, much less why she'd come to Wolf Creek in the first place. But then, I'd never even asked her.

"Say something."

"I—I don't know what to say."

"Do you hate me?" she whispered.

"Hate you? Why would I hate you?" She was afraid that my feelings for her would change. I could see that, but I was glad she'd told me. "So you sexted with your boyfriend. So what?"

"Yeah, but then he broke up with me the very next day and sent it to all his friends. Who sent it to their friends. Before I even knew what he was doing, the whole school had seen it. And then someone sent it to my mom. Anonymously, of course."

"Damn," I said. "What did she do?"

"Before or after she called me every foul name you could think of?"

"Oh, Shaniqua, I'm so sorry." When I moved to put my arms around her, she put her hand on my chest and held me at arm's length.

"So now you think I'm easy, don't you?"

"What? No! I would never think that about you."

"But you expect me to sleep with you now, right?"

That pissed me off. I got up off the bed and walked to my bedroom door. "You're crazy." Reached for the doorknob.

"Don't go. I'm sorry. It's just—"

"Look." I turned around to face her again. "I'm not what's-his-name."

"William."

"Whatever. I'm not him. I love you, but neither one of us is ready to have sex. At least I'm not. I know I'm supposed to be all macho and stuff and pressure you into it, but that's just not me. No way I'm going to be a teen father. I have enough of my own things to deal with without having to change poopy diapers and stuff." What I didn't tell her was that I was actually *afraid* to have sex—with anyone, not just her—until I could completely control the wolf. I didn't know what I would do if the wolf hurt her.

"Me, neither. And just for the record, I never did it with William, or anyone else. I don't even know why I sent that stupid text in the first place. Not only did it get me exiled to this place, but I was almost arrested for distributing kiddie porn. Can you believe that?"

"What? Kiddie porn?"

"Yeah, even if you send a nude text of yourself, if you're under age, they can throw you in jail."

"That's the dumbest thing I ever heard of. You sent it of yourself, not some little kid you were trying to sell or something."

"I know. That's what my dad tried to tell them. The only reason they didn't lock me up was because my mom used to work for an attorney who was friends with the cop who investigated it, and he talked him into giving me a second chance."

"Thank God for that."

"Yeah, but I don't think my parents will ever forgive me. They sent me here because they couldn't even look at me." She put her head in her hands. "I wish I'd never sent that stupid thing."

I sat next to her. Put my arm around her shoulders. "Well, I for one am glad you did."

Her head whipped up, anger flaring in her eyes.

I held up my hands defensively. "Hear me out. If you

hadn't, you'd never have ended up here, and I would never have had the chance to meet you. And I'm glad you told me about it. Thank you for trusting me."

"You're glad? Honest?"

"I are. Honest."

She cocked her head, her eyes a little wide. "So now that I've told you my deep dark secret, you got anything you want to share?"

My stomach plummeted into my toes at light speed. What did she mean? Did she know about the wolf? "Like what?" I stalled.

"Really, James?" She leaned forward and put one knee up on the bed, the other leg with her foot on the floor. "That all you got to say?"

"Okay, you caught me. When I was about ten or eleven, Logan and Chase said they'd let me into their club if I stole a VCR and—"

"I know. You already told me, and like I said before, it sucks that they did that to you." She brushed her fingers across my cheek. Her touch was electric and I almost forgot what I was saying. "Anything else you have to say?"

I shook my head. "Nope, that's it."

A weird look flashed across Shaniqua's face, and I wondered what she was thinking. She was quiet for a few moments. "Well," she said with a shrug, "I guess neither one of us will ever be president, huh?"

"As if."

"And is that your biggest secret? Stealing?"

The volcano erupted in my stomach again, and I couldn't help but wonder again just how much she really knew about me. And what she planned on doing about it.

□

Shaniqua left right after I told her that getting arrested had been my darkest secret. I got the feeling that she knew there was something more, something terrible. But did she only suspect what I was, or did she actually know? And should I come clean and admit it to her?

I was so confused.

"You tell her?" Dad snagged a cookie and was munching on it in the living room when Shaniqua ran down the hall and out the door. I'd followed her, trying to get her to stop, but she bolted away from me. By the time I reached the front door, she was long gone. I stood there, watching the place where she disappeared.

"No."

"Then why's she so upset?"

I shrugged, not wanting to get into it. "Dunno."

"You're going to have to tell her, you know."

"But, you said—"

"I know what I said, but circumstances sometimes change, and you have to do the right thing." He slung his arm across my shoulders and guided me to the couch. "Sit."

I sat.

"Look," he said. "Normally, I'm all for keeping your true identity secret. Most humans won't understand. You know that."

"Yeah, I know." I ran my fingers through my hair. "Dad, what am I going to do? What if she freaks out? What if—"

"James." He had that "Be Calm and Maintain" voice that I hated. "Do you love her?"

That caught me off-guard. Since when did Dad notice things like that? Mom, maybe, but Dad? He was as oblivious to things like that as Sheldon on *The Big Bang Theory*. I wasn't sure what to say, so I gave the old one-shoulder shrug and didn't say anything.

Neither did my father. I hated that, that silence that

always meant something. Finally, when I couldn't stand it anymore, I looked up at him.

He was smiling, a goofy grin I'd never seen on him before. "You do, don't you."

I ran my fingers through my hair. "Yeah, I think I do."

He patted my shoulder heavily. And grinned even bigger. Got a far-away look in his eyes. "I remember the day I first met your mother. We were just about your age—"

"Dad."

"—she was waiting on a customer at—"

"Dad!"

His eyes came into focus and he looked at me again. "What?"

"Me. Shaniqua. Remember?"

"Oh, sorry." He scratched his leg, right above the ankle. "Does she love you?"

"I think so."

"Then you owe it to her to be honest."

"But what if—"

"James. You're going to have to trust her."

He was right. But it was going to be almost as hard as controlling the wolf.

▢

Shaniqua was so disappointed in James. She went over and over their conversation. She'd been nothing but truthful with him, told him everything. And all he'd told her was about being arrested. Again. Big deal. Not only had he already told her all about it, but it was nothing compared to being a werewolf. She needed to know if what she thought she'd seen that night in the woods was what really happened. What was it like? Was he born that way? Or did he get bitten? She wanted to know every-thing.

And what about that woman he supposedly killed? What was that all about? She'd heard the rumors, but didn't believe them.

But what if they were true?

Was it accidental, his shooting her, or did it have something to do with being a werewolf?

And dammit, why wouldn't he tell her about it?

She'd been so sure he would trust her, like she trust-ed him. Maybe he didn't care about her as much as she thought. Could Uncle Roshaun be right? Had she made another huge mistake? She shook her head, refusing to believe she'd misjudged their relationship so badly.

Not again.

Her cell phone chirped and she pulled it out of her purse, thinking absently that it was probably Aunt Lydie checking up on her.

~ *U ok?* James asked.

Shaniqua frowned. *Do you even care, James?*

~ *Im fine.*

~ *U sure? Didn't seem like it.*

"That's because I'm not fine," Shaniqua muttered. "I'm most decidedly *not* fine." ~ *Y do u evn care?*

~ *So U R mad @ me.*

"No shit, Sherlock," Shaniqua said as she typed, her thumbs flying angrily over the keyboard. But before she hit Send, she paused, remembering what Watts had told her about the silent game shrinks liked to play, how it made the other person so uncomfortable that they'd talk just to fill the silence. "Yeah, let's see how that works." She deleted the text and continued walking toward home. It didn't take more than a minute or two for James to text her again.

~ *Meet me @ Diane's?*

Knowing full well where he meant, she decided not to make it easy on him and texted back, *~ Who's Diane?*

~ Sorry. I meant PJ's. U no? The diner.

~ I no. JK. C U N 10?

~ Gr8. C U then ☺♥

Maybe there was hope for them, after all.

☐

I pulled up in the Le Mans and parked. I didn't think Shaniqua was here yet, so I trotted across the street and ducked into the flower shop. Most girls liked flowers, my mom once told me, and even though Shaniqua was definitely not "most girls," I figured she'd at least appreciate the gesture of a single rose.

After all, it worked for *The Bachelor*.

And she said she and her aunt both liked the daisies I sent her.

"Hey, James," Diane called as I entered the diner, the rose tucked safely under my shirt, and headed for a booth in the back. "Haven't seen you around for a while."

"Sorry. Been really busy."

The bell above the door dinged as I slid into the booth and we both looked at the door. Shaniqua smiled and waved to me. I waved back.

"Yeah, I can see that," Diane said, her eyes twinkling.

Shaniqua slipped into the booth across the table from me but didn't kiss me. Not a good sign.

"Hey," I said.

"Hey," she replied. I handed her the rose. She accepted it, twirling it between her fingertips, but didn't say anything.

"So, I guess you're wondering why I asked you here."

Shaniqua sniffed the flower. "Really, James?"

"What?"

"Forget it." She started to get up.

"Okay, okay," I said hurriedly. "I got it. I'm sorry."

She sat back down and looked at me expectantly.

I took a deep breath. It was now or never. I had to tell her what was going on or risk losing her. I couldn't let that happen, at least not without a fight. "You've been here for a while, so I'm sure you've heard the rumors by now."

"Rumors?"

Normally, Shaniqua wasn't one to play games. It was one of the many reasons why I liked her. I couldn't figure out if she was now or not, but even if she was, I still had to tell her the truth. "Two years ago, when I was fourteen, my cousin and I—"

"Beth, right?"

"Yeah." There was no way to know how she was going to react to what I had to tell her. "Anyway, there was a serial killer running around town, murdering people on the nights when there was a full moon." I paused and risked a glance at her. She wasn't laughing at me. It didn't seem like she thought I was crazy, either. Maybe this would all work out, be okay. She might even believe me. "So Beth and I decided we'd have to figure out how to trap and kill it."

"It?"

"Yeah. We were pretty sure what it was, but no one would believe us."

"So what was it?"

Another deep breath. And another. And—

"So what can I get you two?" Diane's timing sucked.

"You want anything?" I asked Shaniqua.

"Can I get a Diet Cherry Coke?"

"Sure thing, hon." She turned to me. "And what can I

get you, sugar? You haven't had a float in a while, less you been cheatin' on me and getting them somewheres else."

"I could never cheat on my favorite server, Diane. You know that." I grinned at her. "I feel like some fries." I turned to Shaniqua. "You want some fries?"

"Sure."

"A basket of fries and a root beer."

"No float, huh?"

"Maybe next time."

I watched her walk into the kitchen. When I turned back, Shaniqua was smiling at me like nothing bad happened.

"You're really something, you know that?" she asked.

"What?"

"Just the way you treat people, like they all matter."

I shrugged. "Don't they?"

"So you were saying?"

Oh, yeah. That. "Where was I?" I asked, stalling.

"You and Beth knew what was killing people, but no one would listen to you."

"Yeah. Right."

Shaniqua reached across the table and placed her hands on top of mine. "It's okay, James. You can trust me."

"I know."

"Besides, I already know what you're going to say."

I frowned. *Oh, God, tell me she didn't follow me when I drove past her house last month and see me transform. Please, no.* "You—you do?"

"It was a werewolf, wasn't it?"

I stared at her in disbelief. "How did you know?"

"Oh, come on, I'm not stupid, you know."

"I know, but—"

"Here you go, kids." Diane plopped our sodas down on the table. "Fries'll be up in a minute. It's nice to have some customers again. It's been kind of dead in here, since, well, since that kid was killed back in September. People think it's happening all over again. The murders and such."

I didn't want to be rude to Diane, but now was not the time to talk about the town's reaction to what was going on. I looked up at her and gestured to the drinks. "Thanks, Diane."

She stood there a second as if waiting for us to say something else, but when we didn't, she pursed her lips and walked away, muttering something under her breath.

I leaned closer to Shaniqua and lowered my voice. "Who told you?" A few people knew the truth, but the bogus story former Sheriff Brazelton came up with was that PJ had been bitten by a rabid raccoon and gone mad, and that's why she'd killed all those people. I shot her in self-defense when she'd come after me. Donna's body had been removed from my house and the story there was that she'd been just another one of PJ's victims. I'd heard all the rumors and such, and every time I did, I wondered if Riggs had been the one responsible for starting them. I wouldn't put it past him.

"No one told me." She unwrapped her straw and stuck it into her glass. "I just figured it out. All the killings happened during the full moon, and what else comes out during that time besides werewolves?"

I shook my head. "You're amazing. I never would have guessed you would believe a weird story like that."

She shrugged and took a sip of her soda. "It's the truth, isn't it? Why shouldn't I believe you? Besides—"

Diane appeared with our fries and placed the basket on the table between us. "Here you go. Dig in."

"Thanks, Diane." Shaniqua picked up a fry and bit

into it. "Hot!" She grabbed her Diet Cherry and took a huge sip. Then she sat back and closed her eyes. "Oh, wow, those are perfectly salted and yummy." She smiled up at Diane. "I'll definitely be ordering more of those bad boys."

Diane giggled. "Well, enjoy."

As she headed back to the counter, I smiled and shook my head. "Yeah, talk about knowing just what to say and how to treat people. You are now one of her favorites, I guarantee it."

"Like you said, it doesn't take much." She glanced over at Diane, who was busy wiping down the counter. "As I was saying…"

"Yeah?" I squirted catsup all over the fries.

"Eew, gross," Shaniqua exclaimed. "What are you doing?"

"Putting catsup on the fries. What's wrong with that?"

She sighed heavily and pushed the basket toward me. "I didn't really want any anyway."

"Sorry. Want me to get you some more?" I looked around for Diane, but she must have gone into the kitchen.

"No, that's okay. I was going to tell you why I believe you."

"Yeah, why do you believe me?"

"Because my Aunt Lydie told me once about something she saw as a kid when she lived in Texas."

"What was it?"

"She and her parents were living in a little town close to the Mexican border. They were dirt poor. Had to walk a mile and a half down a dusty dirt road to fetch water from the town well. No indoor plumbing. Barely enough food. That sort of thing."

"Wow, that's rough."

"Yeah. So one day, she and her little sister were lugging two heavy pails of water each down this dirt road. They'd left later than normal and it was nearly dark, and they were still only about half-way home when they heard something behind them. They turned around but didn't see anything at first. Then they heard this low growling, like a dog but deeper and kind of gravely. It rushed out of some bushes at them. It wasn't very tall but it had kind of gray skin, scaly like a lizard, fangs and some really nasty quills on its back. And it ran at them like a person, on two legs."

"Oh, crap. What did they do?"

"They dropped their buckets and ran screaming down the road. Luckily, their mother had sent a neighbor to find them and he came along in his truck and scared it off."

"What the hell was it?"

"Ever heard of the Chupacabra?"

"Chupacabra? I thought those were a myth."

Shaniqua gawped at me for a second before she burst out laughing.

"What?"

"Do you—do you—" She wrapped her arms around herself and held her stomach. "—realize how—ridiculous that sounds?" She was laughing so hard, she nearly fell out of the booth. It was infectious, and I caught it, too.

Diane flashed us a curious look, so I put my finger up to my lips.

"Shh, shh." We weren't all that successful at quieting down. It felt good to laugh like that. It had been a long time.

"You want to know what the really funny thing is?" Now was as good a time as any to spill it.

Shaniqua sat up, still chuckling, and dabbed under her eyes with a napkin from the dispenser on the table.

"What's that?"

"PJ wasn't the only werewolf around here."

"Oh, yeah?" Shaniqua snorted. "So who else? Oh, wait. Mr. Petrellis is certainly weird enough. And he does have all that hair growing out of his ears."

I just looked at her. Maybe now wasn't the best time, after all.

She quieted down when she finally looked at me. "James?"

I took a deep breath. *Here goes...*"Me," I said quietly. "I'm a werewolf, too."

▢

"Well, finally."

"What do you mean, "finally"?"

"Well, first Watts told me about when you killed that woman, PJ. Said the rumor was that she was actually a werewolf. Plus, you never seem to be around on full moon days. Or nights. *Lifetime* movies with your mom. Yeah, right." She picked up a fry, shook off as much of the catsup as she could, and grimaced. "That's why I followed you the other night." She popped the fry into her mouth.

I just about choked on my own fry. "You what?"

"I followed you. Or at least, I *think* it was you. Remember the leaf I took out of your hair that day?"

Unable to speak, I simply nodded.

"That came from you running through the woods the night before, didn't it?"

I nodded again.

"So I've known since then what you were. Or what I thought you were." She plucked another fry from the basket. "It doesn't matter, you know."

"It doesn't?" How could a guy like me be so lucky to

have found someone like Shaniqua?

"Nope." She nibbled on the fry. "Not even when you go off with Mr. Hansen at lunchtime but won't tell me why, or what you do with him. What's up with that, anyway?" She tilted her head. "Is he a werewolf, too? You guys plotting something wolfey?"

I leaned toward her. "I'm not supposed to say. I promised." I glanced over my shoulder and lowered my voice more than it already was. "But yeah. Yeah, he is." I turned back to Shaniqua. "And no, we're not plotting anything wolfey. He's teaching me how to control it. But you can't tell anybody, okay?"

"Who'd believe me, anyway?" She reached across the table and took my hands in hers. "Tell me everything."

"You sure you want to know?"

She nodded, so I explained about how my parents and their friends left their homes right after high school and settled in Wolf Creek. About how they wanted to live peacefully among humans, not eat them. And how everything had been going along just fine until PJ contracted the always-fatal Moonspell.

"It's kind of like rabies," I added.

"Huh." She stuck a finger into the fries and flicked them around without actually taking any. "So, you were born a werewolf?"

"Yeah, but we don't actually transform until we're about fifteen. I didn't even know about it until after what happened with PJ. It actually kind of pissed me off, my parents not telling me before that. I mean, it's what I am. Shouldn't I have known it from the very beginning?"

"How come they didn't tell you?"

I shrugged and jammed several fries into my mouth. "Don't know. I guess they figured it was better I didn't know about it until I was old enough to keep it a secret."

Shaniqua nodded and sipped her soda. "That makes sense." She was quiet for a long time, and I thought it best to just let her process this. I wondered how I'd feel in her spot. Would I even be able to handle it?

Would she?

After what seemed like forever, after all the fries were gone and our glasses empty, I asked Shaniqua if she wanted another soda. She nodded without looking at me.

That scared me. What was she thinking? Was she going to dump me? She'd made such a big deal about honesty, and seemed so disappointed when I told her about my being arrested, like she'd known there was something more. Something darker.

But now that I'd been honest with her, was my secret too dark for her?

I picked up our glasses and the empty basket and took them over to the counter. Diane was at the register finishing up with a customer I didn't recognize. A lot of people left town after what happened, and a whole new crop moved in. In a way, it was kind of nice being mostly anonymous, although I also missed the way everyone used to know everyone else. I felt bad about her not having many customers anymore. People were just sort of holing up these days, waiting for things to pass. No one was even talking about the murders much. The whole town seemed to be in denial. I couldn't really blame them, though, not after what happened last time.

The worst part of the whole thing—other than the actual murders, of course—was that since no one was willing to talk about it, Riggs was in no danger of being fired.

And that really sucked.

"Earth to James," Diane said. "Come in, James."

"Huh?"

"There you are. You went away for a bit there."

I shook my head and smiled ruefully at her. "Oh, sorry."

"What can I do you for?" she asked.

"Can we get some more sodas?" I handed her our glasses.

"Sure." She gestured with one of the glasses toward Shaniqua. "Your girlfriend seems nice."

"I like her." I leaned an elbow on the counter and turned to look at Shaniqua. Our booth was empty. My stomach dropped to the floor. Panic set in. Whipping my head around, I turned to the door. The bell hadn't rung, except when Diane's only other customer left. Could Shaniqua have snuck out with him?

"Relax." Diane filled our glasses from the soda fountain, talking to me over her shoulder. "She went to the ladies room."

"Oh, I knew that." *Smooth. What a doofus.*

"Yeah. Sure you did. That's why all the blood left your face and you're white as a sheet."

The heat rose up my neck to my scalp faster than a NASCAR could complete a lap at Daytona, and I knew I was blushing.

"It's okay, kid. We've all been there." She set fresh sodas down on the counter in front of me. "Here you go."

"Thanks." I took them over to the booth and set them on the table. Just as I sat back down, Shaniqua came up behind me, put her hand on my shoulder, leaned down and kissed my cheek before tapping my arm.

"Scootch," she said simply, and there she was, sitting next to me again, like she hadn't just gotten the most disturbing news in the world. "So what's it like?"

"What's what like?"

"Transforming, silly."

I squirmed a little, not sure I wanted to talk to her about that. Not yet, anyway. It might be too much.

"Well…"

"It's okay. I want to know." She reached across the table for her soda. Took a sip. "Really."

"To be honest, it hurts like hell. First, the moon pulls on you until you think you might go crazy. Then your skin feels like you're about to spontaneously combust and the hair grows so fast that it itches beyond belief. Your bones snap, and—"

Talk about white as a sheet. I guess I should have realized that when she said she wanted to know, she didn't really want the gory details. Should have stuck with my "feelings." That's what girls always seemed to like.

"Sorry, I didn't mean to be so…explicit."

"No, that's okay. I asked, didn't I?"

"Well, anyway, I'm learning how to keep it from happening. It'll take a long time, from what I understand, but Mr. Hansen is teaching me some techniques I can use so that eventually, one day, I'll barely even have to think about it."

"Like your parents?"

"Yeah, like them. Dad says it's a good idea to go somewhere once a year, into the woods or something, and transform. Otherwise, it could lead to some sort of health issues or something."

"So how many of you are there?"

"You mean here, in Wolf Creek, or everywhere?"

She took another sip. "Both, I guess."

"I'm not really sure. I think there are about ten or fifteen families left in town. Most of the original settlors left over the years and started other colonies."

"Colonies? I thought werewolves traveled in packs."

"They do, when they follow the Old Ways. It can be dangerous to be a Lone Wolf without the protection of the Pack. But for those of us who choose our own path, we don't believe in the Old Ways, or in Pack Rule. There is no Alpha here. Just a bunch of people trying to live their lives as best they can."

"What about the rest of the world? How many packs are out there?"

"More than you even know."

◻

After we finished our fries and drinks, I walked Shaniqua home. She was quiet most of the way, and I respected that. It was a lot to take in, and I wanted to give her as much time to process it all as she needed.

Finally, she turned to me. "You didn't—hurt Logan and the others, did you? I mean, I wouldn't blame you if you did, but—you didn't, did you?"

I frowned and shook my head. "No, of course not! I would never hurt anyone like that." I took hold of both her hands and searched her face. She didn't seem scared of me, so that was a good thing.

Then she smiled and I knew everything was okay. She stroked my cheek and ran her fingers through my hair. "I didn't think so. But I had to ask. You know?"

I chuckled softly. "Yeah, I probably would have asked me too, if I were you."

We walked the rest of the way holding hands, not saying anything but just enjoying being together. When we stopped in front of her house and she turned to kiss me goodbye, I got the same fluttery feeling in my belly that I always did, and I thought she did, too. At least the kiss felt as real as it had the first time.

When she pulled back from me, her hand rested against the back of my neck, her thumb stroking just under my hairline. Chills went down my back, and she giggled. "Cold?" she teased.

"Freezing." We smiled at each other for a second but then she turned serious on me. A tear formed in the corner of her eye, and I was worried that she'd changed her mind about me. Had she decided I was a monster after all?

"Hey," I said gently. "What's wrong?"

"Nothing. I…just…thank you."

"For what?" Sometimes, Shaniqua could be a real head-scratcher.

"For trusting me."

"That's okay."

"No, I mean it. That's a pretty serious secret, what you are. I want you to know that I'll never tell anyone. Not even if we break up." She shook her head. "Not ever."

I took her by the hand. "And I'll never tell about what happened back in Chicago." I crossed my heart, never taking my eyes off hers. "I promise. No matter what."

The porch light flashed on and off and on again, Shaniqua's signal to go in. She leaned against the door and closed her eyes. "Gah," she muttered.

"Guess you'd better go in."

She sighed heavily. "Guess so." She opened the door and paused. "See you tomorrow?"

"Sure. Text you later?"

"No, better not." She jerked her head toward the inside of the house.

I nodded. "Gotcha. Night."

"Night." She kissed me lightly on the cheek and headed inside. Her aunt was standing there, apparently watching us through the window, her arms crossed tightly against her chest. She wasn't exactly glaring, but I could tell she said something about me from Shaniqua's body language. I hoped she wasn't in trouble for some reason, but at least now I kind of understood why they kept such a short leash on her.

Shaniqua turned and blew me a kiss, maneuvering around her aunt to do so. I jammed my hands in my pockets and headed back to PJs to pick up my car.

□

The talk with Shaniqua had gone better than I'd expected. She was an awesome chick, and I knew how lucky I was that she was so understanding. It was hard to believe that she hadn't been freaked out by what I'd told her.

For some reason, I thought about Riff as I walked back to my car. I liked to think he would have approved of Shaniqua. For sure he would have loved her green eyes. He had a thing for green eyes. The last Labor Day he was alive, I remembered there was this girl setting up one of the booths at the festival with a dragonfly belly ring that he had the hots for. She had green eyes.

It's a wonder he liked Gwen Stefani as much as he had because she had brown eyes. Or maybe blue. I couldn't remember. But what I did remember was that his favorite song was *I'm Just a Girl* by No Doubt. He would have died of embarrassment if he'd known I knew, but he was my best friend and I knew all his secrets. Even if he hadn't known all of mine. Sometimes I wondered if that made him a better friend than me.

I bopped along, singing quietly to myself. "Oh, I'm just a girl, all pretty and petite—"

"More like a little whore, butt ugly and dumb."

Startled, I whirled around. Riggs. I shook my head and closed my eyes. Great. Exactly what I needed, Riggs hearing me sing that particular song.

He stood there, in that way he had that my mom called his holier-than-thou stance: one hand resting on his gun, the other on his duty belt, elbows facing outward.

Except he was dressed in civies, and his fists were curled in at his waist. He seemed to be balancing on the balls of his feet. There was an old picture of the Justice League I'd seen on the Internet once where the Flash was standing the same way, and I almost laughed out loud. It wouldn't surprise me if Riggs thought he *was* the Flash.

"So, you just a girl, huh? Like that athlete guy?" That horrid grin of his crept onto his face again, and it was all I could do not to shudder.

"Look, Riggs." He scowled. "I mean, Sherriff. I'm on my way home." I gestured across the street, towards the parking lot of PJs and the Le Mans. "Just gotta get to my car."

Riggs glanced over at my car, then back at me before gesturing towards it. "That car, over there?"

Why was he asking me that? He knew what my car looked like—it was the only 1969 Le Mans in town.

Frowning, I nodded.

"Well, then," he said. "I guess you'd better go home, then."

Something was wrong. Since when had he ever been nice to me?

It put me on my guard.

Riggs nodded and gestured vaguely towards my car again. "Go on, now."

I looked at him sideways a second then shrugged and turned my back to him. That was a mistake, and I quickly learned why he'd kept his fists curled at his waist.

He kidney-punched me with the brass knuckles he'd kept hidden, and I fell to my knees. The pain was incredible, like nothing I'd ever imagined. I couldn't breathe. I couldn't see anything but red spots. The world went silent around me.

"Don't ever disrespect me again." Riggs kicked me in the side and I went completely down. "Ever. You feel me, little girl?"

My blood started to boil, and my skin felt like a colony of wasps was stinging me over and over again. I glared up at Riggs and growled. The wolf was waking up, and I wasn't sure I could hold it back.

Or that I even wanted to.

☐

"So," Aunt Lydie said the second the door was closed. "You tell him?"

Shaniqua shot Uncle Roshaun a nasty look. He put up his hands, palms to her, and backed up a step or two.

"Hey," he said, "I didn't say a word."

Shaniqua tossed her purse onto the couch and crossed her arms. "So, what, you were listening?"

"I didn't have to," Aunt Lydie said. Her voice softened. "I remember being young and in love." She looked at Uncle Roshaun and smiled. "It wasn't that long ago, you know." She brushed Shaniqua's hair back off her shoulder. "I just don't want to see you get yourself into another fix."

"I know what I'm doing, Auntie."

"I know you think you do, sweetie. But not everyone is as honest and trustworthy as you are."

"I trust James. Implicitly."

"Well, I guess we'll see if he's worthy of that trust, won't we?"

"I'm going to bed." Shaniqua hung up her purse and headed down the hall to her room. The looks her aunt and uncle gave each other didn't escape her notice, but they didn't really understand. Sure, they loved her. But did they have to be so over-protective? Everything was such a hassle with them.

She flipped on her iPod and put on a little Sam Smith

before she changed into her uncle's comfy, oversized Bears tee shirt and flannel pants and pulled down the comforter on her bed. It was a boring beige with olive green palm trees and something orange that might have been a sun or a sand dune. It was so faded that it was hard to tell. Sometimes she missed having her own things, but she'd been forced to leave nearly everything at home. It made her feel like a refugee, but at least she'd had somewhere to flee to.

And there was James.

He was truly something. Sure, there was the whole "He's a werewolf" thing, but really, who didn't have issues these days? The important thing was that he was learning to deal with it in a peaceful and non-violent way, and she knew he would never hurt her.

When the song "Lay Me Down" came on, Shaniqua sat back against her pillows and closed her eyes. The soulful sound of Sam's voice stirred something deep inside her, and she thought, not for the first time, how much he reminded her of James. They didn't look anything alike, but there was something about their mannerisms that was similar. They had the same aquiline nose and well-defined eyebrows, which amused her. *Who would have thought a werewolf would have nice eyebrows? You'd expect them to be bushy and wild, wouldn't you?*

It had been a mistake to get naked for William, she knew that now. She supposed she even knew it then. But he'd been so popular. All the guys wanted to be him and all the girls wanted to be with him. And he'd picked her. She'd never been quite sure why, but when he started pressuring her into going further than she'd wanted to, she'd panicked. Thought that sending him a naked picture would hold him off for a while.

Boy, had she ever been wrong about that. By the next day, everyone in school had seen it.

Shaniqua shook her head and rolled over onto her stomach. She had to stop dwelling on the past. She was with James now, and he treated her nicer than anyone ever had before. He would never do anything malicious, like William had.

Would he?

☐

Riggs took a step back. "What the hell—"

I could tell by the look on his face that my eyes had been glowing red, so I shut them as tight as I could and did my best to visualize the most ginormous stop sign ever. Of all the people in town, he was the one I was most scared of what would happen if he discovered my secret. The full moon had been two days ago, but its pull on me was still fairly strong, and it was a real struggle. Eventually, though, my skin cooled and my temperature dropped.

I was me again.

Blood trickled out of my mouth, and I wiped it away with the back of my hand as I struggled to get to my knees.

Headlights splashed across us, and, after a brief pause, Riggs reached down, grabbed me by the arm, and yanked me to my feet.

I coughed.

Riggs patted my shoulder and pretended to brush me off, then waved as the car passed us. As soon as we could see its brake lights, he pushed me. "What are you?" he asked. "Some kind of freak?"

"What are you talking about?" I rubbed my side where he'd kicked me, and winced. If he hadn't broken at least one of my ribs, it would be a miracle.

"Your eyes."

"What about them?" So he had seen them glow.

"They—they were red."

"My eyes are brown." I pointed to my left eye and opened them both as wide as I could. "See?"

"I know what I saw."

I shook my head. "You're crazy. Can I go now?"

"Fine. But if you so much as step one inch out of line or tell anyone about this, I'll haul your ass in. Do I make myself clear?"

"Crystal."

He walked across the street and into the diner. I headed to the Le Mans, wondering where he'd parked his car, and how he'd known where I'd be.

CHAPTER 27

Friday, December 4, 2015,
Twenty-Two Days to Full Moon:

The cold wind reminded Shaniqua of the breeze off the lake back home: freezing. It was the only thing she hated about Chicago, never being able to get completely warm during the winter. Her dad said she must be cold-blooded because she only seemed to get warm enough when the sun was shining and she was out in the middle of it.

She and James had just left school and were walking home when a shiny new Fiat pulled up beside them. The window rolled down and a slender hand with French-tipped nails shot out and waved at her. She could hardly believe who had driven up.

"Hey," Nicole said.

"Um, hi?" She sounded like a total tard, but she couldn't help it. Why was Alexis's Number Two Mean Girl all by herself, much less talking to someone like Shaniqua? Didn't they always travel in gaggles, like geese?

Shaniqua exchanged glances with James, who seemed just as confused as she was.

"So," Nicole quipped. "Having car trouble?" She

cocked her head and smiled guilelessly. At least, that's what Shaniqua thought *she* thought it looked like. But Shaniqua was wary, and just shrugged. She wouldn't put it past Alexis to have had one of her toadies play some sort of trick on her. "Oh, that's right. You're only sixteen."

Shaniqua turned to James, her brows furrowed. *Huh?*

"You have to be seventeen before you can drive anyone under twenty," he explained.

"Oh, yeah," Shaniqua said.

"You need a ride?" Nicole looked pointedly at James. "Shaniqua."

"No, she doesn't. I'll get her home. Thanks." James pulled his phone out and dialed. Nicole sat there and watched, blowing a bubble with her gum every once in a while.

Shaniqua watched her out of the corner of her eye and wondered when she was going to leave.

"Mom," James said. "Is Dad there?" He glanced over at Shaniqua and shook his head. "Oh, well, when will he be back? It's freezing out here. I was hoping he could drive us home…Shaniqua, Mom…Yes, Mom, I know…I know, Mom…Can you just tell him, please?" He disconnected the call and shoved his phone into his pocket. He gave her a one-shoulder shrug. "My dad's not home."

Shaniqua grinned at him. "Really?"

"Should be home in about half an hour or so."

"Oh." She stuffed her hands in her coat pockets and slunk down in the seat. "Brr. Why's it so cold? I thought it was always sunny and warm in California."

"Hey." Nicole climbed out of her car and leaned against the door. "Looks like you could use that ride after all."

"Well…" Shaniqua looked at James pleadingly. She blew on her hands, trying to warm them up. She honestly didn't know if she'd last out here another half hour or so. She couldn't even feel her toes anymore.

James sighed. "It's okay." He nodded toward Nicole. "Go on. Get warm. I'll call you later."

"You sure it's okay? I'll stay if you want."

"No sense in both of us freezing our asses off. Go on."

Shaniqua threw her arms around him and hugged him tight. "You're the best. Thanks!" She kissed him quickly, grabbed her backpack and trotted over to the Fiat. She and Nicole climbed in, and when they closed the doors, Shaniqua felt the blast of hot air from the car's heater and thought she'd died and gone to heaven.

"Thanks, Nicole." She held her hands in front of the nearest heater vent in an attempt to warm them, at least enough to get some feeling back. "But aren't you afraid someone will see us together and tell Alexis?"

Nicole drove with both hands on the steering wheel. She glanced at her passenger before returning her gaze to the road. "I couldn't care less what Alexis thinks." Her fingers tightened around the wheel. "Or anyone else."

CHAPTER 28

Monday December 7, 2015,
Nineteen Days to Full Moon:

Nicole and Shaniqua barely said two more words to each other on that long drive home. The whole thing left Shaniqua puzzled. But not nearly as much as at school, when Nicole ran up to her in the hall. They had Biology together, but so did Alexis and the rest of her brownnosers, so Shaniqua wasn't surprised when Nicole didn't speak to her. But when she'd come up to her and Watts during lunch and asked to sit with them, Shaniqua hadn't known what to think. All she could do was nod. She glanced over at Watts and wasn't at all shocked to see her blanch and nearly choke on her spring roll.

After that, Nicole'd eaten lunch with them all week. Sometimes, James joined them, but other days, he went to talk to Mr. Hansen. That Friday, Nicole'd simply plopped down next to Shaniqua and started eating like it was the most natural thing in the world. When Watts saw that she'd beaten her to the table, Shaniqua noticed that she'd veered away and disappeared around the side of the building.

"Guess what?" Nicole said, after a few uncomfortable minutes.

"What?" Anything to break the silence.

"My parents want to meet you."

Shaniqua nearly spat out her water. As it was, she swallowed it wrong and just about coughed up a lung.

Nicole pounded on her back, a look of concern on her face. "You okay?"

"Yeah," Shaniqua croaked. "Just—swallowed down—the wrong pipe." She wiped her eyes with her sleeve and coughed a final time. "They really want to meet me?"

Nicole nodded. "They really do."

"Why?"

Nicole frowned. "What do you mean, why? Because you're my friend, that's why." She sighed heavily. "It's a thing with them. They have to meet all my friends."

"Oh."

"So what do you say? Next Saturday good?"

And that's how Shaniqua came to believe her luck might actually have changed.

CHAPTER 29

Wednesday, December 9, 2015,
Seventeen Days to Full Moon:

Two years ago, today, a rogue werewolf killed the only adult who had believed me when I said a werewolf was stalking the town. I'd managed to kill PJ when, as the werewolf, she'd crashed through my living room window and attacked us, but not before she killed Donna.

It felt like my fault.

I knew it wasn't, not really, but it still felt like it sometimes. Once in a while, I lay awake at night, going over everything that happened, wondering how I could have changed things, what I could have done differently to make sure Donna survived. But it always came out the same, no matter what different scenarios I came up with.

Donna always died.

So every December ninth, on the anniversary of her death, I went to the cemetery and put a silver bullet on Donna's headstone as a kind of memorial. Last year, I'd gone alone. This year, Shaniqua went with me. At first, it felt weird, like I was somehow disrespecting Donna, but Shaniqua actually insisted that we bring flowers along with the bullet.

"It will show that she is missed," she explained.

"That's why I bring the silver bullet," I told her as I paid for the flowers. After Donna'd died, I'd found her hidden stash of silver bullets and kept them underneath the floorboards in my room. I figured by the time I ran out of them, I'd be able to get some more.

Shaniqua slipped her hand through my arm and we left the flower store, heading for the cemetery. It wasn't very far from the center of town, and we strolled along in companionable silence. That was one of the good things about Shaniqua. She didn't feel like she had to talk all the time to fill up the silence.

When we got there, the gates were locked, but I knew they would be. Toby, the crypt keeper, kept them chained shut with an enormous lock, like something you'd see in a horror movie, but there was plenty of room to slip through the gap.

I hoped Shaniqua was game, but I didn't need to worry. She was up for just about anything. We slipped through and walked along the street that cut the graveyard in half. It was cold and damp, and Shaniqua pulled her jacket collar up over her ears in an attempt to keep warm.

Donna died sometime after four in the morning, and last year I'd come to the cemetery about the same time, but this year was a daylight moon, so it had set shortly before four in the afternoon. Because Shaniqua wanted to come with, I couldn't very well ask her to meet me at four o'clock in the morning, even though it wasn't a full moon, so we'd come out here about seven. That way she didn't have to lie to her aunt and uncle or sneak out in the middle of the night. She just told them we were on a date and left it at that.

A crow cawed above us. "It's kind of creepy in here," she said, hugging herself as she looked around.

I shrugged. "Yeah, I guess so. Okay, here it is."

We walked up to Donna's grave. Clouds passed over the moon and the nearest light post was about fifty feet away, so it was hard to see, but it looked like there was something sitting on the grass in front of her headstone. I squinted and approached slowly. "What the—"

My silver bullet from last year was gone. In its place was a shot glass with a Scottish crest on it, and the words "Quiet Riot." On the grass was a ratty old stuffed Unicorn. I had no idea who could have left them.

"What's Quiet Riot?" Shaniqua asked. "Some kind of rave or something?"

"That was Donna's bar," I said quietly, and knelt beside the grave. "After she died, it was closed down." I laid the flowers against Donna's headstone and patted them gently. The paper they were wrapped in crinkled.

"Is that what the empty storefront on Wolf Creek Road is?"

I nodded.

"What's up with the Unicorn?"

I shook my head. "Not sure. Donna once told me that the Unicorn was the national animal of Scotland, where her ancestors were from. Apparently they were some of the very first werewolf hunters.

"She was a hunter?"

"Yeah."

"But—"

"I know, right? But at that time, neither one of us knew what I was."

She laid her hand gently on my shoulder, and we stayed there like that, quiet, for several minutes. In my mind, I was talking to Donna, telling her again how sorry I was that things worked out the way they had. Shaniqua seemed to be getting restless, shifting back and forth and looking over her shoulders, so I was about to wrap it up when she leaned down and whispered in my ear.

"Do you hear something?"

"What do you mean?" I whispered back. "I don't hear anything."

"Listen." She whirled around. "There it is again!"

I followed her gaze. "I still don't—"

Something moved, something deep in the shadows several rows away.

"I think we're being watched," she said.

"Yeah, I feel it now, too."

"Can we go now?"

"Sure." I took her by the hand and squeezed it gently. "Come on, I'll buy you some fries."

"Chili cheese?"

I chuckled. That girl sure could eat. "Extra cheesey."

We headed for the gate. The shadows seemed to be following us, so we sped up a little.

When we got to the gate, I pulled the two halves apart and held them while Shaniqua slipped through. Just as I started to follow her, something howled from deep inside the shadows, an angry yet mournful sound.

Once through the gate, we stuck to the middle of the road and hurried back to town.

Neither one of us ever mentioned what happened that night, but I wondered who—or what—had followed us.

It wasn't long before I found out.

CHAPTER 30

Saturday, December 12, 2015,
Fourteen Days to Full Moon:

The Morningside mansion was even more beautiful on the inside than it was on the outside, which had richly manicured lawns, complete with a fountain of an angel in the center and a circular driveway that wound its way through a well-tended rose garden. No drought here, apparently. Two-story arches ushered visitors into a glass-enclosed terrarium that it would take hours to wander through before you could be sure you hadn't missed anything. It was as if a tropical wonderland had been transplanted from the lush jungles of Bora Bora, or wherever there were jungles.

It made the surrounding woods seem pedestrian by comparison.

When Shaniqua felt sufficiently recovered from her shock and delight at how lovely everything was outside, she rang the bell and giggled when the chimes played the opening chords to Lady Gaga's *Poker Face*. Not one of Shaniqua's faves, but still cool as a doorbell.

The door opened and Nicole pulled her into the vast foyer. Ivory marble floors lead to twin spiral staircases, the likes of which she'd never seen except on television and in movies.

"Hi," Nicole said breathlessly. "I thought you'd never get here."

"I'm sorry," Shaniqua said. "Am I late?"

"No, not at all." Nicole took both Shaniqua's hands in hers. "I couldn't wait for you to get here. Come on."

Shaniqua let herself be led while she gawked at one priceless object after another. She'd never seen such extravagance, much less been invited in to it. The floor was made from what she could only guess was fine Italian marble. Through huge floor-to-ceiling windows, the woods that flanked the town appeared slightly menacing with darkened boughs that crisscrossed overhead. Then she blinked and the sunshine sparkled off the window, highlighting the vegetation so that it looked like a picture in a fairytale.

They stopped suddenly in front of a heavy wooden door, and Nicole knocked.

"Daddy?" she said quietly. "Daddy, Shaniqua's here."

The door opened suddenly and made Shaniqua jump. "Come in, come in." Dr. Morningside, a large man with an equally large voice, motioned them inside what Shaniqua could only assume was The Library. Because in a house like this, it had to be capitalized, didn't it? Framed photographs were peppered in between rows and rows of books. Legal books, leather bound books, first editions, classics. Basically, anything a girl could want. If she lived in this house, she'd spend all her time pretending to be Belle from *Beauty and the Beast*, happiest when she was reading. She hoped she'd get a chance to get a closer look.

In the meantime, she glanced around the room at the photos. Dr. Morningside holding a huge pair of scissors at some ribbon-cutting ceremony; Dr. Morningside shaking hands with President Obama; Dr. Morningside with his arm around Mayor Willoughby. Dr. Morningside with more famous people than she could ever believe.

They sat on an uncomfortable couch that seemed more like it belonged in a museum somewhere than in someone's house, and made small talk until a woman with platinum blonde hair and a wide smile poked her head in the door.

"Lunch's ready," she said. Her face lit up when she spotted Shaniqua. Extending her arms, she approached so swiftly, Shaniqua was somewhat alarmed and stood up in a hurry. "You must be Nicole's friend. Hi!" She grabbed her around the shoulders and gave her a hug before pushing her gently away. "I'm Nicole's mom."

"Nice to meet you, Mrs. Morningside."

"Oh, please." She waved her hand at Shaniqua. "Call me Monica."

"Come on, let's eat." Dr. Morningside rubbed his hands together. "You're in for quite a treat." He threw his arm across his wife's shoulders. "It's pot roast day." He kissed Mrs. Morningside's cheek. "My wife makes the world's best pot roast."

"True story," Nicole agreed.

"Thank you, family," she said, flashing a smile so white that Shaniqua nearly threw her arm up in front of her eyes to avoid being blinded. For about the hundredth time since coming here, she wondered if sparkling white teeth were a requirement in Wolf Creek. Seemed like everyone had them.

Dr. and Mrs. Morningside left the library with their arms wrapped around each other, and Nicole trotted along behind them. Shaniqua took a final look around the room, hoped she'd get another chance to skim through the books even as she wondered about a family that ate dinner for lunch, and followed them down the hall.

The dining room was huge, and the glass-topped table was just as massive. It was set with the most gorgeous china Shaniqua had ever seen. Dr. Morningside sat at one end and Mrs. Morningside—Monica—sat at the other. The girls sat facing each other at the sides. Shaniqua looked out the floor-to-ceiling windows at the panoramic view of Wolf Creek and the forest beyond. Sunlight flowed in through the glass and hit the prisms in the chandelier above them. Rainbows fell on the crystal water goblets and made them sparkle. Shaniqua felt as though she'd fallen down the rabbit hole and into some magical world of beyond.

"We're so glad you could join us today, Shaniqua."

"Thanks for having me."

Dr. Morningside raised his glass. The rest of the family followed suit. They looked at Shaniqua expectantly. She hurriedly lifted her glass.

"Here's to new friends," Dr. Morningside said.

"To new friends," the family repeated. They sipped their water.

"To new friends," Shaniqua mumbled. She was beginning to feel uneasy. All this attention was creeping her out.

The rest of the meal was fine. They chatted about school, about some of the doctor's exploits when he travelled with Doctors Without Borders, and about some of the crazy pet owners Mrs. Morningside dealt with at the vet clinic where she worked part-time.

And they never once asked about Shaniqua's past. For which she was eternally grateful. It was just too embarrassing.

Dr. Morningside was right. His wife did make the world's best pot roast. Shaniqua was about to mention this when the doctor pushed his chair back from the table.

He wiped his mouth with his napkin—his cloth napkin—and announced that he had work to do.

"Nice to meet you," he told Shaniqua. "I'm glad to know that we'll be seeing more of you around here." Then he left the table and went back into the library.

Shaniqua looked at Nicole quizzically. They'd be seeing more of her? Really? It was news to her.

"You girls go on, now," Mrs. Morningside said. "I'll take care of the dishes."

"Come on," Nicole said. "Wanna watch a movie?"

Shaniqua looked at her watch and couldn't believe they'd been sitting at the table discussing current events and what-not for nearly three hours. "No, I'm sorry, I have to get going. But thanks for inviting me. It was…fun."

"You sure? We have a lot of DVDs."

Shaniqua shook her head. "Sorry, I have to help my aunt." They stopped at the front door. "What did your father mean back there? When he said they'd be seeing more of me?"

"Oh, that was just his way of telling me that he approves. He's done that with all my friends, ever since I was little. If he didn't like you, he would have excused himself and left the table without saying anything to you." She threw her arm around Shaniqua's shoulders and squeezed. "So you're in! Yay!"

Shaniqua smiled weakly. "Yay."

But something didn't feel right. And it wouldn't be long before she found out why.

CHAPTER 31

Friday, December 18, 2015,
Eight Days to Full Moon:

arty flyer." Nicole was striding down the hall with a red and yellow stack of papers in her hand. She handed one to just about every person she met. With the exception of the geeks and nerds, Shaniqua noted.

"Party flyer. Party—Oh, hey. Hi!" Nicole stopped when she saw her, reached into her tote bag, and handed her a bright fuchsia piece of paper. "I was hoping to run into you." She grabbed Shaniqua's wrists and pulled her away from Watts, giggling. Shaniqua thought she was acting especially girly, but she put on her happy face and grinned back before reading the flyer.

"So is this…"

"Yeah, it's for my birthday. The big eighteen." Nicole leaned in and got real close to her. "It's BYOB. That's bring your own—"

"Bottle. Yeah, I know."

"So will you come?" Nicole looked at her pleadingly before glancing at Watts and scowling. "You can bring someone, if you want."

Shaniqua looked over at Watts, who stared back at

her like a startled rabbit, and shrugged. "I don't know…"

"Oh, please? Please say you'll come. It's a cosplay party. Isn't that cool? I always wanted to throw a cosplay party."

"Well…"

"Good." Nicole let go of her wrists. "It's settled. It's going to be epic. See you then!" She hurried off down the hall, still passing out flyers. If even half the people who were given flyers went, it was going to be epic, all right.

Shaniqua and Watts watched her until she disappeared around the corner of the lockers. The faint sounds of laughter floated back to them.

"You aren't really going to go, are you?" Watts asked. She adjusted her backpack and they headed to class.

"Sure, why not?"

"Why not?" Watts's voice rose. "Why not? Because she's part of Alexis's pack of hyenas, who have done nothing but make your life miserable since school started, that's why not."

"Nicole's not like that."

"Are you kidding me? She's just as bad as the rest of them."

"How can you say that? She ate lunch with us all last week and never once said anything mean." Shaniqua looked pointedly at Watts. "To either one of us. I think she's changed."

"I don't trust her. And I don't see how you can, either."

Watts didn't know Shaniqua'd gone to Nicole's for lunch, that she'd met her parents, and that Nicole sincerely seemed to want to be her friend. Shaniqua was tempted to tell her, but at the last minute, something told her not to. She shrugged. "Well, I still want to go. Just to see what it's like."

"All right, but I think you're crazy."

"You want to go with me?"

Watts snorted. "Not on your life. You're on your own, pal."

"Don't call me pal, buddy."

"Don't call me buddy, mate."

"Don't call me mate, friend."

They burst into giggles and walked into Trig.

CHAPTER 32

Monday, December 21, 2015,
Five Days to Full Moon:

Shaniqua's aunt and uncle had gone Christmas shopping and told her that I could come over but that we'd have to sit outside on the porch until they got home. I guess they still didn't trust me and thought something might happen while they were gone. I couldn't blame them, after what Shaniqua told me happened with that asshole at her other school, but I wished they'd give me a little credit and realize I'd never hurt Shaniqua. Or at least realize she'd learned her lesson.

They were what my mom called helicopter parents, always hovering around her. I don't think they actually snooped through her things or eavesdropped on our conversations, but she had to ask them for permission to breathe.

It made me realize how lucky I was to have the parents I did. They pretty much let me do what I wanted because they'd taught me early on how to make good choices and that there were consequences for the bad ones.

Plus there was the whole killing-a-werewolf thing.

Shaniqua was bent over her sketch pad, working on

yet another drawing of Meilikki. The tip of her tongue was sticking out of the corner of her mouth and her brow was furrowed in concentration. It gave me the warm fuzzies to watch her, knowing that I contributed in some small way to her happiness when I bought her those watercolor pens. Sure, it meant I had to work a little longer—okay, a lot longer—to earn the money to get my car painted, but I didn't mind so much.

Shaniqua continued sketching. "What?"

"What, what?"

"You're staring at me."

"Am not."

She looked up at me, eyes twinkling, and giggled. "Oh, yeah. Right."

Heat blasted up my neck and spread across my face in about a millisecond flat. How was she able to read me so easily when she was such an enigma to me?

"Sorry."

"S'okay." She chewed on the end of her pen.

Now it was my turn to wonder what was up. I cocked my head and shook my finger at her. "You're up to something, aren't you?"

She tried unsuccessfully to hide her grin. "I don't know what you're talking about."

"Yes, you do. Come on, spill it."

After looking up and down the street, I guess to make sure her aunt and uncle weren't coming, she reached under her pens, pulled out a postcard-sized paper, read it and giggled.

I reached across the table and wriggled my fingers. "Gimme see."

She giggled again and shyly handed it over. There was a brightly-colored animated figure that I didn't recognize on one side. I flipped the card over and read. "'If you have the talent, ambition and drive, you could win a summer internship with a major publisher of graphic novels. Just bring your portfolio, attend the FREE workshops, and have your work reviewed by top industry professionals.'" I looked up at her, my smile so wide it felt like it extended well past my ears and off the side of my head.

"Do you think we can do it?" Shaniqua asked. "I mean, how would we get there? I don't have a license, you can't drive anyone else, and it's not like I can just ask Uncle Roshaun to drive us all the way in to LA." She shook her head. "No, it's impossible. They'll never let me go."

"I know. It sucks. But you definitely have the talent. Your drawings are amazing. You could even bring some pictures of the sculpture of Wolfsbayne you made. I'll bet that would make their eyes pop out of their heads. Probably give you a scholarship." I smiled. "God, this would be so good for you."

"For us," she said. "It would be so good for *us*. Maybe we could even get Meilikki actually off the ground and published." She got a far-off look in her eye. "Just imagine."

I was imaging it. Being the artist for a series of best-selling graphic novels was her dream, and while I still wanted to be a novelist, the idea of working with Shaniqua on a series of stories, no matter how small my contribution might be, appealed to me. I was even warming to the idea of it being about a werewolf hunter.

I had to figure out a way to get her there.

The card was ripped out of my hand. "Ow!" I frowned and put my hand to my mouth. She'd grabbed the card so quickly that it gave me a serious paper cut in the webbing between my thumb and palm. "What the hell?"

She gestured with her head and shoved the card back under her pens. "They're home."

Her aunt and uncle drove into the driveway and pulled into the garage. "That was close," she whispered. "We'll talk more later."

CHAPTER 33

Tuesday, December 22, 2015,
Winter Solstice, also known as Midwinter's Night,
the year's shortest day and longest night.
Four Days to Full Moon:

Watts finished her hot chocolate and tossed the paper cup into the trash before heading into the bathroom. She wasn't much into coffee like so many people these days were, but Cuppa Joe had the best hot chocolate in town, and she couldn't resist splurging on a cup. After finishing up her Christmas shopping with a cute knit cap shaped like a lion's head for Shaniqua and a poster of Freddie Mercury for James, she'd popped into the coffee house to get warm and spend her last few dollars on her favorite drink.

She needed to use the restroom before she got on the bus for the long ride home. She wasn't looking forward to it because it was likely to be crowded this time of day and this close to Christmas.

But it was a necessary evil, so she pushed open the door and went inside.

Fortunately, it was empty. She hated using a public bathroom, but at least there weren't a ton of people in it. She went into a stall, closed and locked the door, then grimaced when she heard the door to the room open and several girls, giggling loudly, walked in.

"I can't wait," one of them said.

"I know," another one said. "It's going to be off the chain."

Watts immediately recognized the second voice, and peeked through the crack between the stall wall and its door—Cheyenne and Destiny, part of Alexis's lemmings. She watched while they applied yet more lip gloss—how shiny did their lips need to be, anyway?—and checked themselves out in the mirror.

"Can you believe the little skank fell for the whole cosplay thing?" Cheyenne asked. "I mean, as if."

"Whatever they have planned for her will be epic, that's for sure." Destiny wiped gloss from the corners of her mouth with a pinkie. "Teach her to be a hater."

"Can't wait. It'll be so epic."

They left giggling and sounding to Watts like a hybrid of a laughing hyena and a braying jackass.

Emphasis on jackass.

Watts came out of the stall to wash her hands. She couldn't believe what she'd just heard, although it didn't really surprise her.

The only question was, how was she going to tell Shaniqua?

CHAPTER 34

Wednesday, December 23, 2015,
Three Days to Full Moon:

We were sitting at the kitchen table, a plate of Mom's world famous peanut butter cookies between us. I'd poured some milk and we'd had several of the cookies and most of the milk when I caught Shaniqua looking at me funny.

"What?" I asked, pinching my nostrils together. "I got a booger hanging out of my nose?"

She laughed that laugh of hers, the one that gave me butterflies. "No, silly." She reached into her backpack and pulled out a bright pink piece of paper. It was folded in half and a little crumpled. She put the paper on her lap and ran it across her leg, trying to flatten it out, I guessed. For some reason, I didn't think I was going to like whatever it was she wanted to show me.

I cocked my head and waited.

And waited some more.

"You going to let me see it?" I eventually asked. She sighed and handed it over. After I read it, I read it again, just to make sure I'd read it right the first time, and frowned at Shaniqua. "You're kidding me, right?"

"What?"

I held the flyer out to her. "You really want to go to a birthday party for Nicole?" I was puzzled. "You realize that Alexis and the rest of the Terrible Toadies will be there, right?"

"Of course I do. I'm not stupid."

"Seriously? Why?"

"Why not?"

I was incredulous. "Why not?" I asked. "Why *not?* How about, they've been making your life miserable since the day you got here. Or how about, they're just going to find some way to humiliate you if you go? How about that?"

"Aren't you the least bit curious?"

"About what?"

"About how the other half lives. Don't you want to see the inside of one of those McMansions on the hill?"

I shook my head. "No, I don't."

"It's really pretty, you know," she told me. "Stuffy, but still…"

"How do you know?"

"I went to lunch there the other day. Remember?"

"Oh. Yeah."

"So will you come with me?"

I grabbed a cookie and stuffed it in my mouth so I wouldn't have to answer her.

"Come on, James. You know you want to."

I sat back in my chair and brushed some crumbs off my shirt.

Shaniqua leaned across the table and put her hand on my arm. Grinned. I looked away.

"Ja—ames," she wheedled. "Pleeze?"

I couldn't help it. I smiled. Tried to hide it from her, but she saw it anyway.

"Thanks. I knew I could count on you." She got up and threw her arms around my shoulders, pulling me close. "It'll be okay," she whispered into my ear. "You'll see."

I rubbed her forearm. Her skin was so silky smooth. Taking her hand in mine, I kissed her palm. "Okay," I told her, even though I didn't believe it. I'd have to check my calendar to see when the full moon was. It had to be soon. I could already feel it pulling at me.

"I got to go." She folded the flyer, put it back into her purse and zipped it shut. Slinging it over her shoulder, she leaned down and kissed me. "We still on for tomorrow?"

"Yup."

"Good. I can't wait to give you your present. See you about eight?"

"Sure. You want me to ask my dad to drive you home?" I was nervous about letting her walk home without me. Thoughts of Riff kept nagging at me, but Shaniqua was nothing if not independent, and I didn't want to scare her off by smothering her. I actually couldn't believe her aunt would let her walk around town by herself, what with everything going on, but Shaniqua had once mentioned that they didn't have any friends in town and never really talked to the neighbors, did most of their shopping close to where they worked in the next county, and rarely watched the news on TV, so chances were they didn't even know about the murders.

"No, it's still early. I'd rather walk." She squeezed my hand. "I'll be okay. Promise."

I walked her to the front door and stood there, watching her skip down the walk before heading toward home. She turned and waved when she reached the corner. I waved back and watched until she disappeared.

I couldn't help but wonder if I'd ever see her again.

Winter takes a firm grasp and temperatures plummet. The nights are the longest and the darkest, and the moon spends more time above the horizon opposite a low sun.

CHAPTER 35

I was getting ready for my date with Shaniqua when that now-familiar burning sensation filled my gut. I tried to shake it off, telling myself that everything was going to be okay, that I could hold the wolf off until after the party, but I knew that was a lie.

Dad stuck his head in my door. "You about ready to head out?"

I turned toward him slowly, struggling to keep from showing him how conflicted I was about tonight. But he knew me too well.

He took a step into my room and frowned. "What's wrong?"

I shook my head. "Nothing."

He didn't buy it. "James."

I plopped down on my bed and sighed. "I'm supposed to take Shaniqua to a party tonight."

"Oh, James." He sat down next to me. "You can't go to a party tonight. Not with a full moon. You know that, right?"

I nodded. "I know."

"And you know you don't have enough experience at taming the wolf yet to risk going to that party, don't you?"

"Yeah, especially when it's full of Beautiful People."

"Beautiful People?" Dad scratched his cheek and frowned.

"You know. Jocks, Mean Girls. Logan O'Shaughnessy…"

"Oh, right." There was a strange expression on his face when he turned to me. "You've told her, haven't you?"

"Yeah."

"And it went okay? She didn't freak out and run screaming into the night, did she?"

I chuckled. The thought of Shaniqua being that dramatic seemed hilarious. "No, she was okay about it. I think she already kind of knew."

"So she'll understand when you tell her why you can't go tonight, won't she?"

"Yeah, I guess."

Dad stood up and patted my shoulder. "Then you'd better give her a call. On your way out to the woods."

"Okay, Dad."

I hated the idea of disappointing her, but I figured it was better to be safe than sorry.

❑

Shaniqua was trying to decide how her hair would look best with the cat ears she was wearing to the party when her phone buzzed. She pulled it out of her back pocket to see who was texting her. James. She smiled, until she read the text.

~ Meet on the crnr n 5.

Shaniqua frowned as she texted him back. *~ What's up?*

~ Just meet me. Plez. Its mportant.

Shaniqua sighed. *~ Fine. Have 2 sneak out. B there ASAP.*

Shaniqua grabbed her jacket and walked down the hall, pausing outside the kitchen and checking again to make sure she hadn't been seen. Her aunt was reading a book while Uncle Roshaun watched TV.

Her aunt and uncle knew nothing about the party, and she wanted to keep it that way, just in case something bad happened. Once they realized she'd snuck out to go to the party—and she knew they'd find out—she'd be in big trouble. That was okay. It was just something she had to do. But if they caught her sneaking out to meet James, it would be impossible to make it to Nicole's.

She tiptoed past the doorway and over to the front door then slipped outside and ran across the yard and down the street. When she neared the corner, she saw James and waved. He waved back.

"Hey," he said. "How you doing?"

"Good," she replied. She kissed him on the cheek. "I can't stay long. The party—"

"I know. I can't either." He looked around nervously. Scratched behind his ear and then practically contorted himself to scratch underneath his shoulder blade. She was pretty sure she knew what was going on.

"You okay?"

"Yeah, I'm fine. I just—I can't go. I'm sorry."

A slight smile played across her lips. "It's okay." She didn't have to ask. She knew why.

"Listen, Shaniqua." He glanced up at the sky, scratched, then levelled his gaze at her. "Watts told me that this whole party thing is a set-up. The whole point is to humiliate you."

"I know."

"What do you mean, you know?"

"I know. She told me."

James shook his head. "You know? You *know* and you're still going?"

She took his hands in hers and looked at him. He had such beautiful eyes, she sometimes felt like she could lose herself in them. But tonight, she saw a flash of something, something close to anger. For the first time since she'd realized that the boy she loved was not human, she was actually a little frightened.

"I have to. Don't you see? If I don't go, I'll always wonder if I could have handled whatever they plan to throw at me." She ran her hand through his hair, brushing it out of his eyes. "If I back down now, not only will things get even worse at school but it'll be that much easier to run away the next time something bad happens. I have to stand up for myself. You can see that, can't you?"

"Yeah, I guess so." The fire went out of his eyes. "But I don't like it."

"That's because you're so sweet." She leaned against him and wrapped her arms around his neck, drawing him close. "And I love you for that," she whispered into his ear.

He pulled back a little. "Promise me that you'll text me when you get there, and again when you leave."

"I promise."

"You know I'd be there if I could, don't you?"

"I know. It's okay." She gave him a quick peck. "I got to go. If my aunt and uncle find out I snuck out, it'll be a moot point anyway, because they'll kill me. *And* ground me for life."

They would, too. She hurried down the street, turned when she got to the corner and waved, then jogged home.

She managed to sneak back in without being seen, and Watts arrived shortly afterwards, knocking on her bedroom window so Shaniqua could let her in without her aunt and uncle knowing she was there. Watts had volunteered to come and help Shaniqua get ready for the party.

Watts used her black eyeliner to turn Shaniqua's eyes into cat eyes. When she was done, she stood back and looked critically at her work. "You sure you want to do this?" she asked.

"I'm sure. Can I see?"

Watts touched up the corner of Shaniqua's left eye and shrugged. "Sure." She put the cap back on the liner. "What do you think?"

Shaniqua took a final look at herself in the mirror. "Perfect."

"I don't know why you insist on dressing up when you know it's all a set up."

"Because I have to prove to them—and to myself—that they can't hurt me." She turned to her friend. "What do you think?"

She'd chosen a simple yet classic costume. A black cat, complete with leotard and tights, cat ears on a fancy headband studded with rhinestones, which matched the collar she wore around her neck. She'd snuck her aunt's black stilettos out of her closet last week when she'd been home alone, and she'd spent hours practicing walking in them to make sure she didn't fall and make a fool of herself at the party.

"Incredible," Watts said. "James's eyes are going to fall out of his head when he sees you."

"He won't see me." She turned back to the mirror and adjusted her cat ears.

"What? Why not?"

"James can't go."

"But I thought—"

Shaniqua turned to her friend. "Full moon."

"Oh. Right. I—I'm sorry." Watts put her hand on Shaniqua's shoulder. "You okay? You need me to go with?"

"Thanks, but you'd be miserable the whole time. Besides, I need to do this alone." She turned back to the mirror and took a deep breath. "Wish me luck."

"Luck. Text me when you get home."

☐

I watched Shaniqua run back home, still totally amazed that the chick had chosen to be with me. I'd expected her to be pissed when I backed out of the party, but instead, she was cool about my not taking her, like she'd expected it. She was cool about my being a werewolf. She was cool, period.

And I was one lucky dude.

It didn't seem possible, but there you go. My parents found each other in high school. Maybe I'd found my soul mate, too.

But first things first. Checking in on Shaniqua and the party seemed like a good idea. I wouldn't stay long, just long enough to make sure no one hurt her, and then I'd head for the woods. Controlling the wolf for that long seemed…doable.

Heading for Nicole's, I glanced up at the moon. It had actually been up since this morning, and even though it was almost completely down, the pull on me was still tremendous. And yet, I thought I might have the easiest time yet controlling the wolf. Mr. Hansen's tricks seemed to be working. It was all a matter of putting yourself into a perpetual Zen-like state and carrying it over into your day-to-day life until it felt natural.

A year ago, even as soon as last summer, I would have laughed at that. But it was true.

The party was already in full swing as I parked the Le Mans at the end of Nicole's street. It seemed like the Mean Girls told Shaniqua to get there later than everyone else, probably to make sure that there would be plenty of party-goers around to witness her humiliation, whatever that might be. I wondered if I'd be able to stop it before it got out of hand.

As I walked up the street, I could practically feel the beat of the bass line of the music they were playing thrumming through my veins along with the pulsing of my own bloodlust, and I half hoped one of the neighbors would call the cops to come and raid the place before anything nasty happened.

My plan was to sneak up on the house and hide in the bushes until I spotted Shaniqua and made sure she was okay. But there were way too many kids milling around outside for that. The only thing I could hope for was that no one would stop me from checking things out.

And then Chase showed up.

"What the hell are you doing here?" He took a step away from me. "No one invited you."

Remembering how scared he'd been in the locker room that day my eyes went red, I crossed my arms and just looked at him. He shifted uneasily and glanced around for his buddies, but lucky for me, he was alone.

"The flyer said everyone welcome." It didn't but I was betting he was one of the ones who got a personal invite. He was part of their collective posse, after all, even if he hadn't been around them much lately.

"Everyone but you." Chase shifted again, bouncing on the balls of his feet like they were spring loaded.

"Look, Chase." I uncrossed my arms and reached out to him. I only wanted to reassure him that I wasn't going to hurt him, but his eyes went wide and he stumbled backward. I sighed and stayed where I was. "I'm not going to hurt you. I don't know what you think you saw in the locker room that day—"

"Your eyes went solid red. I saw it. I saw it!"

"Whatever you think you saw…"

"It was you," he whispered, and backed away again.

That confused me. I had no idea what he was talking about. "What was me?"

"That day I was followed, the day I thought the Wolf Creek Shredder had come back. She didn't come back. It was you!"

"What are you talking about? I never followed you anywhere."

"Just leave me alone!" Chase turned and sprinted down the street, got into his car and sped off. I thought about going after him, but if something happened and the wolf took over, it could be disastrous. Besides, it was no use trying to talk to him when he was so hyper, anyway.

I turned back to the party and searched for a good spot to check things out without being observed. There were some magenta bougainvillea shrubs alongside the house that weren't too tall, and it seemed like a good place to hide while I looked through a window. I just wanted to check things out, make sure Shaniqua was okay, but it felt kind of like being a Peeping Tom. In a way, I suppose I was, but my intentions were good.

Then the yard went silent, and I knew Shaniqua had arrived in her costume. I got ready for trouble.

□

Shaniqua stood on the sidewalk in front of Nicole's house. It was totally obvious that her parents weren't home, and probably weren't expected back any time soon. All the lights in the place must have been blazing. Music blared out the front door, which stood wide open. It seemed like every kid in school was there. Everyone who mattered. Well, everyone Alexis and her entourage thought mattered, anyway.

She steeled herself for whatever awaited her and

headed up the walkway. Her heels clicked on the tile steps. Kids who were outside smoking and drinking stopped what they were doing and stared at her. When she got inside, everything was pretty much the same as it had been the other day. Crystal vases held gorgeous flower arrangements and sat on what she could only assume were expensive antiques that lined the entryway. The floor was a swirly patterned marble that mimicked the swirly cloud formations painted on the cathedral ceilings. They'd put a huge table at the end of the hall between the twin staircases and there were more brightly-colored gifts than she'd ever seen piled so high she wondered why they didn't tumble off the table and litter the floor.

Liam and two other guys she didn't know were huddled over a foosball table. Funny how, even though their supposed best bud had been savagely murdered not long ago, they were sufficiently over their grief and ready to party. Same with Alexis, her posse, and Hannah. Shaniqua shook her head, and her mother's favorite saying blasted through her mind: *'With friends like that, who needs enemies?'*

Shaniqua snorted. *For once, Mom was right.*

"O-M-G," someone said, and everyone in the room gawked at Shaniqua. She could feel the heat rising in her face and forced herself to remain calm. After all, she'd known humiliation was the plan. She just hadn't realized it would begin the instant she stepped inside the door.

It turned out being the only one dressed in a costume was not the main event.

Shaniqua walked up to Nicole and Alexis, who were sitting on the sofa—sorry, *divan*, as Monica Morningside had informed her, not couch or sofa. That was so "gauche." The girls were gossiping, no doubt. Shaniqua stood with her hands on her hips and waited for them to turn to her. When they did, Alexis spit her drink out all over Nicole.

"Thanks for inviting me, Nicole," Shaniqua said. "This party is super fun."

They snickered and put their heads together before Nicole turned to her and pointed. "Nice outfit. It's…um…fierce."

"Hey, thanks," Shaniqua said, trying not to bite her tongue off. "I like your outfit, too. Only when I dress up as the Queen Bitch, I try not to look so constipated." She handed Nicole the bottle of prune juice she'd brought. *BYOB, my ass.* "Maybe this will help."

Shaniqua turned on her heels and walked swiftly toward the door, but not before she saw Nicole's face turn bright red. She giggled, nearly bursting out into full-blown laughter when she heard Alexis laughing, too.

"What a va jay jay," Nicole muttered.

"Still have a problem with the video?" Alexis asked.

Nicole shook her head, her eyes narrowed. "Not in the least." She turned towards one of the boys, who lurked near the entrance to the living room, waiting for his cue. "Now."

The sound of a thousand text messages being received rang throughout the house. And that's when Shaniqua knew that the real humiliation had just begun.

▢

Shaniqua looked hot in her cat costume, but I had to wonder again why she'd decided to wear it when she found out it was all a joke. A big, mean joke.

Even though I was peeking in through the window directly at Nicole and Alexis, I couldn't hear exactly what happened when she saw them, but by the looks on their faces, Shaniqua'd gotten off a good one. I was getting ready to leave, figuring the worst of it was over, when my cell phone chirped. I ducked back behind the bushes and pulled it out of my pocket. It was a video, just about the worst thing I'd ever seen.

Shaniqua was naked, laying on a bed in a seductive pose. She had thick black mascara on her eyelashes and purple make up above her eyes. Her cheeks were flushed. "This hot enough for you?" she said. She'd told me all about the sexting, but to actually see it was something else entirely.

I had no doubt about who sent it. Alexis and her skanky pack of hos. But where did they get it from?

The rage boiled my blood, and I lost it.

The wolf came on me before I could stop it. Not that I wanted to.

□

The next thing I knew, the moon was almost completely down. What was left cast an eerie silver glow over everything. My head ached, pulsing with the remnants of the transformation, like always.

I couldn't figure out where I was. Maybe I was in my bed at home, and everything—the party, the crappy way the Mean Girls treated Shaniqua, whatever must have happened after I transformed—had all been a terrible nightmare. Maybe I was fourteen again, before anything bad had happened. Before I'd killed my first monster.

Before I found out I was one, too.

For that one welcome moment of sweet relief, there'd been a reprieve from the horror that had become my life. But it was all just wishful thinking.

I was in the woods, far away from Nicole's house and the rest of town, but beyond that, I had no clue. The last thing I remembered was watching that stupid video on my phone and the sound of everyone at the party laughing.

And how pissed off it made me.

Maybe that's why the transformation had come on so suddenly, so unexpectedly. After all, I was still learning how to control it. Normally, things went okay, as long as I was able to run in the woods that bordered Wolf Creek.

But what about last night? What had I done?

It was as if someone—some*thing*—flipped a switch in my brain. It was true. It happened. It had all happened. The party. The text. The transformation. My transformation. The only thing I could hope for was that I hadn't hurt anyone.

Clumps of twig-encrusted mud, stones and dead leaves dug into me and I realized that I couldn't sit there any longer. I had to find out what happened. My clothes were in tatters, and I was practically naked. I scrambled to my feet and immediately stumbled over a tree root. I was close to hyperventilating, and leaned against a tree for a moment, trying to slow my breathing and quiet the pounding in my chest. After a bit, I realized I was in Cailleach Canyon. Wolf Creek had been named after the creek that ran through the canyon, which was about seven miles outside of town. The canyon itself was named after the Scottish goddess who brought destruction and winter with her, and ruled the dark half of the year.

It seemed appropriate.

Heavy forest rose all around me, the limbs of the trees nearly—but not quite—blocking out what was left of the full moon. Night birds called mournfully as they wound down and prepared for sleep. Crickets chirped continuously.

The creek was dry, and I remembered when I was a little kid my dad used to take me hunting for bullfrogs. Where did they all go in the drought?

I had to get back to Nicole's to see what happened. To see what I had done.

I didn't know exactly where I was, but I figured that if I kept to the creek bed, I'd eventually end up back near Nicole's. I followed it for miles. How far had I run, anyway? What little light there was reached me sporadically through the trees, but mostly there were long stretches of shadow. The trail was narrow and hard to see. Rocks and sticks constantly jabbed into my feet. Unseen creatures skittered along in the underbrush.

And it was cold. So cold. It seeped into my skin and made me shiver. Every time I left the path along the creek to try and climb up into a clearing, I had to fight my way through tangled branches and vines. Tree roots seemed to reach out and trip me at every turn. Branches tore at my face and arms. Finally I just plodded along the creek and forgot about trying to climb out of the creek bed.

Eventually, the woods thinned and I could see the sky above me. I'd make it out of the woods if I could only hike up the hill to where the ground levelled out.

It wouldn't be long now.

□

There was a clearing ahead of me, and I could make out the dim shape of a house. Nicole's house. My heart beat wildly in my chest, and I was panting like a dog.

My nose went into hyper-drive, and it felt like it was going to explode. The mustiness of the damp leaves on the ground beneath me, mixed with the odors floating off the trees and the underbrush, whizzed up my nose like someone was shoving a pine cone up it. But the worst thing, the stench that turned my stomach, was the coppery-sweet smell that permeated through all the other scents.

Blood.
My only hope was that it wasn't human.

                                    ☐

I moved slowly along the tree line, skirting from one tree to the next, edging closer to the house. No one was around, and everything was quiet. Too quiet. The crickets weren't chirping. The night birds had gone silent. My head felt fuzzy, and it was all I could do not to hurl.

What would I find inside the house? I had never felt so afraid. Not even the night I killed the werewolf.

I made sure I was alone and that no one would see me. Slowly, I snuck onto the grass, and was pleasantly surprised at how soft and cool it felt on my feet after walking barefoot in the forest for so long. But I didn't dare stop to enjoy the feeling. Someone might see me.

A little dazed, I stumbled toward the house, worried about what I would find there. When I got close, I loped across the driveway, barely feeling the sting of the gravel on my feet. I barely felt anything by now. I went over to the place where I'd hidden last night. Was it only last night? It seemed like forever ago.

I crouched beneath the window and immediately felt a prick of pain in my foot. Shattered glass from the window dug into my heel. As I pulled out the shard, I realized that the window must have busted out violently.

Oh, God, no. Please God…

I glanced through the broken window, but all I saw was the living room. Everything seemed okay. But by now, I was pretty much sleepwalking through everything. It wasn't until I got inside that I saw what the place really looked like. I went to the front door, which was not only unlocked—weird for this time of night—but standing slightly ajar.

Please, God…

I wanted to turn back. I wanted to get back into my car, drive home, burrow into bed and pretend like nothing happened. But that was impossible. Something major *had* happened. So I went inside, through the fish bowl-like entry way, into the foyer.

A few of Nicole's birthday decorations were hanging haphazardly from the string of lights that she'd hung them on. But everything else seemed in order. Hoping that I was wrong, that I had transformed far away and that everything was okay, I passed through the archway into the living room.

I slowly looked around. The last thing I remembered was Nicole and Alexis laughing at Shaniqua, and so was everyone else. But that's where my memories ended. There was no sign of the party-goers. My gut had been clenched so tightly, the relief that flooded through me felt like a tidal wave. I licked my dry lips. Maybe I hadn't done anything after all. Maybe everyone was safe and sound, tucked in their beds for the night.

I dared to hope that I wasn't going to find what I knew I would find. Hope died when I came to the couch where Nicole and Alexis had been gossiping and saw that the back of it had been ripped to shreds. The fabric lay in pieces. The oak legs were splintered into dozens of shards, like wooden shrapnel.

Sticking out from under the remnants of the couch lay what was left of my clothes: bits and pieces of my jeans and jacket, an old sweatshirt, the remains of my kicks, my wallet. And my cell phone. They all lay in a weird circle of sorts, and it looked like I had simply exploded.

Which I suppose I had, in a way.

Nicole had apparently tried to escape out the door into the hallway, but hadn't made it more than a few feet from the couch. She lay there in a pool of drying blood.

What was left of her, anyway. Which wasn't much. She was now little more than a red smear from one end of the blue-walled corridor to the other. She looked like a big pile of raw hamburger, a matted hank of chestnut hair clinging to the bloody corner of what was left of her mouth.

Alexis had actually made it into the hall before she'd been torn apart from behind. She'd been sliced in half, pieces of her bones sticking out at odd angles, and her blood was smeared all the way across the white marble floor. Her body lay crumpled at the foot of one of the twin staircases. The only thing left of her face was a single eye hanging out of the socket, where it lay against her cheek. It stared at me accusingly.

As I went further into the house, I found remnants of the guys who'd been at the party: Liam's bloody Letterman's jacket, Brody's Fedora and Mickey's Celtic cross. My stomach roiled and it was all I could do not to puke. But it wasn't just the bloody carnage that made my gorge rise. It was the full knowledge of what I'd done. My moral understanding that I alone was responsible for the violent deaths of my classmates.

I had done this terrible thing.

These kids were not the nicest people in the world, it's true. They were so full of themselves, so sure they were entitled to all the good things in life simply because their parents had money. They'd thrived on tormenting me and people like me. People like Shaniqua. I hated what they'd done to her, but even still, they didn't deserve to die. Not like this.

Once living, breathing kids with dreams and ambitions, I had turned them into nothing more than a pile of flesh and bones, pools of viscous blood and gore. And for what? Because they'd humiliated the girl I liked. I remember thinking that they had to pay, that I had to protect Shaniqua somehow, save her from further shame and embarrassment. Then I guess I'd given in to the bloodlust and rage and done this horrible thing.

How could I ever make it right?

□

That knowledge, the understanding of everything I was responsible for, made me stagger to the bathroom, where I barely made it to the john before hurling. When I thought I'd brought up everything I possibly could, I dry-heaved several times before collapsing onto the cool marble floor.

I rested there a few minutes as the realization of the carnage, the horror of what I'd done, settled into my soul. I had to turn myself in. There was nothing else to do. I could never bring them back, so spending the rest of my life in jail was the only way I could possibly make things right. The nightmare of my existence, of what I'd become, had been sealed forever by my actions.

James Manarro was gone forever.

In his place was a monster.

And that monster was me.

□

"You didn't do this, you know."

I turned toward the voice and scrambled to my feet. Shaniqua stood in the doorway to the bathroom. Her face and arms were scratched, her hair was wild—more so than normal, I mean—and she was dirty, but it was so good to see her.

"You're alive!" I leaped across the bathroom before remembering that my clothes were lying in pieces in the living room. Heat soared up my neck and across my face as I grabbed a towel off the rack and wrapped it around my waist. "I was so worried about you."

She giggled and pulled me to her, plucking a few leaves and twigs out of my hair. She handed me my backpack. The one I kept in the trunk of the Le Mans on full moon nights.

"How did you…"

Her eyes twinkled. "Girl's gotta have some secrets." She gestured at the towel around my waist. "You might want to change into something a little more…fashionable." She giggled again as she turned around and stood with her back to me while I pulled my day-after clothes out of the backpack and got dressed. "I know you think you went all crazy and shit, but it wasn't you."

"How can you be so sure?"

"Because the beast that did this had reddish brown hair with a bunch of black running through it." She reached out and gently took a strand of my hair between her fingers. "Yours is golden brown. And beautiful."

I frowned. "You saw who did it?" Being human, that had to be one of the most terrifying things she would ever see, and I wondered how it would ultimately affect her.

And what it would do to our relationship.

She shook her head. "No, I was gone before anything happened. But as I was walking down the street, I heard all these people running and screaming behind me. So I ran back to the house to see what was going on."

"Wait. Everyone was running *away* from the noise, and you ran toward it?"

"Uh huh. Why?"

"Why? *Why?* Because I had no idea what was happening and you could have gotten hurt, that's why."

"I didn't even think about it. All I knew was that it

was a full moon and I was afraid you might get hurt, somehow."

It occurred to me that she was lying. Especially since she couldn't look me in the eye. "You sure you don't mean you were afraid I was the one doing the hurting?"

Anger sparked in her eyes. Her nostrils flared and she snorted loudly. "That's not what I meant at all. What I *meant* was that I was afraid that someone saw you in your werewolf form and wanted to kill you." Tears pooled in her eyes as her anger abated. "I didn't want anything bad to happen to you," she whispered.

There I was, being a jerk again. "Oh, baby, I'm so sorry." I wrapped my arms around her and stroked her hair. She leaned against my shoulder, trembling, and I held her.

"Well, well, well. What do we have here?"

My stomach plummeted. I'd been so busy comforting Shaniqua and worrying about what had happened that I hadn't heard Riggs drive up. He was standing in that Popeye stance again, surveying the carnage around us.

He seemed unfazed.

If Sheriff Brazelton were still on the job, he might have barfed on his shoes again, like he did when they discovered what was left of Riff's body. But maybe not, since he'd already seen something similar. Even so, compassion would have been apparent.

Riggs's face was completely blank.

"So, I finally caught you."

"Caught us?" Shaniqua asked.

"Not you, sweetheart. Your lover boy there." He gestured towards me with his head, a malicious grin spreading across his face.

It chilled me.

She took a step toward him. I tried to stop her but she shook off my hand. "What are you talking about?" she asked. "James didn't do this."

Riggs regarded her curiously, his head tilted to one side, his eyes widening gleefully. "And I suppose you just happen to know who did."

She shook her head vehemently. I prayed she wouldn't say it. *Don't tell him what you saw, baby. He won't believe you.*

"No, I don't know. But I do know that it wasn't James."

Riggs chuckled. "Oh, yeah? And just how do you know that?"

"Because he was with me." She took a deep breath. "All night."

CHAPTER 36

Thursday, December 31, 2015,
New Year's Eve,
Twenty-Four Days to Full Moon:

New Year's Eve, and Shaniqua was stuck at home. Her aunt and uncle were pretty upset when they found out that she had snuck out to go to the party and been there when the massacre happened. Sheriff Riggs questioned her extensively about it, going so far as to insinuate that James was somehow responsible, but so far, at least, she'd been able to convince him that James wasn't even there. That they'd been together all night. He seemed to believe her. At least, she hoped he believed her.

And through it all, through all the hard questions, insinuations, implications and whatnot, reliving the horror over and over ad nauseam, Riggs had never once cracked. Never once had he indicated that he was the least bit troubled by what happened, by all the blood and gore left in the terrible aftermath of the massacre.

She had to wonder just what kind of monster Riggs was.

But what really worried her was why she hadn't been honest with Aunt Lydie and Uncle Roshaun in the first place. She'd admitted to her uncle that it was a stupid thing to do. And as it turned out, it had been, given what happened.

But the worst thing about it was the look on Uncle Roshaun's face when Riggs told them that Shaniqua had admitted to being with James all night. They had, of course, drawn the typical conclusion, and how could she deny it without telling them the truth?

She was stuck with her uncle's disappointment in her, maybe forever. She only hoped he'd one day forgive her, that she hadn't damaged their relationship permanently.

She would never forgive herself if that happened.

But for now, here she was, sixteen years old, grounded like she was five. And on New Year's Eve to boot.

Her cell phone chirped.

Watts. ~ *Hey, S. Sup?*

~ *Bored.*

~ *Me 2. Still grounded?*

~ *Yep.*

"Gee, that's too bad."

Watts stood in her doorway. "What are you doing here?"

Watts shrugged and plopped down on the bed next to her. "Where else would I go on the last day of the year?"

"But, how…" Shaniqua lowered her voice and frowned. "You didn't…break in, did you?"

Watts pointed to her chest. "*Moi*? Why, I can't believe you'd even ask me that." She grinned and bumped against Shaniqua. "No, dude. I just called and asked your aunt if it was okay if I came over and hung for a while."

"You asked my aunt?"

"Yeah."

"And she said it was okay?"

"Dude, chill." She curled her fingers into her palm and blew on them. "I do have a way with the older set, you know."

Shaniqua laughed again and shook her head. "Oh—kay."

Maybe New Year's Eve wasn't going to be such a drag after all.

CHAPTER 37

Thursday, January 21, 2016,
Three Days to Full Moon:

A solitary figure crept down the darkened corridor. School wouldn't start for a couple of hours, so the place was deserted. Still, the werewolf, in its human form, stayed in the shadows, just in case. *Fools. They have no clue. I'll get that little punk Manarro, and his girlfriend, too.*

Walking quickly, it hesitated when it heard the shriek of the wind as it rattled the panes of glass next to it, then continued on to the lockers lined up against the side of the building. When it got to number L1427, it reached into its hoodie pocket and pulled out a note that it'd folded into quarters. The wolf snickered, a deep, throaty guffaw, and slipped the note through the air vents in the locker door, waiting with its ear against it until it heard the note land on something inside.

It won't be long. The werewolf licked its lips and longed for the rise of the full moon. *No, it won't be long at all.*

I was glad to be back in school. For a while there, I didn't think I'd ever make it. Riggs had grilled me for days, and several times I thought he was going to arrest me.

But eventually, with no real evidence against me and no coherent eyewitnesses, he'd been forced to let me go. The media had reported it as a wild animal attack, and I guess people must have chosen to believe that.

I was thinking about that, wondering how long it would be before Riggs pieced together what I really was, when I went to my locker to put my stuff away before meeting Shaniqua and Watts for lunch. When I opened my locker, there was a folded note sitting on top of my Biology book. At first I thought it was from Shaniqua, and I eagerly opened it up and started to read.

I know what you are. If you want the killing to stop, meet me in the meadow a mile and a half east of Cailleach Canyon. There's a large oak tree at the entrance. A wolf's head is carved into the trunk. Meet me there on Sunday at 6:00. ***DO NOT BE LATE*** *or you will be sorry.*

It didn't seem possible. Who could have figured out my secret? Had Shaniqua told someone? Why would she? Everything was great between us. No, I couldn't believe it. It had to be someone else. But who was left, after the massacre at the party. Brody, out for revenge for his brother's murder? Or maybe Cheyenne, that chick who tagged along after Alexis but never really seemed part of her posse. All she ever did was mumble unintelligibly. Could be Logan's cousin Handy, but he'd never really been a part of Logan's group, even when they were all little, and in fact, seemed to avoid him as much as possible.

And why would someone write a note anyway? Why not just tell me to my face? I wondered if Logan being gone had taken away their cajones. It wouldn't have surprised me, that was for sure.

But it was also for sure that I was going to have to meet whoever it was and see what they wanted.

I just hoped they didn't bring a gun with them.

Especially loaded with silver bullets.

Food provisions are running low. Amid the frosty cold, the bottomless snow of midwinter gathers deep in the woods, and the howling of wolves with hunger in their hearts and their bellies can be heard echoing in the still, bitter air. This is the time when the wolf is strongest.

CHAPTER 38

This was it. I was on my own. For truly the first time in my life, I had to take things into my own hands, like a man. Sure, once upon a time I'd killed a sick werewolf, but I'd had help. Even though Donna died and Beth had lain unconscious in the hospital, they'd still played major roles in ridding Wolf Creek of the rogue werewolf. But this time, I couldn't risk any more lives. Shaniqua was human, after all, and had no experience, other than me and what happened at the party, with werewolves. I couldn't let anything happen to her.

I had to do this all by myself.

When I pulled into Cailleach Canyon, the first thing I noticed was that there was a car parked in the lot. Not just any car. A gold, 1969 Le Mans. Nearly identical to my own. What was going on? Was someone playing a really bad practical joke on me? As far as I knew, mine was the only Le Mans in town, gold or any other color. So who owned that one? I parked next to it, peeking through the windows for any clue about the owner's identity, but it was super clean. Not even a water bottle or fast-food wrapper had been left behind.

Shrugging, I headed toward the entrance to the park and followed a narrow dirt path that snaked deep into the woods. My footsteps crunched over the fallen leaves and crackled on the dead twigs. I had to keep constant watch to make sure I didn't trip over the tree roots and vines that littered the ground. Trees closed in around me. Night had overtaken the daylight and seemed to compress the air against my skin. Darkness settled down around the overhang above me and crept in through the gnarled branches of trees that seemed to turn into something scary as I watched.

As I got closer to the clearing where the note told me to go to, a night bird cried out. I could hear the creek below gurgling and I remember being happy that the recent rains had brought enough water to the land to actually make the creek flow again. The croak of a bullfrog made me grin. I swatted at a gnat that buzzed my ear.

The sun finally went down, its hazy beams dissolving quickly. The trees blocked any remaining light, and the trail disappeared into the trees. I switched on the flashlight I'd brought from home, but the battery must have been weak because it didn't really help much. It only reached about three or four feet in front of me.

From what I could see of the trail, it seemed to take a slight left, and I followed it until it ended in a meadow of sorts. Oak, maple, and some other kind of trees lined the clearing but the meadow itself was clear so there was a little more light. Enough so that the trees were silhouetted against the fading blue of twilight.

This had to be the clearing I was supposed to meet whoever wrote the note in. There was a large oak that seemed to guard the opening. A wolf's head was carved into the trunk, just like the note said there would be. I ran my fingers over its smooth face and wondered who had carved it, and why. Shrugging, I wandered into the clearing and listened to the croaking of the frogs and the chirping of the crickets.

And underneath it all, silence. An eerie silence.

A slight breeze picked up and the fallen leaves rustled on the ground. The branches of the trees lining the clearing creaked and moaned as the wind blew through them. I squinted and tried to see through the gloaming, but night draped the woods and the individual trees vanished into a dark and twisted wilderness. Even the closest shrubs became mere suggestions of themselves.

There was a strange glow in the eastern sky, just over the treetops. It took me a minute or two to realize just what it was—the moon. The Wolf Moon. The time of year when the wolf is the strongest.

And the hungriest.

I shivered, even though adrenaline was keeping me warm. I could feel it heating my blood. It was there in the tingling of my skin, and the thumping of my heart.

It wouldn't be long now.

〇

I watched another few moments while the moon rose farther in the sky. The silver crescent that appeared above the trees became first a half circle then a bright, beautiful full circle. It lit up the silhouetted trees and scrub oak surrounding the meadow, and kept rising from its place behind the trees and woods beyond. It was glorious, and made the woods surrounding the meadow seem somehow magical. I was transfixed.

But then, across the meadow, something moved. I squinted to pick the figure out of the shadows, but could only see a shape rather than any specific features. It was impossible for me to say who it was, although he or she did seem familiar.

Whoever it was, was observing me. I could feel their eyes on me. But I also knew that they were just as drawn to the rising moon as me. So I wasn't surprised that, when I was finally able to tear myself away from my fascination with the lunar orb to look at the other werewolf, it was facing away from me, raptly watching the moon rise. It was an optical illusion—the moon didn't actually rise that fast—but it was still fascinating, and neither one of us could resist watching it.

I turned back to it. Its pull was intense and I wondered how anyone ever successfully fought off the wolf. Or why they would even want to. The moon was so beautiful, so intriguing and mysterious.

Reluctantly, I pulled myself away, drew a deep breath, and turned to speak to the dark figure.

It stepped out of the darkness into the sparse light of dusk. "You came," it said.

I was so startled, I dropped the flashlight. It was PJ all over again.

I never would have guessed who the killer really was. Not in a million years.

☐

"Mr. Hansen! What are you doing here?" It couldn't be him. Not Mr. Hansen, everybody's favorite teacher. The dude who said he wanted to help me learn how to control the wolf. The one I'd confided everything to. My mentor. My friend.

"What do you think?" He raised his lip and snarled, a very animalistic sound, as he circled around me.

"But…I thought you were my friend." We circled another quarter turn. "If you hated me so much, why teach me to control the wolf?"

"Control it?" Mr. Hansen spat. "You naïve little simpleton, I wasn't teaching you to control it, I was teaching *it* to control *you*." He growled and bared his teeth at me.

"You remember a little incident about two years ago?"

I frowned, not sure what he was talking about. A tiny glimmer of a thought skittered in the back of my mind. But it couldn't be. Not that. No way. Not *that*. "Two years ago? I didn't even know you two years ago."

"No, but you knew my sister." He kept circling, and I turned with him.

"Your...*sister*?"

"She once told me how you loved root beer floats and fries." He growled, a savage, animalistic rumble, a cross between a feral snarl and a low moan. "You were one of her favorites. Did you know that?" He was only two or three steps away now.

"You mean, PJ was your *sister*?"

"That's right," he yelled. Fetid spittle foamed up on his lips and sprayed me in the face. "And you killed her, you little prick!"

He was right in front of me now, and I realized he was already transforming. Before I could gather myself, he lashed out with unimaginable speed and tore open my chest.

I flew backward, my body shredded. Smashed into the ground with such force, it knocked all the air out of me. I could feel the life-force flowing out of me, and I choked on the blood that rose in my throat. It made me cough, and I turned my head so that it flowed over my chin rather than pour back into my mouth.

Weakness overtook me. I could barely move. So this was it. This was how it was going to end. My head fell to the side, lank and lifeless, and I caught a brief glimpse of the moon as it broke into the clearing in a strong and luminous beam.

That was all it took. Mr. Hansen wasn't the only werewolf here. How could I have forgotten? That primal knowledge of who I was, of *what* I was, gave me the impetus to transform. It was like my insides had detonated, a gut-wrenching eruption that caused my bones to strain against my flesh and turn it to fire. My skin was punctured from the inside by thick golden fur that sprouted wildly over every square inch of my body.

Muscles stretched and bones splintered as my arms and legs lengthened and thickened. My head elongated, my nose turned into a lupine snout, and my teeth became fangs, dripping with hot saliva. My clothes shredded as my arms, massive and furry, expanded until they burst from their sleeves. My dagger-sharp claws whipped out and sliced into the beast that raged against me in the silvery glow of the moon.

The transformation was complete. I was no longer James Manarro. I had become the great, furry beast that I was born to be. I was a massive monster, raging against one of my own.

I was the wolf.

I reared up on my hind legs, tilted my muzzle up to the sky, and howled. Instinct took hold of my brain and I charged the other wolf. It roared, in surprise and anger, and sprang at me. Its ragged teeth sank into the flesh of my lower leg, spearing my calf and nearly shredding it. I howled in agony.

The dark beast dragged me across the ground, shaking its head voraciously and ripping my flesh. I twisted around. Its eyes were enormous, blood-red pools of destruction. Its paw swung down to swipe the life out of me, but I managed to get out of its death grip. I screamed in pain again when the beast's claws ripped chunks of my flesh off the bone. I bared my fangs and lunged, instinctively clamping down on its throat.

I held fast while it thrashed and battered its body against the ground. I tightened my grip as the life-energy flowed out of the beast's crushed larynx. Viscous blood pooled beneath us. Turning a bit, I looked into the dark wolf's eyes and thought I saw, for the briefest of instances, some sort of recognition there, some piece, some left-over bit of Mr. Hansen. Then the red eyes blinked, and that spark was gone.

The body stilled, and I realized that the great wolf, the second—and hopefully last—serial killer to haunt Wolf Creek, was finally gone.

☐

I headed back toward my car. Normally during a full moon, I raced through the woods for most of the night, until the moon's gravitational pull lessened and my humanity returned. With each cycle, the time of the wolf becomes shorter as I learn to control it.

With any luck, it wouldn't be long before control would be easier, and I wouldn't feel the urge to transform every month. Especially if I wanted to be with Shaniqua. "She seems to understand, but she's never actually seen me transform," I told myself. Would things change between us if she ever did?

As I mulled this over, I heard a faint cry coming from the far side of the meadow. I paused, listening intently. It seemed to be getting louder, more frenzied. I ran toward it, plunging through the scrub oaks and underbrush.

And couldn't believe what I was seeing.

THE END

To find out what happens to James next, read *Moon Shadows*, the third and final book in The Wolf Creek Mystery series.

About the Author

After sixteen years as a paralegal, Lisanne Harrington staged a coup and left the straight-laced corporate world behind forever. Now she panders to her muse, a sarcastic little so-and-so who delights in getting the voices in her head to either all speak at once in a cacophony of noise or to remain completely silent. Only copious hamburgers and Diet Cherry Dr. Peppers will ensure their complicity in filling her head with stories of serial killers, were-wolves, and the things that live under your bed.

When not writing, she watches reruns of *Gilmore Girls*, horror movies like *Sharknado* and *Fido*, and Investigation Discovery crime shows. She likes scary clowns, coffee with flavored creamer, and French fries. Lots and lots of French fries.

She lives in SoCal, in the small town she fashioned Wolf Creek after, with her beloved husband and persistently rowdy but sweet miniature pinscher, Fiona.